JUSTICE for HIRE

Rayven T. Hill

Ray of Joy Publishing
Toronto

Books by Rayven T. Hill

Blood and Justice
Cold Justice
Justice for Hire
Captive Justice
Justice Overdue
Justice Returns
Personal Justice
Silent Justice
Web of Justice
Fugitive Justice

Visit rayventhill.com for more information
on these and future releases.

Published by Ray of Joy Publishing
Toronto

Second Edition

ISBN -13: 978-0-9938625-2-6

JUSTICE for HIRE

CHAPTER 1

Monday, August 22nd, 8:05 a.m.

THE BLACK Cadillac Escalade pulled to the curb. Its darkened windows concealed all but the shadowy outline of the driver as the vehicle sat motionless, the engine purring.

The sidewalk was deserted except for an old man, ambling along, working his cane. Soon he was safely away, and the back door of the SUV swung open and a girl stepped out. She carried a small handbag, clutched at her side, a strap over her shoulder holding it in place. She stepped forward as the vehicle pulled out and eased away.

As she turned and went up the sidewalk, if any of the few pedestrians who hustled past looked her way, they may have noticed her blank expression and her vacant eyes. But they hurried about their own business and paid no attention as she walked two blocks, turned into a plaza, crossed the parking lot, and approached a single glass door. She swung it open and stepped into a small lobby.

A wall plaque listed the names of business tenants who occupied suites on the second floor. She glanced at the sign, stepped through another door into a larger lobby, and took the elevator up.

On the second floor, she stepped from the elevator into a

long hallway extending in both directions. She turned to her right, continued down the corridor past three suites, and stopped at the fourth. A sign on the door said "Bonfield Development." She twisted the knob, opened the door, and stepped inside.

A long desk blocked the way to the large room beyond, where expensive prints hung on the rich oak-paneled walls. The hardwood floor reflected the sunlight that poured through wall-to-wall windows. The luxurious room looked more like a showcase than a suite of offices. Several doors along one side, and the back wall, led into other rooms, probably offices, studios, and boardrooms. Music washed from overhead speakers, loud enough to camouflage the gentle hum of the central air conditioner that cooled the room.

A gray-haired receptionist behind the barricade beamed at her. "May I help you?" she asked.

"I'm here to see Charles Robinson." Her voice was expressionless, her gaze still blank.

"May I ask your name, please?"

"Cheryl Waters."

"Just a minute." The receptionist consulted a ledger and poked an intercom button. "Cheryl Waters to see you, sir," she sang.

The intercom squawked, "I'll be right there."

"If you'd like to take a seat, Mr. Robinson will be with you in a few minutes."

Cheryl didn't respond as she lifted her emotionless eyes and gazed toward the back of the room.

The receptionist curiously watched the girl a moment, and then went back to her paperwork. The phone rang, and she answered it, arranged an appointment for one of the other executives, and jotted the information in the calendar.

Cheryl didn't move.

In a few moments, a door at the back of the room opened and a man stepped out. In his midfifties, with silver-gray hair, he wore a pleasant smile. He strode across the room toward her.

Cheryl turned and stepped around the long desk to meet him.

He extended his hand. "I'm Charles Robinson."

Cheryl ignored his outstretched hand, reached into her handbag, and removed a small pistol.

Robinson lost his smile. His mouth fell open, and he raised his hands.

Gripping the weapon, she pointed the shiny barrel at his chest.

"What do you want?" he managed to ask.

She didn't answer. Her finger tightened on the trigger, the cold look still in her eyes.

He stepped back, too late, as the gun exploded, hurling lead into his heart. Before he could react, there was a second blast. As he crumpled to the floor, a third shot, this time in the head, made sure he would never breathe again. Cheryl studied him a moment, and then the pistol slipped from her grasp and clattered on the wooden floor.

CHAPTER 2

Monday, August 22nd, 8:15 a.m.

THE RICH SMELL of fried bacon filled the house, and for a moment, Annie Lincoln paused and gazed out the kitchen window. The cloudless sky promised to bring another beautiful summer day. She was thankful, as harrowing as the last few days had been, that her family was safe. She would be lost without her husband.

After many years as a construction engineer, Jake had become one of many cutback casualties. Because of Annie's extensive experience in freelance research, they decided to extend her expertise and take a shot at private investigations. Lincoln Investigations was born, and she was pleased she could work alongside her husband. However, she'd never expected their new vocation would lead from the safe world of research into a recent brush with a murderer. Everything had eventually turned out fine, they were safe, and she was grateful.

"Mom, the potatoes are burning."

Annie, shaken from her thoughts, looked down at the sputtering pan. She laughed and flipped the potatoes. "They'll be all right," she said. "I know you and your dad like them crispy."

She dumped the bacon from another skillet onto a sheet

of paper towel and cracked a half dozen eggs into the pan. Three for Jake, one for her, and two for Matty. At eight years old, Matty was growing fast, and threatened to be big like his dad someday.

She heaped the plates and brought them to the table. Matty was hungry and waiting, his fork in his hand. Jake dropped his iPad and turned his attention to the still-sizzling meal.

Matty couldn't wait to dig in, but Jake cautioned him with a look. Matty obediently bowed his head, peeking up with one squinted eye, as Jake thanked the Lord for the food.

Then they attacked the morning feast.

Jake poked a couple of potatoes into his mouth and looked at Annie. "What are your plans for today?"

Annie set her fork down. "Nothing real exciting," she said. "I thought I would do a little more studying. Those books on police procedure and crime scene investigations are rather interesting." She paused and suggested, "Maybe you could take a look at them as well."

Jake shrugged. "You can fill me in on the important points when you're done."

Annie laughed. "That could take a while." She sat back and studied Jake. Finally, she said, "I thought I might buy a small pistol."

Jake's mouth stopped working. He looked at her, wrinkled his brow, and stared as if trying to figure out if she was serious. He sat back, wiped his mouth on a napkin and set it beside his plate before looking up. "Do you think that's a good idea?"

"Why not?"

He shrugged. He seemed to be thinking as he observed her, and then nodded slowly. "Yeah, maybe you're right. It might be a good thing."

Matty's mouth dropped open, his eyes wide as he stared back and forth at his parents.

"It doesn't mean I have to use it," she said. "It's just in case. You know things can get dangerous sometimes. Maybe I won't ever use it, but it would make me feel more secure."

"You'll have to get a license if you want to carry it," Jake said.

"I know. That could take a few days, but if you're good with it, I thought I might go this afternoon."

"Go for it," he said as he leaned back in, picked up his fork, and poked the last potato in his mouth.

She didn't think he would object much. Once he got over the mild shock, he would agree keeping her safe was a good thing. She brushed back a stray golden hair and asked, "Do you have any plans today?"

Jake crunched a piece of toast. "I just have to change the oil in the Firebird," he said. "And maybe give it a quick tune-up. That's about it."

"You might want to take a look at my car while you're at it," Annie said. "The motor has been making a scratching noise lately."

Jake laughed. "Scratching? Engines don't scratch. They bang and whistle and scrape, but they don't scratch."

Annie shot him a wry look.

"I'll look at it," he said.

"Are you really gonna get a gun, Mom?" Matty asked.

"Yes, I believe I will. And Matty, make sure you don't tell anyone. It's just not a good idea for anyone else to know."

"Sure, Mom. No problem. I'll keep it shut and throw away the key."

Jake set his fork down, sat back, and stretched. "I may give the lawn a mowing later as well. Haven't had much time the last few days."

"I'll do it, Dad. After school."

Jake reached out and tousled Matty's hair. "Maybe I'll let you try in another year or so. I don't know if it's a good idea yet."

"I've watched you, Dad. It doesn't look that hard." He flexed a small bicep. "I think I can push that thing around."

Jake laughed. "Yeah, I'm sure you could, but it's a little dangerous."

"You could get hurt," Annie put in, and then wondered if she was a little overprotective.

Matty shrugged one shoulder and took the last bite of his toast. "Thanks for breakfast, Mom," he said as his fork clattered onto the empty plate. He charged from the room to get ready for school.

Jake helped Annie clean up the table and put the dishes in the sink. At six foot four inches, he towered over her by a foot as he leaned and gave her a quick peck on the lips. It became an extended kiss as she held onto him, thankful it had been her luck to meet such an amazing guy.

Without notice, Matty popped back into the room and whipped open the fridge. He grabbed his lunch from the middle shelf, flipped open his backpack, dropped the bag inside, and slung it over his back. "See you later, guys," he said and turned to leave.

"Hey, come back here," Annie said.

Matty trudged over to his mom, looked up, turned his head, and waited while she planted a kiss.

"You can go now," she said.

Annie watched as Matty wandered from the room. She frowned. "Do you think he's getting too old to kiss me?"

Jake shrugged. "Maybe." He pulled her a little closer. "But I'm not."

CHAPTER 3

Monday, August 22nd, 2:45 p.m.

JAKE WAS FINISHING an afternoon snack when the office phone rang. He wiped his hands and dashed from the kitchen, through the living room to the office. He dropped into a chair behind the desk and swooped up the phone.

"Lincoln Investigations."

"Hello, are you the investigator? I was told to call you ... my daughter ... it's my daughter. They ... they said she killed someone, and I don't know what to do. It's not true. I know it's not. Please help—"

Jake cut her off. "Ma'am, calm down, ma'am."

Silence on the line, and then Jake continued, "We'll do our best to help you. Everything will be all right, but please, take a deep breath and explain what happened."

Jake heard her breathe, and then, "My name is Cara Waters. My ... my daughter was arrested and they said she killed someone, but she couldn't have."

"We'll certainly look into it for you, and do what we can, but perhaps you would be better off with a lawyer?"

"Yes, yes, we've talked to a lawyer, but we're sure Cheryl, my daughter, didn't kill anyone. We need you to find out what this is all about. They say there are witnesses, but it just doesn't make sense."

Jake paused. "My wife and I will come and see you. When would be a good time?"

"As soon as possible, please."

"Then we'll come right away."

He made a note of her address and arranged to be there by 3:30. His brow wrinkled in thought as he hung up the phone. If there were solid witnesses, how could the girl's mother think her daughter hadn't killed anyone?

Annie was next door at her friend Chrissy's. He dialed her cell and filled her in. "You may want to ask Chrissy to watch for Matty. He'll be home from school soon and we won't be here."

Matty and Chrissy's son Kyle were the best of friends, and Chrissy was always eager to watch Matty if the Lincolns needed an urgent babysitter. Matty and Kyle hung around together most of their free time anyway, and Matty knew if he came home and his parents weren't there, he should go next door.

Jake slouched back in the swivel chair, dropped one foot on the desk, and twiddled the pen. Another murder case. He'd hoped they would have something a little safer to do for a while, but a client was a client, and she sounded desperate.

The small office was sparse. A couple of bookcases contained a set of encyclopedias as well as a few law books and manuals, gathering dust, the Internet being their main source of research now. An iMac sat on the desk, Annie's favorite tool. A filing cabinet with a printer perched on top, and a couple of extra chairs made up the rest of the room's contents.

When Jake heard the front door open, he stood and went to meet Annie.

"Just let me grab what I need," she said as she went to the kitchen and returned with a handbag. Jake knew it contained her notepad and pen along with a small digital recorder and other items she couldn't live without.

"We'll take your car," he said. "The Firebird's in the garage, and we're only going a few blocks."

Annie flipped her keys from a ring by the front door and followed Jake out. They jumped into her Ford Escort and she turned the key. She looked at Jake with a teasing smile. "The engine doesn't scratch anymore."

Jake laughed. "I just adjusted your fan belt. That's all it was."

Annie dropped the shifter and they pulled from the driveway. Jake gave her directions as they drove, and in a few minutes, they pulled in front of the Waters' house and stepped out.

It was a typical Canadian home. A single-car garage in front, a well-kept lawn with a few flowers and bushes sprinkled up the edge of the pathway and along the front of the house. A red Subaru sat in the driveway.

They walked up the short stone walkway to the front door and rang the bell.

The stress Mrs. Waters had endured for the last few hours was obvious when she opened the door. The strain shrouded her pudgy face as she asked, "Are you the Lincolns?"

Annie nodded. "We are."

She invited them in and motioned toward the front room. Mr. Waters stood and approached as they entered. "I'm Harold Waters," he said as he gestured toward a couch under the front window. "Have a seat."

Jake and Annie sat while Mrs. Waters perched on a straight-backed wooden chair and crossed her legs, her hands working nervously. Mr. Waters dropped into an armchair and leaned back comfortably.

Annie slipped the recorder from her bag. "Do you mind if I record this?" she asked as she set it on the coffee table in front of them.

Mr. Waters nodded and waved his hand. "Sure."

Jake studied Harold Waters. Though not as big around as his wife, he could afford to drop a few pounds. He had short reddish hair, and his matching beard was ragged and probably hadn't been trimmed for several days. He looked to be in his midforties, perhaps a couple of years older than his wife.

"Tell us what happened with your daughter," Annie said.

The distraught couple exchanged a glance. Mr. Waters spoke. "Our daughter went missing eight months ago. She's nineteen now, and for the last three or four years she hasn't lived here with us. She has always been rather flighty and irresponsible, and would be away for long periods, without a word from her, but usually only for a few weeks. When she disappeared eight months ago, we began to be concerned after a couple of months, so we reported her missing. The police were unable to find any trace of her."

"Until today," Mrs. Water interrupted. She seemed to be on the verge of tears. "They said she killed someone. But she didn't. I know she didn't."

Mr. Waters reached out and touched his wife's hand. "It's okay, dear, we'll get to the bottom of this."

Mrs. Waters sighed and dropped her head a moment, and then looked up again, but remained silent.

"So now your daughter is back?" Jake asked.

"Yes, yes," Mr. Waters said. "She's been arrested. We haven't been allowed to talk to her yet. They only let us look through a window, and it's her." His voice quivered as he continued, "She's in jail. According to the police, two witnesses said she walked into an office and shot someone. They called the police and she was arrested."

Jake crossed his arms and looked thoughtful. "Your wife mentioned you've seen a lawyer?"

"Yes, a legal aid lawyer, a public defender. He talked to Cheryl briefly, and she gave him her name, and he called us," Mr. Waters said with a quick glance at his wife. "I'm afraid we can't afford a real lawyer."

Jake sat back. He knew public defenders were real lawyers, but they could only put up a basic defense, with no resources to do in-depth investigating.

"Our daughter has always been somewhat of a free spirit," Mr. Waters continued, "but she's a good girl. She has never shown any tendency toward violence of any kind. Rather the opposite. She loves kids, animals, and everything else. This isn't like her at all. There has to be another answer."

"We'll talk to your daughter," Annie said. "That's our first step. We'll see what she has to say, and then we'll get a copy of the police report and talk to the witnesses."

"Can you get this sorted out?" Mrs. Waters asked.

Annie gave her a calming smile. "We can't promise anything, Mrs. Waters, but we'll give this top priority. We'll know more after we talk to Cheryl."

"Is there anything else you can tell us?" Jake asked.

"That's all we know," Mr. Waters said. "Like I said, we haven't been able to talk to Cheryl yet." He moistened his lips. "I hope they'll let you see her."

"They will," Annie said. "Cheryl is entitled to the best defense possible." She flashed a smile. "Besides, we know a lot of the police officers."

Jake leaned forward. "If there's nothing else, we'll get on this right away."

"That's all I can think of," Mr. Waters said.

Jake stood and dug a business card from his top pocket. He handed it to Mr. Waters. "If there's anything else, give us a call."

Annie leaned forward and picked up the recorder. She snapped it off, dropped it in her handbag and stood.

They shook hands and Mr. Waters followed them to the door.

"We'll let you know what we come up with," Jake said, as they stepped outside. The door closed behind them and they made their way down the driveway and climbed into the Escort.

"It looks pretty grim," Jake said as he glanced at Annie.

Annie started the engine and nodded. "Very grim, indeed."

CHAPTER 4

Monday, August 22nd, 3:35 p.m.

DETECTIVE HANK CORNING had never seen a more curious case.

He dropped the report on his desk and slouched back, gazing vaguely across the precinct, unaware of the constant buzz of bustling officers occupied with their tasks. An air conditioner rattled nearby in a useless attempt to cool the air. The ringing of phones and the tramping of duty boots on the wooden floor went unnoticed as Hank contemplated the facts.

He'd interviewed Cheryl Waters extensively and was convinced she was either a good liar, or telling the truth and unaware of what she'd done.

He'd been puzzling over this case for the last four hours. He'd talked to Cheryl's parents, and neither of them knew Charles Robinson. He couldn't find a motive, and he couldn't find a connection between Robinson and the killer.

But the facts were clear. Cheryl Waters had killed a man in cold blood. She didn't fit the profile of a cold-blooded killer, and Hank was puzzled.

A light vibration at his hip brought him out of his thoughts. He slipped his phone from its holder and looked at the caller ID.

"Hey, Jake. What's up?"

"Afternoon, Hank. How's everything?"

"Good," Hank replied. "I bet I know why you're calling. It's Cheryl Waters, right?"

"We just got back from interviewing her parents. How'd you know?"

"I gave Cheryl's parents your number and recommended they call you. They're going to need all the help they can get on this. I don't know what you can do, though. There's no disputing, Cheryl killed the guy, but her parents were adamant there's more to this."

"I don't think they're disputing it," Jake said. "But they want to find out what it's all about. They've been unable to see their daughter, and they don't expect much of a defense from their lawyer."

"I need to get out of this place for a while. I can drop a copy of the police report over to you if you want. That may give you somewhere to start, but it's a tough one."

"That would be great," Jake said. "We're at home now if you want to come by."

"See you soon."

Hank dropped the phone back into its holster and leaned forward. He scooped up the papers from his desk, dropped them into a file folder, stood, and carried them across the room to the photocopier against the back wall. He made a copy of the report, returned to his desk, and slipped the copies into his briefcase.

When he stepped outside, he was greeted by a refreshing breeze, a welcome change to the stifling atmosphere inside the precinct. He went behind the building and climbed into his 2008 Chevy. The engine cranked a couple of times when he turned the key, then settled into a steady purr.

As he drove across town, he considered the circumstances of this case. As head of Richmond Hill's robbery/homicide division, he knew he must pursue any solid leads, but the captain would only cut him a limited amount of slack. His job was to report the facts and let the crown prosecute. He wasn't free to pursue unfounded leads in the search for exculpatory evidence. That would be up to the defense.

He hoped Jake and Annie could come up with something. Though the Lincolns were rookie investigators, Hank had confidence they could do better than most in digging out the truth. He'd known them for more years than he could remember. He and Jake had been teammates on the high school football team, and had been friends since. Annie and Jake had been seeing a lot of each other at the time, and they'd both decided to go to the University of Toronto while Hank had wanted to be a cop.

In a few minutes, he turned onto Carver Street and spun into the driveway behind Annie's Escort. He grabbed his briefcase, hopped out, and went to the front door.

Jake answered his ring with a grin. "Come on in." As Hank stepped inside, Jake slugged him on the shoulder and pushed him toward the kitchen. "If you're feeling brave, I just made a fresh pot of coffee. You can let me know how it tastes."

Annie greeted Hank and poured three steaming cups, while the guys made themselves comfortable at the table. She passed the coffee around, brought some cream and sugar, and then sat at the end and leaned forward, her arms resting on the table.

Hank fixed his coffee, took a swig, and then looked at Jake. "Not as good as Annie's, but it's okay." He snapped open his briefcase. He withdrew the papers and dropped them on the table. "There's not a lot here," he said. "It's fairly straightforward, but you're welcome to do what you can with the information."

Annie browsed the report and sipped her coffee thoughtfully.

"Hank," Annie said, "do you have any indication why Cheryl killed ..." She consulted the paper and continued, "Charles Robinson?"

Hank shook his head. "I can't get anything from her, and her parents have no idea what this is all about. When she was arrested, she had no identification on her. Nothing at all in her pockets, only the handbag she apparently used to carry the gun. It was otherwise empty. She gave me her name, I checked it out, and her parents IDed her. That's how we knew who she was."

Annie asked, "Did Cheryl admit she did this?"

"She said she didn't remember anything about it."

Jake frowned and set his cup down. "How can she not remember?"

Hank shook his head slowly. "I don't know what to make of it. Though she claims she doesn't remember, it doesn't make a whole lot of sense. She doesn't seem to be lying."

"What about a polygraph test?" Jake asked.

Hank shrugged. "That's something the defense should look into. It's not admissible in court, however, but it wouldn't hurt, just so you know where you stand."

Annie nodded. "That sounds like a good idea," she said and then asked, "So what'll happen with Cheryl now?"

"I expect she'll be arraigned in the morning," Hank said. "There's no way she'll be granted bail. She's been gone for eight months and now she's back, but she's too much of a flight risk. She'll probably be dumped into the women's detention center until the trial."

Annie looked at Jake. "We have to go and see her this afternoon."

The back door clattered and Matty charged in, shadowed by Kyle. "Hi, Uncle Hank," Matty said as he came over to Hank and greeted him with a fist bump.

Hank messed up Matty's hair. "What're you up to, Bud?"

"Not much. Just teaching Kyle a couple of wrestling moves."

Hank laughed. "He couldn't have a better teacher."

"Yeah, maybe. Anyway, I just wanted to say hello. I guess we should get back at it. Come on, Kyle." Matty grabbed his friend by the arm and the back door slammed as they left.

"Where were we?" Annie asked.

"You wanted to see Cheryl this afternoon," Jake said.

"It would be less red tape to see her now, rather than when she's locked up in the detention center," Hank said.

"Then we'll go right away."

Hank guzzled the rest of his coffee. He sat back and ran his fingers through his short-cropped, slightly graying hair, then stretched. "I guess I better get going," he said. "I have some other things to take care of today." He stood and headed for the front door. "I hope you can get something out of Cheryl."

Jake walked him to the door. "I hope so too," he said as Hank left.

Hank walked to his vehicle and jumped in. He started his car and drove away, wondering if there was more to this case than appeared.

Whether Cheryl was a callous killer, or there was some other explanation, he knew from experience what kind of heartache there could be when it came to children, no matter what their age.

He was married once, a long time ago. They'd had a daughter, Beth, but her heartbreaking death from a brain tumor at six months old had been devastating. His wife, Elizabeth, had never recovered from their loss, and it had been the catalyst that had driven them apart and ended their marriage.

He sympathized with Cheryl's parents and hoped Jake and Annie could come up with something, but he wasn't feeling all that optimistic.

CHAPTER 5

Monday, August 22nd, 4:00 p.m.

ANNIE GAVE CHRISSY a quick call and asked her to watch Matty while they went to the precinct to interview Cheryl. Chrissy agreed, and Annie poked her head out the back door, where the boys were kicking around a soccer ball. She called Matty, explaining they had to go out awhile.

"No problem, Mom. See you later."

She flipped open her handbag and checked the batteries in her digital recorder. Lots of power. She hung the bag over her shoulder and met Jake at the front door.

"All ready?" he asked.

She nodded, and they stepped outside. Jake had pulled the Firebird from the garage, and the motor rumbled as they climbed into the vehicle, and then roared as they pulled from the driveway.

In five minutes, they turned into a visitor's slot at the rear of Richmond Hill Police Precinct. They hopped out, made their way to the front of the ancient building, climbed the concrete steps, and went through the double doors into the bustling room.

At the duty desk, an officer leaned forward out of a slouch and grinned. "Hey, Jake. Hey, Annie."

Annie smiled. "Hi, Yappy."

"Haven't seen you guys around for a while."

Officer Spiegle was called Yappy by almost everyone. No one knew how he got the name, but he seemed to like it. He wasn't much of a cop, though. Normally, he would've been passed over during the hiring phase, but his daddy had been a well-respected sergeant who had been killed in the line of duty, and so Yappy was tolerated.

"We're here to see Cheryl Waters," Jake said.

"Sure, she's downstairs." Yappy came around the desk. "I just have to check your stuff first."

He gave Annie an obligatory search by peeking in her handbag, and then looked at Jake. "You carrying any weapons?"

Jake laughed and held up his massive fists. "Just these."

Spiegle shrugged. "I had to ask. You know how it is." He motioned toward the back of the room. "This way."

They followed him across the precinct floor to a secure door. Spiegle fiddled with some keys and finally swung it open. "You know the way," he said.

"Thanks, Yappy," Jake said as they entered into a short hallway, opened another door, and descended the stifling stairwell to the holding cells beneath the precinct.

As they approached the central control desk, a young deputy looked up.

"I'm Annie Lincoln. We'd like to see Cheryl Waters."

The deputy turned to an idle cop slouching at his desk. "Bring Waters out." He turned back and fiddled with some papers. He drew an *x* at the bottom of a page and flipped it around. "Sign here."

Annie signed the sheet and the deputy grunted and slipped it into a slot beside him. "She'll be ready in a minute."

Jake and Annie sat, occupying the only two seats in the waiting room.

Except for the occasional faint shout of an unhappy prisoner, which could be heard coming from behind a thick metal door at the far side of the room, it was deathly quiet. The solid door, with a bulletproof window, led into the area where the holding cells were. There were six cells, three on each side of a passageway. Prisoners were held there awaiting arraignment, or temporarily before transport to prison, or sometimes the cells were used as an overnight "drunk tank."

Far away, the banging of a metal door echoed. The sound reverberated for a moment, and then all was quiet.

In a couple of minutes, the cop returned and approached them. "She's ready for you."

They followed him through another doorway and down a short hall to a room guarded by an officer. He swung the door open, allowing them to enter.

The interview room was a small, soundproofed area, with two chairs on the near side of a shiny metal table, and one on the other. Bright overhead lights shone on the barren, blank walls. Cheryl Waters sat at the far side, her head bowed, her wrists cuffed to a ring on the table.

They sat, and Annie snapped open her handbag and removed the recorder. She set it on the table, switched it on, and leaned forward, resting her arms on the cold metal surface.

The frightened young girl raised her head. The redness in her eyes showed she'd been crying. Her long dark hair was in disarray, dripping down below her shoulders onto the bright orange jumpsuit. She fidgeted with her hands, and her body trembled.

Annie spoke softly. "I'm Annie Lincoln, and this is my

husband, Jake. We're private investigators. Your parents hired us to find out what this is all about."

"I ... I don't know," Cheryl said. "They told me I killed someone, but I don't remember." She closed her eyes and took a deep breath before continuing, "Please help me."

"We'll do our best," Jake said. "But we need to know exactly what you do remember."

"I was out west," Cheryl said. "I was in Calgary for a few months, and then decided to come home for Christmas. I got back to the city about the twentieth of December." She frowned, looking confused. "But that was last year, and now they tell me this is August."

"Where have you been for the last eight months?" Annie asked.

Cheryl shook her head slowly, her eyes squinting in thought. "I ... I don't know. It doesn't make sense to me."

"Did you come back from out west alone?" Jake asked.

"Yes. I took the bus."

"Did you meet anyone on the bus?"

"I talked to a few people. I was sitting with a nice old lady, and we talked a lot."

"Did anything happen on the bus, or after you got here, that seemed out of place? Anyone suspicious you may have talked to, or met?"

Cheryl shook her head. "Nobody."

Annie sat back and looked into Cheryl's pleading eyes, trying to understand. The girl was doubtless confused. Was it possible she had amnesia, and was telling the truth?

"Did you see your parents at Christmas?" Annie asked.

"I saw them a couple of days before." Cheryl frowned as if deep in thought, her hands still working nervously. "But I don't remember seeing them on Christmas Day."

"And that's the last you remember?" Annie asked.

Cheryl nodded.

Jake spoke. "And you don't remember going into Bonfield Development and shooting Charles Robinson?"

Cheryl shook her head, her voice trembling. "No, I don't remember." She paused. "I would never kill anyone."

"What do you remember about this morning?" Annie asked.

"All I remember is, I was in the office and a woman was holding on to me. A man was ... on the floor ... dead. The police came and arrested me. They said I killed him."

"Do you know Charles Robinson?" Jake asked.

Cheryl shook her head vigorously. "I've never heard of him before."

"And yet, there are two witnesses who said you shot him, and your fingerprints are on the gun."

"I ... I can't explain it," Cheryl said as she dropped her head. "I just can't explain it."

Annie glanced at Jake. He looked back and shrugged his shoulders, a puzzled look on his face.

"A lawyer came to see me," Cheryl said quietly. "He said they would take me to see the judge in the morning, and that ..." Her voice broke, and she blinked in a futile attempt to hold back the tears. "He said I should plead guilty, and—"

"No, no," Annie interrupted. "You must plead not guilty. If you plead guilty, it's over."

"But he said there's too much proof I did it."

"Yes, there certainly seems to be enough proof. However, a trial will give us some time to figure this out and help with your defense."

"But what if he insists I plead guilty?"

"He has to do as you ask. He works for you."

Cheryl nodded slowly. "Okay."

"No matter what he says, plead not guilty."

"I will," Cheryl said, her voice firm, and then hopeful as she asked, "Do you think you can help me?"

"We'll do our best," Jake said. "Is there anything else you can tell us? Anything at all?"

"I ... I'm sorry. There's nothing I can think of."

Annie sat back and studied Cheryl. She needed a lead. Something to look into, but she didn't know where to start. She leaned forward and placed her hand on Cheryl's. "Don't give up hope. We'll do everything we can to help you."

"Okay," Cheryl said softly.

Annie stood, turned, and tapped on the glass window of the secure door. The guard opened it for them. She looked over her shoulder as they left. Cheryl was watching them leave, her eyes pleading for some help in this dreadful situation.

As they climbed the stairs to the main floor, Jake asked, "Do you think she's telling the truth?"

"I don't know," Annie said. "But she sure doesn't seem like a killer."

"And yet, she is."

"Yes, she is, but there's got to be an explanation." Annie wrinkled her brow. "It almost seems like she may have been under some kind of hypnotism or something."

"Or maybe drugs." Jake opened the upper door and they stepped into the precinct. He stopped and turned to face Annie. "Where do we start?"

Annie took a deep breath and exhaled slowly. "I don't know."

CHAPTER 6

Monday, August 22nd, 5:15 p.m.

JAKE LEANED AGAINST the fender of the Firebird, folded his arms, and watched Annie pull the police report from her handbag and study it.

"I think perhaps the best idea is to interview the witnesses," she said as she flipped through the pages. "There was one actual witness to the shooting. The receptionist at Bonfield Development. The other one was in an adjoining office and heard the shots."

"Sounds like a good plan to me."

"I'd better give her a call first." Annie dug her cell phone from her handbag, consulted the report, and dialed.

Jake straightened and opened the vehicle door. He climbed in and started the engine, revving it up, and then flipped his sunglasses on and watched as Annie edged around the front of the car, her head down, concentrating on the phone call. He saw her smile and nod, and then click off the phone and drop it in her handbag. As she climbed into the car and fastened her seat belt, Jake looked at her, a question on his face.

"She's rather upset," Annie said, "but she's eager to talk to us."

"You have her address there?"

Annie nodded.

Jake pulled the gearshift into first and touched the gas pedal heavier than was necessary, considering the power under the hood. The tires squealed as the car leaped forward and sped across the lot. "Just tell me which way to go," he said.

"Her name is Sally Flint. She lives a few blocks away. Take a right and go down to Main."

Jake waved to a cop, who'd stepped from the precinct, frowning as the Hurst mufflers roared and the Firebird spun past him onto the street.

Annie guided Jake, and after a few minutes, they pulled in front of a small bungalow on a street lined on both sides with uniform houses. Towering trees shaded the cobbled street and well-trimmed lawns in front of the tiny clapboard dwellings.

They stepped from the vehicle and took the short path to the front door. Jake rang the bell and it was answered almost immediately.

Sally Flint was a pleasant-looking woman, maybe in her midsixties, with graying hair tucked into a neat bun on the back of her head. As they introduced themselves, she managed a weak smile and invited them in.

The small front room she led them to looked like an antique shop. Fading pictures hung in ornate frames, outdated wallpaper covered the walls, ancient wooden chairs were scattered about, and tables were littered with knickknacks and photos of moments long past. A tattered rug covered most of the sturdy hardwood floor.

She motioned toward a florid sofa with elaborately carved arms and legs. Jake and Annie sat as Sally perched in a matching chair on the other side of a crowded coffee table. She leaned forward, hands folded in her lap, her face tense.

"Thanks for seeing us," Annie said.

"I don't know how I can help," Sally said, her voice breaking. "I told everything to the police."

"I realize that," Annie said as she felt in her handbag and removed a notepad and pen. "But we need to go over it and get a feel for ourselves."

"Such a shocking affair." Sally frowned and shook her head. "A terrible, terrible thing. I've never seen anything like it."

"I realize how hard it must have been for you," Annie said, "but could you go over everything from the beginning?"

Sally nodded. "I'll try." She paused a moment before continuing, "It was such a pleasant morning. Mr. Robinson was such a nice man, you know." Her voice quivered. "He'd been away for a week and got back over the weekend. He had some big deal going on. Bidding on some properties, I think. He was the president and CEO of Bonfield. Forever busy, but he always had time for the people who worked for him."

Jake asked, "Can you tell us a bit about what Bonfield Development does?"

Sally smiled. "Most people have probably never heard of the company, but we've built high-rises all over the city. Bonfield is a booming company, and like I said, Mr. Robinson was always cooking up a deal."

"Would Bonfield Place happen to be one of them?" Annie asked.

"Yes, it sure is. Probably the biggest project, and one of the best-known retail and office complexes in the downtown area."

Jake glanced at Annie. "I've been there," he said. "It's an impressive building."

"Can you tell us about this morning when Cheryl Waters arrived?" Annie asked.

28

Sally cocked her head. "Is that ... the girl's name?"

Annie nodded. "Yes, we spoke to her a few minutes ago."

Sally thought a moment before speaking. "The girl ... she came in, and said she was there to see Charles Robinson, so I buzzed him on the intercom and he came out."

"She had an appointment?" Jake asked.

"Yes, she did. For eight thirty. She was a few minutes early, but Mr. Robinson was able to see her right away."

Annie was writing in her notepad. She looked up and asked, "What was her demeanor? Any unusual behavior?"

"She seemed pleasant enough, but businesslike. Not smiling or anything, just straight to the point."

"Did she have the gun in her hand at the time?"

"Oh, no."

"So she didn't appear to be a threat in any way?"

"Not at all."

"Okay, please continue."

"Well, like I said, I buzzed Mr. Robinson, and he came out to meet her, and then ..." She took a deep breath and closed her eyes briefly. "And then ... she just shot him." She reached into her sleeve and pulled out a tissue, dabbing at her eyes.

"Did you actually see her shoot him?" Jake asked.

"No, she was behind me. She walked past reception and into the main area. I turned back to my desk as Mr. Robinson came out. That's when ... that's when I heard the shot."

"Just one shot?"

"Two shots before I could turn around, and when I saw him, he'd fallen to the floor." She paused and dabbed at her eyes again. Her voice shook. "Then she just pointed the gun and shot him again." She sat back and closed her eyes, dropping her head back. "Dear, dear." She sighed deeply. "What a terrible mess."

Jake waited a moment, allowing Sally to regain her composure. She reminded him of his own grandmother, a sweet old woman who'd left Jake with many fond memories of his childhood. As a boy, it seemed she always had special and interesting things for them to do. He was feeling a touch nostalgic just thinking about her. And so, he felt kindly toward Sally. Finally, he asked gently, "And then what happened?"

Sally brought her head back down and opened her eyes. "And then, Fred came out. I tried to stop the girl from leaving, but she didn't struggle or put up much resistance at all. I called Fred to help me. He came over and held the girl while I called the police."

Jake waited for her to continue.

"The girl seemed confused. She said she didn't know what had happened. She didn't believe us when we told her she'd shot Mr. Robinson."

"Yes," Annie said. "She told us the same thing. That she doesn't remember."

Sally frowned. "How could someone not remember? It seems odd to me."

"Yes, it certainly does," Annie said. "We're trying to understand it as well."

"And then, the police came and arrested her," Sally said. "A nice policeman asked me a few questions and gave me a ride home. I certainly was in no condition to take the bus."

"Mrs. Flint," Annie said, and then hesitated. "Is it possible Mr. Robinson was having an affair?"

Sally seemed offended by the question. "Oh, no. Never. His wife dropped by from time to time. They're such a lovely couple." She shook her head, frowning. "I would find it hard to believe anything like that was going on."

Annie smiled an apology. "I had to ask. We're looking for

a motive." She paused before asking, "Can you think of anyone who would want to harm Mr. Robinson? Any enemies you know of?"

Sally shook her head. "Not that I know of. Everybody loved him."

There was silence for a few moments as Annie jotted in her notepad.

Finally, Jake asked, "Do you live by yourself?"

"Yes, yes. My husband passed on a few years ago. A bad heart. He worked for Bonfield for many years, and dear Mr. Robinson gave me a job after my Billy passed."

Annie looked concerned. "Will you be okay here by yourself?" she asked.

Sally sighed and smiled thinly. "I'll be okay. I've had a bit of heartache in my life."

"Be sure to call if you need someone to talk to," Annie said. "In the meantime, can you think of anything else about this morning?"

"I believe that's all," Sally said, her voice barely rising above a whisper.

Jake stood and offered his hand. "Thanks for seeing us."

Annie stood and dropped her notepad into her handbag and dug out a business card. She handed it to Sally. "Here's our number. Feel free to call."

Sally stood, followed them to the door, and let them out.

After they made it down the walkway to the road and climbed into the car, Annie turned to Jake. "Such a sweet lady. I do hope she'll be okay."

Jake shrugged as he pushed the key into the ignition and started the Firebird. "She'll be all right," he said.

CHAPTER 7

Monday, August 22nd, 7:08 p.m.

OLIVER CRAIG dropped the folder onto his desk and raised his head as he heard a light tapping on his office door. He looked toward the sound. "Yes, what is it?" he demanded, annoyance in his voice.

The heavy oak door inched open, and a middle-aged woman stepped into the office, one hand tucked into the pocket of her simple white uniform. "He would like to see you, sir," she said.

"I'll be right there."

The woman turned, and the soft patter of her comfortable nurses' shoes on the marble floor faded away.

Oliver pushed back his chair, his dark eyes thoughtful, as he stared across the luxurious room. His father was dying; there was no doubt about that. He'd been dying for more than a year, but it now appeared he could be in his last days. When his father had first been diagnosed with a brain tumor, he'd entrusted Oliver with information about certain research—research Oliver was unaware his father had been involved in. Hundreds of files, years of important and valuable research. Research that was now going to make him rich beyond his wildest dreams.

He brushed a hand through his slicked-back graying hair and wondered what the old man wanted this time. Probably the same thing as usual. His father's mind appeared to be rapidly deteriorating, his memory certainly not what it once was.

He didn't want to be disturbed right now. Something had gone wrong with their first operation, and he was trying to figure out why. Perhaps things weren't as prepared as they had thought. He couldn't afford another slip-up like this one. Something had to be done about it.

He sighed, tossed his pen onto the desk and rose to his feet. Better see what his father wanted.

He left the office, made his way down a long hallway, and stopped in front of an open door. He never liked going in there. The room smelled of death, and he hated the taste of the sterile atmosphere in his mouth and the sounds of the equipment as it hummed and pumped, prolonging the old man's life.

He took a breath and stepped inside the room. The nurse was perched in a chair by the bed, a book in her hands, reading by the fading evening sun that lit the otherwise darkened chamber as she kept vigil over the dying man.

"You can leave us for now," Oliver said.

The nurse closed her book and slid it on a stand beside her. She left the room and closed the door quietly.

Oliver dropped into a chair beside the bed and leaned forward. He studied his father, pale and thin, wasting away, a skeleton covered in paper-white skin. His hair was sparse, not much more than a few strands of white protruding in patches from his otherwise bald head.

The old man turned his head toward his son. "Hello, Oliver," he said, his breathing shallow, his voice raspy.

"Hello, Father. How are you feeling this evening?"

The aged mouth forced a weak smile, a strange softness in his voice as he said, "Very weak. But it's good to see you."

That was something Oliver hadn't heard often. The gentleness apparent even through the hoarseness of his voice, and the warm eyes his father now had, were unknown to him. His father always had hard eyes, demanding eyes, piercing eyes. And a sharp voice, never satisfied, always requiring more. Unlike his mother, who'd been weak, submissive, and withdrawn.

The faint voice rasped again, "Oliver, I need you to do something for me."

"Yes?"

The feeble man took a slow breath and his voice labored as he spoke. "My notes. I want you to burn them."

Oliver frowned. "Burn them? But they are your life's work. They contain all of your research and may be important someday."

The old man closed his eyes and shook his head slowly. "No. You must destroy them. Promise me you will. They are dangerous."

Oliver nodded. "I'll destroy them."

The frail man lifted his arm. "Give me your hand, Oliver."

Oliver was repulsed as he reached out and held the dying hand. It felt like the hand of a child. Small, flimsy, helpless, and repugnant. He swallowed the distaste he felt as he looked into his father's pleading eyes. He saw in them a clarity, and a determined sense of purpose he'd never seen before.

"I should've burned them long ago," the frail man continued. "I should never have given them to you. You will destroy them, won't you, Oliver?"

Oliver nodded and repeated, "I'll destroy them."

"We did some terrible things." The old man coughed weakly. "Unspeakable things. The world must never know the full truth of what was done."

"It will never know," Oliver promised.

His father's searching eyes studied his and then, seemingly satisfied he'd heard the truth, he closed his eyes. Oliver dropped the weakened hand and watched as his father rested, his breathing shallow.

Oliver leaned back and contemplated for a moment. His father had taught him well in his better days, and he'd learned much. He'd learned a promise made was as easily broken if the situation demanded it. His father wasn't in his right mind. Oliver knew if he was, he would never have asked for his research to be destroyed. It was important and, if handled properly, would bring him the power he deserved. Money and power.

He'd given up much for that power. He'd been married once. His wife had left him a long time ago, taking his young son with her. It was just as well. He'd had more important things to do and hadn't had time for them. And now, when that elusive power was within his reach, almost in his grasp, he couldn't allow a sudden burst of his father's confused conscience to stand in his way. He couldn't let a promise to a senile old man put a stop to his dreams.

Besides, he had come too far.

He rose to his feet and, turning his back on the sleeping invalid, strode from the room.

CHAPTER 8

Monday, August 22nd, 7:45 p.m.

ANNIE DROPPED INTO the swivel chair and pulled it closer to the desk. She touched the space bar on the keyboard and in a few moments the iMac woke up, the monitor revealing a photo of Matty and Jake in one of their many wrestling bouts.

She booted up Safari, googled Bonfield Development, and was presented with several pages of information on the massive company.

A quick study showed Bonfield owned and developed hotels, resorts, and residential towers in different countries, as well as owning several pieces of high-end real estate in most major cities.

A recent news story stated that the company's president and CEO, Charles Robinson, was bidding on a select piece of land in the downtown area of Richmond Hill. His chief competitor was Sheridan Construction, another large development corporation.

It was estimated the land, not counting any value from the buildings, could be worth more than $20 million. According to the news story, it was expected Bonfield would win the bid. They planned to build another upscale office tower, their third in the city, and it was predicted to overshadow even the prestigious Bonfield Place.

Charles Robinson appeared to be the catalyst in all of the corporation's undertakings. Annie wondered how the bidding would go now that he was dead.

Her thoughts were interrupted by a crash from the living room. She rolled her eyes and shook her head. The guys had broken something else.

"Can't you boys take that outside?" she shouted.

"Sorry, honey," she heard back.

"Sorry, Mom."

She pushed back from her chair and wandered into the living room. Jake was examining a leg of the coffee table, which appeared to have been the latest victim of their carousing. He looked at her sheepishly. "No problem. I can fix it."

"That's the second time you broke that table," Annie said.

"Yeah, and maybe not the last." Jake raised his arm and examined his bruised elbow. "Better to have a broken table than a broken arm."

"You're not as tough as you look, big guy," Matty said.

Jake glared at him. "I'll get you next time."

Annie laughed, dropped onto the couch, and tucked her legs underneath her. She was pleased she could laugh off the incident. It was only a table, but she had struggled a lot with her inclination to be like her mother, who ruled her house with a sharp voice, demanding everyone adhere to her stringent demands.

Matty strolled from the room as Jake plunked into the armchair. "Did you find out anything about Bonfield?" he asked.

Annie nodded. "Quite a bit. They're a pretty large company—" She was interrupted by the doorbell ringing.

"That'll be Hank," Jake said as he rose to his feet.

Matty charged from the kitchen, got to the front door first, and swung it open. "Hey, Uncle Hank. Come on in."

Hank messed up Matty's hair the way he always did. "Hey, Matty."

Jake appeared in the foyer. "We're in the living room."

Hank followed Jake into the room, sat on the couch, leaned back, and relaxed, while Jake returned to the armchair. Matty plopped in between Hank and his mother.

"We dropped by the precinct today and talked to Cheryl," Jake said.

"Did you get anything interesting from her?" Hank asked.

Jake shrugged. "Not really. She claims she doesn't remember anything."

"That's basically all I got too."

"She seems believable," Annie said.

"But she's still a killer," Hank said. "There's no way around that. The thing that escapes me is motive. I couldn't find any connection between Robinson or Bonfield to either Cheryl or her parents."

"I find it hard to believe she could be a hired killer. That seems pretty ridiculous. She's not the type," Jake said.

"Most killers don't seem like killers on the surface," Hank said.

"Who benefits?" Annie asked. "Does Cheryl benefit from Robinson's death at all? If not, who does?"

"Follow the money," Jake said. "It's almost always love or money."

Matty listened intently, his head twisting back and forth as he followed the conversation. In the past, Annie had tried to shield him from any discussions they had regarding murder or crime, but Matty had recently straightened them out about his understanding of what some people did to others. Annie had relented and allowed him to listen in unless things got too gruesome.

"There's certainly lots of money in this case," Annie said. "I did some research into Bonfield Development. They're a multibillion dollar company."

"And I have my guys checking a little deeper into Robinson's background, as well as his wife's. I talked to her. She's distraught, of course, but if there were any affairs going on, we need to find that out."

"According to her receptionist," Annie said, "they were a lovely couple, and she was adamant neither one of them would have an affair."

"If that's the case," Jake put in, "then it's the money. Again, who benefits?"

Hank flipped a notepad from his inner pocket and consulted it. "Besides his wife, he has a son, Richard. He's on the board of directors at Bonfield. We're checking into him, as well as all of the other board members, but he's not a priority suspect."

"Sheridan Construction," Annie said.

Hank glanced over at her. "Who?"

"Sheridan Construction. They're Bonfield's chief competitors in a bidding war going on for a prime piece of land downtown. They would certainly benefit by his death."

Hank thought a moment. "It's a possibility," he said. "But big land deals go on all the time, and people don't usually get killed over them."

"Just a thought," Annie said.

Matty seemed to be getting bored with the conversation.

He slid off the couch, left the room, and disappeared down the hallway toward the kitchen. Annie heard the back door slap shut as he went out to the backyard.

Hank spoke. "I'm going to push the crown to ask the judge for a mental health hearing. If the prosecuting attorney is convinced Cheryl is unable to proceed because she has a serious mental issue, he must bring this to the court's attention. I expect the judge will order a competency examination be conducted and appoint a psychiatrist or psychologist to conduct it."

"At least that should give us a diagnosis of her mental condition," Annie said.

"And whether or not she's faking it," Jake added. "But she's still a murderer."

"Yes, she is," Hank said. "But we want to find out why. I've questioned a lot of suspects in the last twenty years, and I have a pretty good idea if someone's lying or not. And my gut tells me Cheryl is seriously confused."

"So you hope a psychiatrist can get something out of her you can't?" Annie asked.

"Exactly. I don't expect she'll be found incompetent to stand trial. That's not the issue with me. I want to get at the truth."

"Yeah, so do we," Jake said. "We're just not sure what our next move is."

"We'll see what tomorrow brings," Annie said. "Today was a pretty eventful day."

Hank looked at his watch. "I have to get going in a minute. Amelia's expecting me by eight o'clock or so."

"Another big date?" Jake asked.

Hank grinned. "Something like that."

Amelia was the mother of a victim in a recent case Hank

had worked on with the Lincolns. Everything had turned out well, and she and Hank had hit it off after that.

Hank continued, "We thought we might check out that new place, Tommy Marino's. I hear the food is pretty good there."

"How are Amelia and Jenny?" Annie asked.

"They're both doing great," Hank said. "And still putting up with me."

"That's a miracle," Jake said, then looked over toward Annie. "You still didn't get that pistol you were talking about."

"We've been pretty busy. I didn't have time to look into it."

"Yeah, we have been."

"Maybe tomorrow," she said.

"Yeah, maybe."

"You're buying a gun?" Hank asked.

"I thought I might get a small one. For protection."

"Do you realize Canadian law doesn't allow private investigators, even licensed ones, to carry a pistol?"

Annie's mouth dropped open a moment. "I didn't know that."

"Yeah, anyone can own one if they pass a test and don't have a criminal record. Then they need to get the proper license, but they still can't carry it, except to and from a firing range. And even then, there're a whole lot of rules about what they have to carry it in. And private investigators are treated no differently than the general public."

"So what good is owning one?" Jake asked.

"Not much good. Just for sport."

"So much for that idea," Annie said.

"Why didn't you know this before?" Hank asked.

Annie shrugged. "I've never thought about it. We're still pretty new at this investigating thing. Originally, it was all research and background checks. Nothing dangerous. I never thought I would need one, but lately we've been running into a whole lot of bad guys."

Jake added, "And bad guys don't care about a license to carry a gun. If they're caught, carrying a concealed weapon is the least of their worries."

Hank laughed. "You're allowed to carry handcuffs and a baton, if that makes you feel any better."

"Not much protection from a guy with a gun, is it?" Annie said. "Hey, you, put that gun down and hold still there, fella, while I hit you with my baton and then handcuff you."

Jake chuckled and held up his massive fists. "It's a good thing I have these."

CHAPTER 9

Monday, August 22nd, 8:03 p.m.

OLIVER CRAIG's months of preparation and planning had resulted in a situation less than ideal. Sure, the outcome had been as planned, but the girl was a loose end that wasn't supposed to exist.

He leaned forward in his chair, picked up the telephone, and dialed a number from memory.

"Yes?"

"Wolff, it's Craig."

"Yes, Mr. Craig."

"You messed up," Craig said. "What happened? The girl survived."

"I don't know how that happened, sir. We thought we had her fully prepared. All the tests were positive, and there was no indication whatsoever there might be a complication."

Craig thought a moment before speaking. "We don't have the resources to deal with her. Will she be a problem?"

"I don't believe so."

Craig thought he heard apprehension in the voice. He sat back and took a deep breath. "Is the boy ready?" he asked.

"I believe so, sir."

Craig wrinkled his brow. "You don't sound so sure."

The voice on the phone hesitated. "He's ready, sir."

"Wolff, I know you're the best there is. I have complete faith in your abilities, but we can't afford the next operation to go wrong. Do you hear me?"

"Yes, sir. The boy has been thoroughly tested, and we're satisfied he's ready." Silence on the phone, and then, "The girl had a strong will. It was evident at first; however, we were convinced it had been overcome." More silence. "It seems we were mistaken."

"That'd better be the only slip-up. Are we on schedule for tomorrow?"

"We're all ready to go," Wolff said, and then paused and asked, "How's your father?"

"Not so good. He won't last much longer."

"He was a genius, and I learned a lot from him," Wolff said. "But that was a long time ago, before the operation was abandoned and he pursued other things."

"And now I've given you a chance to resume your research. We'll all benefit from this."

Wolff hesitated. "I appreciate the opportunity; it's just that … well, it's important research, but …"

Craig raised his voice slightly and said, "We've been over this before. I've given you an opportunity you never would have had otherwise. Don't go soft on me now."

"I'm not going soft. It's just that my original research, many years ago, was for the ultimate benefit of mankind. Not for personal gain."

"What's the difference?" Craig asked. "The people we use are the dregs of society, the outcasts and the deadbeats. And they are benefitting us, and we're making the world a better place. Your father would've approved, and your grandfather."

"Yes, they would have. They were faithful to the cause,

and I'm not questioning my involvement. I'm in this all the way," Wolff said. "And tomorrow will be a success."

"I'm counting on it," Craig said. "And, I'm counting on you."

"Yes, sir."

Craig leaned forward and thoughtfully replaced the telephone receiver. He knew he could depend on Wolff. Even through his intermittent pangs of conscience, Wolff was committed to him because of his father. At least he had that much to thank the old man for.

Tuesday, August 23rd, 3:25 a.m.

THE SCREAM OF heavy metal music blasted in Cheryl Waters's head. Her own screams couldn't drown out the sound of the noise as she lay frozen, finding it hard to breathe. She couldn't think, couldn't see anything but total darkness in her cell.

Suddenly the sound stopped and her body was jolted with excruciating pain—an intense electrical shock. And then again, over and over. Then, the torture stopped, and she lay still in the darkness, trying to catch her breath, struggling to sit upright, but the straps that bound her arms and legs held her firmly.

An intense light was switched on and she heard the sound of the door to her cell opening, and then footsteps drawing closer. She turned her head and watched as the man came toward her. She waited quietly as he undid the straps.

"Sit up," he said.

Cheryl struggled to sit, drawing her legs up. She wrapped her arms around her knees and stared quietly at her tormentor.

"I am the Wizard," he said.

The Wizard disappeared. The room was quiet now, and she lay on her back. A light was on, and she heard a banging. She sat upright and turned to see a police officer tapping on the bars of her cell with his baton.

"Are you all right?" he asked.

Cheryl stared at the officer a moment, trying to clear her head. Her body shivered uncontrollably. Her voice shook and she finally managed to say, "Just ... just a dream."

The officer frowned as he observed her. "It must have been a pretty bad dream. You were screaming."

Cheryl nodded. "It ... it was."

The cop watched her a moment, then turned and walked away. She heard the corridor door slam shut, leaving her alone again with memories of the nightmare in her head. It had been so real. The face of the man who called himself the Wizard was familiar to her in some vague way, and the pain she'd felt still seemed to fill her body as though the scenario in the nightmare had actually occurred.

She lay on the metal cot in a fetal position, her knees drawn up, afraid to sleep, shivering with fear in the warm room. Finally, drained and overcome with exhaustion, she fell asleep.

CHAPTER 10

Tuesday, August 23rd, 9:04 a.m.

BOBBY SULLIVAN could barely make ends meet. The gas station, where he pumped gas for impatient customers, was about the best job an ex-con like him could hope to find. And he was lucky enough to have this job only because the guy who owned the place had been a friend of his father. That was a long time ago, when his parents were still alive.

Orphaned ten years ago, and fifteen at the time, he was fortunate his widowed aunt had taken him in. In hindsight, he was grateful to her, and grateful that even after his stretch in prison, she'd welcomed him back. In fact, she'd stuck with him throughout his ordeal, and was the only one who'd come to visit him. Not often. It was a long trip to Kingston from Richmond Hill, but her few visits, and her letters, had helped him get through his five years of incarceration.

Bobby finished cleaning the windshield of a sedan and dropped the squeegee into the bucket of cleaning solution. Walking around to the driver's open window, he leaned over.

"That'll be fifty dollars, sir."

The man handed him a hundred. Bobby ran to the booth and returned a moment later with the change, handing it back. Without a word from the occupant of the vehicle, the car sped away. Bobby watched as it turned onto the street and melded into the morning traffic.

He took a seat on the curb by the gas pump and waited for the next customer. It might not be the best job in the world, but at least it wasn't hard work.

At times, he accepted his lot in life. This was one of those occasions, and he slipped off his cap, leaned back against the pump and turned his face toward the morning sun, enjoying the warmth.

At other times, however, he was angry at the way things had gone. Society called him a rapist. He knew he wasn't. He'd been seventeen at the time, and she was fifteen. They were in love, and had been seeing each other for several months before finally succumbing to temptation. They'd made the mistake of consummating their relationship in her father's house. In her bedroom. And when her parents came home and caught them, it was all over for him.

Gone were his dreams of being a star baseball player. He'd been touted as the next big hope, a golden boy, probably destined for the big leagues. The world soon forgot about him after his conviction.

Her father was rich, and he wasn't. His pathetic defense hadn't stood much chance, and so he was locked away.

He never saw her again after that, and he never heard from her while he was in prison. He still thought about her, of course, but by the time he was released, she was married and had moved away with her new husband. Somewhere back east, he'd heard.

Bobby stood and watched as another car wheeled into the station. It was a brand new SRT Viper. He admired its sleek red lines with a bit of envy as it pulled to a stop at the pump. He didn't figure he ever had a chance of owning anything like that. Not with this dead-end job.

He plopped his cap back on, went to the driver-side window, and leaned down. The window zipped open and the guy inside turned his head. "Fill 'er up, and watch the paint." The guy tried to talk tough, but his high-pitched voice and his geeky appearance belied his attempt to be cool. He looked more like a rich snot spending Daddy's money.

Bobby was careful of the paint as he poked the nozzle into the filler. What he really wanted to do was put a scratch on the guy's car for being such a jerk, but out of respect for the beautiful machine, he didn't.

"I'm looking for Bobby Sullivan."

Bobby spun his head as he heard the voice. A young guy was approaching, his hands tucked into the pockets of his jacket. "Are you Bobby Sullivan?"

Bobby nodded. "Yup. That's me," he said, and then his jaw dropped as he saw the boy remove his right hand from his pocket, his fist wrapped around a pistol.

The hose fell from the tank, spilling gas down the side of the shiny red vehicle. The nozzle clattered on the concrete, splashing fuel at Bobby's feet as he ducked.

The boy lowered the pistol and fired. Bobby heard an explosion and a bullet whizzed past his ear. On all fours, he scrambled around to the back of the car, and then to the opposite side, where he was out of range.

He heard a curse from inside the vehicle, and then rubber smoked as the car bolted away, leaving Bobby fully exposed. The shooter took a step forward and aimed the gun, holding it steady.

A second shot caught Bobby near his left shoulder. He dropped to the ground, and then attempted to stand, but fell again, landing on his back.

The killer stood over him, the gun now pointed directly at

Bobby's head. He fired again. A hole appeared in Bobby's forehead and he fell to the ground, too dead to see what happened next.

The killer stood a moment, the gun still in his right hand, which now hung at his side. He observed his handiwork and appeared satisfied his victim was dead.

One more shot exploded as he raised the gun to his own temple and squeezed the trigger. The weapon slipped from the dead hand and clattered on the pavement as his body crumpled to the ground. The sound of the Viper faded in the distance, and then all was quiet and still. The assassin lay beside his victim, their blood trickling from their warm bodies, mingling as one on the hot concrete.

CHAPTER 11

Tuesday, August 23rd, 9:35 a.m.

DETECTIVE HANK CORNING was settled firmly in his chair in the precinct, poring over the notes, reports, and evidence of the murder of Charles Robinson, when Yappy approached him.

"There's been another murder, Hank."

Hank dropped the papers onto his desk, leaned back, and looked up.

"Two guys dead at a gas station," Yappy continued and handed Hank a note. "Here's the address."

Hank sighed as he stood. "Thanks, Yappy," he said as he took the note and scanned it. He sighed again, then grabbed his briefcase and strode from the precinct.

Crime scene investigators were already on the scene when Hank arrived at Full Power Gas Bar. He pulled his Chevy to the curb behind a haphazardly parked cruiser and stepped from the vehicle.

A crowd of onlookers gathered in groups of two or three, trying to get a better view, wanting to see what all the commotion was about. Officers were kept busy, making sure the rubberneckers stayed well back.

Hank moved closer and scanned the scene. Red and blue lights flashed. An ambulance was parked nearby, and another one was turning into the lot. The familiar yellow tape was being stretched around the area. Investigators milled about. The police photographer's camera clicked, taking shots at a variety of angles.

Hank glanced around the gas station. A man was on the far side, leaning against the front fender of his vehicle. Could be a witness.

He approached the pair of bodies lying on the pavement beside the gas pump. A pistol lay a couple of feet away. Looked like a 9mm Glock. Two or three bullet casings were nearby. Evidence cones marked critical pieces of evidence.

He turned his attention to the victims. Both had been shot in the head, and one of them also had a bloodstain on his shoulder. Probably a gunshot wound as well.

He looked across the lot. The lead crime scene investigator, Rod Jameson, was talking to a uniform. He held a clipboard in his hand. Hank approached him. "Hey, Rod," he said.

Rod spun around. "Hey, Hank. What brings you here?" he asked, chuckling at his own joke.

Hank smiled weakly and asked, "All these people watching, did anyone see anything?"

"Nope. We talked to them all. They arrived since, and never saw a thing."

Hank nodded toward the man leaning against the fender of his car. "That a witness?"

"He wasn't here when it happened," Rod replied. "He got here later. He's the guy who called it in."

"Thanks, Rod," Hank said as he turned and walked over

to the man. He slipped out his badge and displayed it. "I'm Detective Hank Corning."

The man nodded slightly.

"You called this in?" Hank asked.

Another nod.

"Did you see what happened?"

The man finally spoke. "I didn't see anyone around. I pulled in for gas and there they were." He nodded toward the bodies. "And so, I called 9-1-1." He shrugged. "I didn't see a thing."

"There were no other cars around?"

"Nope. The place was deserted."

"Did you see anybody on the sidewalk?"

"Nope. I mean, there might have been … I don't know, but I didn't see anyone."

Hank frowned and glanced back at the bodies. There appeared to be no witnesses, and this guy wasn't much help. He turned back and slipped a notepad and pen from an inner pocket. "I need your name and address, and then you can go."

The man gave him the information and Hank jotted it down. He flipped the pad shut and tucked it back into his pocket. "Someone may need to contact you later," he said, "but for now, you can go."

"Thanks, Officer."

"Detective."

"What?"

"I'm a detective."

The man gave an uncertain nod, as if not knowing the difference, and then climbed into his vehicle. Hank watched him drive across the lot. An officer removed the tape to allow the vehicle to pass.

Hank went back to where Rod Jameson was standing. "Didn't get anything from him," he said.

Jameson raised his chin toward the cooling bodies. "Nancy's here."

Hank turned. Medical Examiner Nancy Pietek had arrived and was bending over the bodies. Hank went over and crouched across from her. "Hi, Nancy."

Nancy looked up. "Nice to see you again, Hank."

"Got anything for me?"

"I just arrived. Can't tell for sure yet, but it looks like either a double murder, or possibly a murder/suicide. Forensics will be able to tell you more about this one than I can."

"It looks to me like a robbery gone wrong." Hank pointed at one of the victims. "This guy's wearing a cap that says 'Full Power Gas Bar' on it. He obviously works here ... but who's this guy? He has no vehicle. Looks to me like he came to rob the place ... but who shot him?" He thought a moment and then looked at Nancy. "But, you think it may be a suicide?"

She nodded. "Possibly," she said as she motioned toward the boy. "It looks like this victim was shot point-blank, either self-inflicted, or by someone who stood close." She pointed with the tip of her pencil. "See those soot marks at the entrance of the wound? And see that star-like tearing in the skin around the wound? When the barrel of a gun is held against bone and discharged, gases from the muzzle can be forced under the skin, causing it to balloon out and tear like that."

Hank whistled.

"Again, I'll know for sure after I get him back to the lab and we check for GSR."

"And the other guy?" Hank asked.

"Two shots. One in the shoulder, and one in the forehead. Both at close range. Probably less than five or six feet away. That's all I can tell you for now," Nancy said as she stood.

Hank took out his cell phone and snapped a few pictures before standing. "That'll do for now," he said. "Thanks, Nancy."

Nancy turned and walked toward one of the ambulances as Hank knelt back down. Without disturbing the body, he felt in the pockets of the victim wearing the cap. He found a wallet and removed it. He flipped it open and pulled out a driver's license. Bobby Sullivan. He compared the picture on the card to the face of the dead attendant, and then tucked the license back into the wallet and returned it to the victim's pocket.

He turned to the other body and searched it as well. He frowned and rubbed his chin. Nothing in any of the pockets. Not so much as a coin, or a key, or even a bus token.

Very strange.

"Hank?"

Hank looked up.

"There's a guy here I think you should talk to."

Hank stood and looked where the uniform was pointing. A red Viper was parked at the curb on the other side of the tape. A young man paced back and forth on the sidewalk beside the car, then looked toward the scene, as if observing the proceedings, and then paced some more.

Hank walked over, identified himself, and showed his badge. "You wanted to talk to someone?"

A vigorous nod.

"What's your name?" Hank had his notepad out.

The boy looked nervous. He stopped pacing, folded his arms, and leaned against his vehicle. "Benjamin. Benjamin

Butler." His voice was high-pitched as he said, "I saw it happen."

"What did you see?"

"I saw a guy shoot another guy."

"Where were you standing?"

"I ... I was getting gas. I was in my car. He was filling my tank."

Hank waited. "And?"

"And a guy came up and started shooting."

"And then you drove away?"

"I ... I was scared. I didn't want to get killed, so I got out of there as fast as I could."

Hank studied him a moment before asking, "Can you identify the shooter?"

"I ... I guess so."

"Do you want to come and take a look?"

Butler frowned. "Can't you ... show me a picture or something?"

"I would sooner you came over, if you don't mind. I would like you to describe how it happened."

"Are ... are they dead?" His voice shook.

Hank nodded.

"Both ... both of them?"

"Both of them."

"I ... I guess I could come over. But not too close, okay?"

"No problem," Hank said. "We don't need to get close. Come on."

Butler followed Hank across the lot. He stopped short as he got near the pump. "That ... that's close enough," he said as he turned away.

Hank sighed. "Look, I realize this is hard. I need you to look at them a moment."

The boy turned his eyes briefly toward the scene, and then looked away. "The guy with the cap. He was pumping gas for me, and the other guy came up and started shooting at him. I drove away as fast as I could. That's all I saw."

"And then you decided to come back?" Hank asked.

Butler shrugged. "It seemed like the right thing to do."

"Yeah, it was," Hank said, and then asked, "There were only the two of them?"

Butler nodded.

"What happened to the shooter?" Hank asked.

"I don't know. He was still there when I left. I don't know what happened to him." He frowned. "What did happen to him?"

"It's too early to tell," Hank said, and then continued, "I need you to go to the station to make a full statement. Is that okay?"

Butler nodded. "Okay."

"Is now a good time?"

"Yes."

Hank beckoned to a uniformed officer and arranged for Butler to follow the cop to the station. He watched them drive away before walking over to Rod Jameson.

"Anything else I should know?" Hank asked.

Jameson shook his head. "Not right now. That's all we got."

Hank took a quick look toward the booth and then scanned the area around the pumps. "Any security cameras here?"

"Nothing. We checked for that first thing."

Hank dialed Jake's number. "Jake, I'm at the scene of what looks like a murder/suicide. I just have a niggling feeling it may be related to the Cheryl Waters case. You might want to drop by." Hank gave him the address, and Jake said he'd be right over.

Hank thought he had a pretty good picture of what had happened here. What he didn't know was why.

CHAPTER 12

Tuesday, August 23rd, 10:25 a.m.

LISA KRUNK considered herself to be the best TV news reporter this crappy little town had ever seen. She knew she was destined for bigger and better things, but for now she had to endure, and eventually, she wanted to be a newspaper journalist and win that Pulitzer she deserved.

The local newspapers and TV stations monitored the police bands, usually quick to respond to anything sensational to boost their ratings. But today, Lisa cursed when she realized she'd missed hearing about a big story. She was starving for news, and had been on the other side of the city trying to corner the mayor in regards to a scandal she had manufactured for the occasion.

When the news had broken about a double homicide, she'd forgotten about this filler story and grabbed her faithful cameraman, Don. They'd jumped in the Channel 7 Action News van and hurried through the city.

It took about fifteen minutes to reach their destination, but as they spun onto Main Street, she could see the flashing lights, crowds of onlookers, and yellow tape flapping in the breeze.

"There. Pull up there." Lisa motioned impatiently toward the side of the street. "Hurry."

Don tucked the van halfway into a small space, shut it down, and jumped out. He went around the vehicle, opened the side door, and retrieved the camera. Lisa was already striding across the sidewalk toward the yellow line of demarcation, her wireless microphone gripped in her hand. She cursed again when she saw what seemed to be a body covered by a white sheet, already being loaded into a waiting ambulance. She saw another ambulance nearby.

Don hurried up behind her and dropped the camera onto his shoulder. It hummed, and a red light glowed as it zoomed in toward the action.

Another body, also covered, was lying on the pavement by a gas pump. "Over there. Get a shot of the other one."

The camera spun around and continued to hum. Lisa scanned the area. She saw Detective Corning chatting with a couple of uniformed cops. Too far away to get to him. Maybe she could catch him later if he came a little closer. She needed to get something juicy. Something she could sink her teeth into. Her viewers wanted that.

A siren screeched as the ambulance pulled out and was guided from the station. The second ambulance backed in a little closer to the pumps and the camera watched the body being loaded inside. The vehicle drove away behind the first, delivering their loads to the city morgue.

Lisa turned as she heard the roar of a vehicle pulling up to the curb a dozen yards away. She smiled as she recognized the car. It was Jake Lincoln. She'd had a few run-ins with him and his ditzy wife in the past.

Time to find out what he was doing here.

She tugged at Don's arm. "Come on," she said. "This way."

She hurried down the sidewalk, Don following, and intercepted Jake as he stepped off the asphalt roadway.

"Mr. Lincoln, you and your wife, as private detectives, have been involved in a couple of high-profile cases lately. Is this incident related to something you're working on now?" She shoved the mike in Jake's frowning face. The camera followed, humming. The red light glowed.

"As far as I know, this is not related to anything we're involved in right now."

Lisa's extra wide mouth flapped, "Then why are you here?"

Jake hesitated. "I really don't know anything about this incident. I just got here."

"Do you know either of the victims?"

He seemed to be getting impatient. "No. Like I said, I just got here and I have no idea what this is all about."

Lisa persisted, looking down her thin sharp nose. "Can you tell the viewers whether or not you'll be involved in this?"

Jake frowned, stepped around Lisa, and strode down the sidewalk. Don spun the camera and followed Lisa as she ran after Jake.

"Just one more question, Mr. Lincoln," she called.

Detective Corning had come over. He lifted the tape, allowing Jake to duck under, and then dropped it and held up a hand when Lisa tried to follow. She stopped short and raised the mike. "Detective Corning," she puffed, trying to catch her breath.

Hank smiled. "Good morning, Lisa," he said.

The camera moved toward Hank, the mike ready. "Detective Corning, can you tell the viewers a little bit about what happened here today?"

"At this point, we know very little. There has been a double homicide, and the investigation has just begun."

"Do you know who the killer is?"

Hank hesitated before saying, "It appears there were no others involved."

That sounded to Lisa like an interesting turn of events. "Are you saying this may be a murder/suicide?" she asked.

"It appears that way. However, we have nothing conclusive yet."

"Were there any witnesses?"

"No. We believe there were no witnesses to the actual shooting."

"Can you tell us who the victims are?" she asked, knowing it was a futile question. They wouldn't release that information until the next of kin was notified, but she was running out of ideas.

"Not at this point," Hank replied.

Lisa needed something juicy for her viewers, but she was at a loss. She asked, "Detective Corning, is Lincoln Investigations involved in this case?"

Hank looked at Jake, who seemed to be a bit peeved. He turned back to Lisa. "I called him. I thought he might be interested, but as far as we know, this case has no relation to anything Lincoln Investigations may be working on at the moment."

"And what are you working on at the moment, Mr. Lincoln?" she asked as she swung the mike toward Jake. She frowned, disappointed, as he turned and walked away.

"That's all we have for now. We'll let the press know when we have more to go on. Thank you, Lisa," Hank said with a smile as he turned and followed Jake.

Don turned the camera toward Lisa. She said, "We will

bring you breaking news as it happens. In an exclusive report, I'm Lisa Krunk for Channel 7 Action News."

She was disappointed. She could edit what she had, of course, but it didn't amount to much. She hoped somehow she could put an interesting spin on the story.

CHAPTER 13

Tuesday, August 23rd, 11:13 a.m.

ANNIE WAS IN THE office going over the notes she had taken regarding Cheryl Waters and the murder of Charles Robinson. There wasn't much to go on, and she was trying to figure out if there was any place to start.

Jake had been delivering some legal papers for a downtown law firm that morning, and he'd called her some time ago and said he might be a while longer. Hank had called him, and Jake wanted to drop by the scene of a double homicide that had just taken place.

She tossed the papers she'd been studying onto the desk, pushed back her chair, and wandered into the kitchen. She expected Jake would be home any minute, and he would want a fresh cup of coffee. She started a pot and sat at the kitchen table, still thinking about the case.

She'd caught the news a little earlier. The reporter had stated that Cheryl Waters had been arraigned that morning, charged with first-degree murder in the death of Charles Robinson. She'd pled not guilty, a date for a preliminary hearing was set, and she'd been remanded to the women's detention center. Because of Cheryl's unstable living arrangements in the past, she'd been considered a flight risk, and the judge had set the bail at one million dollars. Well beyond any amount Cheryl's parents could raise.

Unless the Lincolns could accomplish the impossible and find some exculpatory evidence, the future looked grim for Cheryl and her parents.

Annie was taken out of her thoughts by the sound of a familiar rumble in the driveway. A car door slammed, and in a moment she heard a key in the front door, and then the sound of footsteps in the foyer.

"I'm in the kitchen," she called.

Jake came into the kitchen, followed by Hank.

"Good morning, Annie," Hank said as he took a seat at the table. Jake gave Annie a quick peck on the cheek, then dropped down across from Hank and slouched back in his seat, resting his feet on an unused chair.

"I just made a fresh pot of coffee," Annie said to Hank. "I assume you want some?"

"Sounds good," Hank replied.

"What's this about a double homicide?" Annie asked as she stood and went to the counter.

"Two guys at a gas station," Hank replied. "It looks like a murder/suicide. It appears, at this point, someone shot the attendant and then himself." He explained what the ME had told him regarding the gunshot wound.

Annie finished pouring the coffee and set the cups on the table along with some cream and sugar. She sat and leaned forward, resting her arms on the table. "Two murders in two days. That's rather unusual. Who are the victims?"

"The name of the gas station attendant is Bobby Sullivan." Hank leaned forward. "But here's the most unusual part. The killer had no ID on him."

"Just like Cheryl Waters," Jake added.

Hank continued, "And the gun used was a nine-millimeter

Glock, the same type of gun Cheryl used. Not an uncommon weapon, but it adds up to both murders being eerily similar. And that's why I called Jake." He shrugged. "It may be a stretch, but I'm wondering if the two cases may be related in some way."

Annie frowned. "If they're not related, it's rather unusual."

Hank was pouring some cream into his coffee, along with a stream of sugar. He stirred it thoughtfully and said, "You know what I think about coincidences. I don't like them."

"But the difference is, Cheryl didn't shoot herself," Annie said. She finished fixing her coffee and took a sip before asking, "What do you know about Bobby Sullivan?"

"Nothing yet. My guys are working on it."

"Were there any witnesses?" Annie asked.

Hank explained about the driver of the red Viper. "He got out of there as quickly as he could once the shooting started, so he didn't see much. We took his statement, but it's rather sketchy."

"And no security cameras?"

Hank shook his head. "None."

Annie sat back, holding her cup in both hands. She wondered if there was a connection between the two cases. She had a nagging feeling there was.

Jake finished stirring his coffee and dropped the spoon on the table. "We ran into our good friend Lisa Krunk today." He laughed and took a sip. "She was as annoying as always."

Annie chuckled. She'd had a few uncomfortable occasions to meet Lisa Krunk, and knew Lisa would do just about anything for a story. "I hope you were careful of what you said. She has a way of twisting everything she hears."

"I kept as quiet as possible," Jake replied as he took another gulp of coffee and set the cup down. "Hank did most of the talking."

Hank grinned. "I had to be pleasant with her in front of the camera. Can't give her any chance to make the cops look bad." He glanced down as his cell phone buzzed at his hip. He slipped it from its holder and looked at the caller ID. "It's Callaway. I hope he has something for me." He stood and stabbed at the phone with a finger. "This is Detective Corning."

Annie watched him pace as he listened on his cell. She knew Callaway was a whiz with all things technical. Whether it was computer related or involved installing a wire or other recording device, Callaway was the expert who got the job done.

Hank held the phone between his shoulder and ear and dug a notepad and pen from his pocket. He scribbled in the pad, finally saying, "Thanks, Callaway." He sat back down at the table and studied the pad, frowning and thoughtful. Finally he looked up.

"It appears our gas station attendant was an ex-con," he said. "I remember this. It happened a few years ago. A rather high-profile case and surrounded by a bit of controversy. Bobby Sullivan was convicted of raping Manfred Frost's daughter and served five years in Kingston before he was finally paroled. Apparently he's stayed out of trouble since his release a few months ago."

"Manfred Frost. The Banker?" Annie asked.

Hank nodded. "One and the same."

"Maybe Sullivan rubbed somebody the wrong way while he was in prison," Jake suggested.

Hank shrugged. "Maybe. It may have been a revenge killing, but if so, why wait until he's out? It would be as easy to get him while he was still inside."

"Perhaps he was in protective custody," Annie said.

"Yeah, I'll have to check on that. But if it was revenge,

why'd the perpetrator kill himself as well, if it was indeed a suicide?"

"Any ID on the shooter yet?" Jake asked.

"Nothing," Hank said. "They ran his prints, but nothing showed up. Whoever it is, he doesn't have a record of any kind. Which means we wouldn't have any DNA records on him in the database either, nor would he be in the mug books."

"What about the weapon?"

"A nine-millimeter Glock. Unregistered," Hank replied as he took the last gulp of his coffee and set the cup thoughtfully on the table. "Hopefully, once forensics is done, and we get the ME's report, we'll know a little bit more about what happened. Or at least confirm what we already suspect took place."

"What about Sullivan's friends or family? Any info on that?" Jake asked.

"Apparently, Sullivan lived with his aunt," Hank replied as he consulted his notepad. "A Mrs. Bessie Mitchell. She took him in after his parents were killed in a car crash when he was fifteen. She's a widow, and other than her nephew, she lives alone."

"Has she been notified yet?" Annie asked.

Hank sighed. "Not yet. We just got that information now. That's my next task."

Annie heard the tension in Hank's voice. She knew notifying the next of kin was one of the requirements of his job he disliked the most. The emotional strain of breaking the news of a loved one's death always affected him deeply, and unfortunately there was no easy way to do it. And you never got used to it.

"I have to head over there now," Hank said, and sighed again.

CHAPTER 14

Tuesday, August 23rd, 11:45 a.m.

HANK WAS FAMILIAR with the area where Bessie Mitchell lived, and as he wheeled his Chevy onto Cedarwood Drive, Annie sat in the passenger's seat, watching the house numbers. They were looking for 95.

Annie pointed toward a small bungalow nestled behind a wide bed of blooming summer plants. A freshly cut lawn was split in half by a stone walkway leading up to the single front door.

"There it is," she said.

Hank pulled to the curb and shut down the engine. He turned to Annie. "Thanks for coming," he said. "I've never been good at this." He'd asked her along because he was awkward when it came to breaking the bad news of a loved one's death, especially to women. It wasn't actually in the telling, but it was what to do or say next that was the most difficult for him.

Hank continued, "I know it's not proper police procedure, but ..." He shrugged.

Annie nodded. "I'm happy to help out."

They stepped from the vehicle, and Hank led the way up

the pathway to the front door and rang the bell. It was answered by an attractive woman, probably in her early fifties.

"Mrs. Bessie Mitchell?" Hank asked.

She nodded. "Yes."

Hank held up his badge. "I'm Detective Hank Corning, and this is Annie Lincoln. May we come in for a moment?"

She hesitated briefly, then stepped back and swung the door open. "Come in."

They walked inside and Hank turned to Mrs. Mitchell. "It's about Bobby, your nephew. May we sit down?"

She frowned slightly and waved toward the front room. Hank followed Annie and they took a seat on the couch under a large front window.

Mrs. Mitchell sat in a loveseat across from them and leaned forward. "Is Bobby in some kind of trouble?" she asked.

Hank cleared his throat and glanced at Annie, then back at Mrs. Mitchell. He leaned forward. "Not exactly, ma'am," he said, "but I'm afraid I have some bad news for you."

Mrs. Mitchell waited.

"I'm sorry I have to tell you, Bobby is dead."

Mrs. Mitchell caught her breath. She stared in disbelief, her mouth open, her eyes darting back and forth from Annie to Hank. Finally she said, "But Bobby is at work."

"Yes, ma'am, that's where it happened."

"What ... what happened?"

"He has been shot."

"Shot?"

Hank nodded. "He has been killed."

Mrs. Mitchell sat quiet and still, in shock as she tried to grasp the news. Then, in a hoarse voice, she asked, "Murdered?"

"Yes, ma'am."

"But who? Why? What happened?" Her brow wrinkled. "Are you sure it was Bobby?"

Hank nodded slowly. "It's him, ma'am. We'll need you to make a formal identification later, but there's no doubt, it's him." He watched Mrs. Mitchell, unsure of what else to say.

Annie stood, stepped around the coffee table, and sat on the edge of the loveseat, facing Mrs. Mitchell. She grabbed a few tissues from a box on a nearby stand and pressed them into Mrs. Mitchell's hand. Placing her arm around her shoulder, she attempted to comfort the distraught woman.

Mrs. Mitchell dabbed at her eyes with the tissue as her body quaked, her breath coming in short, quick gasps. "Bobby," she whispered. "My darling Bobby."

Hank sat fidgeting on the couch and watched as Annie tried to comfort the woman. He dabbed at a couple of tears that had broken free, and then gained control, and was thankful he'd asked Annie to come along. He dug out his notepad and pen, flipped through to a blank sheet, and made a notation at the top of the page.

In a few minutes, Mrs. Mitchell blew her nose, turned to Annie, and smiled weakly. "I'll be okay." She cleared her throat, attempting to compose herself, and asked, "How did it happen?"

Annie held the woman's hand and looked into her reddening eyes, her makeup smeared. Annie's heart broke for this grieving woman who'd obviously loved her nephew as her own son. She spoke softly. "We don't know the reason yet, or the identity of the shooter. The police are working on it, and they'll soon find out more."

Mrs. Mitchell nodded. "Did he suffer?" she asked.

Annie looked at Hank. "It's not likely, ma'am," he said.

"And you don't know why?"

"Not yet," Hank replied. "We're hoping you can help with that." He cleared his throat again. "Do you know if Bobby had any enemies, or anyone who might wish him harm?"

Mrs. Mitchell shook her head slowly, the distress she felt evident in her eyes. "No. I don't believe so. Bobby was such a good boy. Well liked by everyone who knew him." She blotted away another tear that had escaped.

"What did he do in his spare time? Did he have any friends you may not know?"

"He came to church with me every Sunday, and then he would go again in the evening. He was there for Bible study on Wednesday as well. He never missed it."

"What's the name of the church?"

"Richmond Baptist."

"I know the place." Hank jotted in his notepad and then asked, "Anything else?"

"He helped out at Samaritan Street Mission once a week, every Tuesday, sorting food and serving meals." She thought a moment before saying, "Other than that, Bobby worked hard and was home every evening. He took care of himself. He didn't drink, or smoke, and he certainly didn't do any drugs. He was trying to get his life back on track after ..." Her voice trailed off, her lower lip quivered, and she drew a deep breath.

Hank nodded. "Yes, we realize Bobby had spent some time in prison."

"He was innocent, you know." Mrs. Mitchell sighed and dropped her head. "My darling Bobby lost five years of his life in a terrible prison, for something he didn't do. And now ..." She sighed again.

Hank knew, technically, Bobby wasn't innocent, but he

was aware of the circumstances of the case, and believed the judge had been harsher than necessary. He was only going by memory, and he made a mental note to look into the case a little further.

Annie moved her arm from around the woman and sat back against the end of the loveseat, still facing her. "Has Bobby lived here since he was released?" she asked.

"Yes, he came to live with me right after his parents, my brother, was killed, and he has been here since he was released from that awful place."

Hank said, "I was wondering if something happened in prison, ma'am, and somebody was looking for revenge. Did Bobby ever mention anyone from there?"

"No, never. He didn't like to talk about that. He was always an optimist, and looked forward to the future. He never dwelt on the past."

Hank looked at his notepad. He would talk to the pastor and anyone who knew Bobby from the mission, but he'd hoped to find some kind of solid lead. He looked up and asked, "Do you mind if I take a look at his room?"

Mrs. Mitchell nodded. "Certainly," she said as she stood. Hank followed her to the hallway entrance where she pointed up the stairs leading to the second floor. "It's up there, first door on the left."

Hank climbed the steps, pushed the door to Bobby's room open, and stepped inside. He flicked the light on and took a quick glance around the sparse, but immaculate room. A look through a dresser beside the door revealed nothing more than neatly arranged clothing: socks, underwear, and t-shirts.

The closet contained a variety of the usual items you would find in a man's closet: shirts, jackets, and pants, along with a well-tailored suit and a couple of ties.

Hank swung open the double doors of a shelving unit along the far wall. It was lined with long white cardboard boxes. A peek inside revealed they contained complete sets of baseball cards, many dating back to the early '80s. Binders on a shelf below contained plastic sheets containing even more cards. Hank recognized many of the star players sheathed safely in the pages. Mickey Mantle, Reggie Jackson, Hank Aaron, Ted Williams, and many of his own boyhood heroes. It looked like a valuable collection.

On the nightstand beside the bed was a Bible. Hank leafed through it. It looked well-worn and often read, with several bookmarks and many portions of scripture underlined. From the top drawer of the nightstand he pulled out a stack of photos held by an elastic band. There were pictures of Bobby taken several years ago, posing in his baseball uniform with his teammates. There were also a couple of pictures of him with a girl, posing and smiling, taken back in happier times.

But there didn't seem to be anything in the room that could shed any light on the reason for Bobby's murder.

Hank flicked the light off and left the room, closing the door behind him. He went back downstairs to the front room. Annie and Mrs. Mitchell talked quietly, the heartbroken woman occasionally dabbing at her eyes, crying softly.

Annie looked up as Hank came in and stood by the doorway. "Thanks, Mrs. Mitchell," he said. "Unfortunately, there doesn't appear to be anything in Bobby's room that can help us."

"I wish I could tell you more," she said.

Hank dug in his pocket, withdrew a card, and held it out. "If you think of anything, you can contact me at this number." She took the card, glanced at it briefly, and tucked it under the edge of a lamp on the stand beside her.

Annie put her hand on Mrs. Mitchell's arm. "Will you be okay?" she asked.

The woman nodded and forced a smile. "I'll be okay."

Annie found a Lincoln Investigations business card in her purse and tucked it under the lamp with Hank's card. "If you need to talk, or need anything at all, call me," she said as she stood.

"I will."

Mrs. Mitchell saw them to the door. "Do you think you can find out what this is all about?" she asked as they stepped outside.

Hank turned back to face the devastated woman. "I'll do everything I can," he promised. "And I'll keep in touch and let you know what I find out."

"Thank you both."

The door closed behind them, and Hank and Annie walked quietly to the car and climbed in. Hank flipped open his pad and looked at his notes. "I'll drop you home, Annie, and then I'll swing by the church and see what the pastor can tell me. Until we find the identity of the shooter, I don't have a lot of leads."

CHAPTER 15

Tuesday, August 23rd, 12:42 p.m.

ANNIE HAD JUST called Jake and informed him she was on her way home and would be there in a few minutes. Jake's stomach was begging for food, so he decided to put together a couple of sandwiches and enjoy a lunchtime snack with Annie when she got home.

He'd just finished piling on the cold roast beef, one sandwich much thicker than the other, digging out a pair of pickles to go with the meal, when the doorbell rang.

He turned and stared briefly down the hallway, then wiped his hands on a towel and headed for the front door. It popped open before he got to it, and he stopped short when a familiar and unwelcome face appeared.

It was Annie's mother.

She bustled in, paying little attention to Jake as she strode past him and into the kitchen. Jake shook his head, rolled his eyes, and followed her.

She spun around. "I was on my way to work, and I wanted to stop by and see my daughter a moment," she said, then called, "Annie, it's your mother. Where are you?"

Jake crossed his arms and glared at her. "She's not here

right now." He hoped she would leave quickly if he didn't tell her Annie would be home soon.

"I saw her car in the driveway." Her tone seemed to indicate she thought he was lying about Annie's whereabouts. "Where is she?"

"She had to go out." Jake wondered how Annie had turned out so well with such an overbearing mother. At nearly sixty years old, Alma Roderick still looked youthful, and if it wasn't for her sour attitude, could still look attractive, maybe even beautiful, on those rare occasions when she actually smiled.

Instead, she gave him a cold stare. "Shouldn't you be out looking for a job?"

"I have a job, Alma," he said calmly, holding back a flood of anger.

"From what I hear, Annie does all the work. It's not right she should have to support you."

Jake's muscles tensed and he raised his voice, "Annie and I are equal partners. We both do what we can and our business is doing fine."

Alma looked at him with contempt and brushed aside his comment with an arrogant wave. "Business? Is that what you call it? Running around, putting my daughter in danger?"

"She's an adult now, in case you didn't notice, and she can make her own decisions."

"Then you should both know enough to leave police matters up to the police, instead of meddling in dangerous affairs." She pointed an accusing finger at him. "You need to be a better influence on my grandson." She sniffed and looked around the kitchen, as if looking for something else to complain about.

Jake dropped his arms and unconsciously clenched his fists. He took a step forward and towered over her. "Look here, Alma," he said firmly. "You have no right to come into our house and tell us how to raise our son."

Alma sniffed again, raised her head, and spun around. She moved to the other side of the table, as if attempting to put a barrier between her and Jake. She gave him a fierce stare, arrogance on her face. "I have to go to work. Tell Annie I dropped in."

"I'm sure she'll be glad to hear it," Jake shot back as he stepped aside to allow her to leave. He watched her stride down the hallway to the front door. He shook his head in frustration, took a deep breath, and dropped down at the table.

He heard the door open, and then, "Hello, Mother." It was Annie. He didn't know whether to be relieved or wish Annie had been a couple of minutes later.

"I dropped by to see you on the way to work," he heard Alma say. "But your husband seems to be in a bad mood today."

Jake glanced down the hallway. Annie was looking his way, and then back at her mother in confusion. Jake waved it off and shook his head. He could see Annie understood the situation was caused by a usual dose of her mother's overbearing attitude.

Annie held the door open. "Thanks for dropping by, Mother. We're always glad to see you, but I wouldn't want to keep you from your work."

Alma leaned forward and gave Annie an obligatory kiss on the cheek. She glanced at Jake, and then turned and strode out the door, her head high.

Annie came into the kitchen, leaned over, and gave Jake a hug.

Jake tried to explain. "I wasn't in a bad mood until she came."

Annie laughed. "I know. She would put anybody in a bad mood." She glanced toward the counter and saw the sandwiches. "Let's eat and forget about her." She went to the counter, brought the sandwiches to the table, and took a seat across from Jake. "These look good."

Jake picked up his sandwich. "Did you find out anything interesting from Bobby Sullivan's aunt?" He took a big bite and waited for an answer.

"Not really. According to Mrs. Mitchell, Bobby stayed completely out of trouble since his release. Went to church, worked hard, and lived clean." She took a tiny bite.

"Anything at all to connect him to the Cheryl Waters case?" Jake asked, crunching a pickle.

"Except for what Hank mentioned before, nothing seemed to stand out." Annie filled him in on the details as they ate. She finished with, "Mrs. Mitchell was so distraught, but I had a long talk with her while Hank was checking out Bobby's room. I promised her we would try to find out why Bobby was killed. So, whether or not his murder is related to Cheryl, I think we need to look into it."

"And that's why I love you so much," Jake said. "And that's why we have no money." He pushed back his plate, wiped his mouth on a napkin, and sat back. "But I'm with you, so what's our next move?"

"Well, there's one more thing."

"What's that?"

"Mrs. Mitchell mentioned Bobby helped out at a homeless mission once a week, every Tuesday after work. Hank will want to check that out as well, but I thought I might drop by and see if I can talk to some of the people he served with."

"Perhaps I'll go with you. I have nothing planned for this evening."

Annie smiled. "It's a date."

CHAPTER 16

Tuesday, August 23rd, 3:05 p.m.

HANK STOOD IN the doorway of Captain Alano Diego's office. "You wanted to see me, sir?"

"Sit down, Hank."

Hank dropped into one of two guest chairs in front of Diego's desk, slouched back, and tucked his feet under the desk. "What's up, Captain?"

Diego sat in his high-back chair, one hand on the desk, the other twiddling with his bristling mustache. He eyed Hank a moment and then sat forward, leaning on the desk. "I need an update on these two murders you're working on. The mayor is after me to see some progress."

"It's only been two days, boss. Less than one day for the second one."

"And?"

"And, I've interviewed everyone who knew the victims and come up dry. My guys are still working on the identity of the second killer, and I'm hoping forensics may have something for me, but right now ..." Hank shrugged.

Diego opened a manila folder lying on his desk and flipped through the pages before looking up. "What about Cheryl Waters?" he asked. "Anything new there?"

"She still claims not to remember anything. There's no doubt she killed Robinson, but I can't find a motive."

Diego consulted the folder. "And Bobby Sullivan?"

"Again, no motive I can find, and the shooter is dead."

Diego closed the folder, sat back, and straightened his navy-blue tie. "The people are getting edgy, Hank. I have to have something. There have been two murders in as many days," Diego reminded him. He had gained a few pounds in the last couple of years, and his jowls quivered as he talked.

As head of Richmond Hill Police Department, Captain Diego had worked his way up through the ranks and was well respected by the men under him. However, Hank knew the captain was under constant pressure from the mayor to perform.

"I'll come up with something soon," Hank said. "Just tell them we're making progress. In the meantime, neither of the killers are a threat anymore. One is dead and the other one's in jail."

"And I see the Lincolns are involved in this?"

"They've been hired by Cheryl's parents."

"I don't have a real problem with that," Diego said. "As long as they stay out of the way. But not everyone in this building likes it when PIs get involved in police investigations."

"I realize that, but they aren't in this just for the paycheck. They're more concerned with helping people, and in getting justice for the victims."

Diego studied Hank a moment before nodding. "I'll leave it with you, Hank. Keep me posted," he said with a dismissive wave.

"I will," Hank said as he stood. He left the captain's office, crossed the precinct floor, and sat at his desk. The two cases were separate and distinct, but he felt there was a strange similarity. He contemplated the facts, considering his next move.

Tuesday, August 23rd, 3:36 p.m.

OLIVER CRAIG SAT like a king in his ivory tower. His suite of offices occupied the entire sixtieth floor in one of the most luxurious buildings in the city: a towering product of inspiration, imagination, and considerable economic investment. From his desk, he could view the whole downtown area through his walls of glass, sitting like he deserved, high above the common people.

The power and money he'd accumulated were exactly what he needed. And he had even higher objectives in mind. Nothing could stop him.

In his rise to the top of the world, he would take with him only those who had earned it. Only those who had shown a willingness to work with him, and to bow at his hallowed feet.

Michael Capella was such a man.

He swept the phone from its cradle atop his handcrafted mahogany desk and dialed a number. He gave Capella's secretary his name and drummed his fingers on the desk until she put him through.

In a moment, Capella's voice came over the phone. "Oliver, it's good to hear from you."

Dispensing with meaningless small talk, Craig said, "We're ready to go."

"Ahhh. Excellent."

"Make sure you're in a public place tomorrow morning. All morning, to be safe. It wouldn't do for you to be a remote suspect in this."

"Don't worry. I'll be in chambers most of the morning, and later, in a meeting with the mayor."

Craig laughed. "Get used to the mayor's office while you're there, Michael. It'll be yours someday soon."

"I'm counting on it."

Craig had plans for Michael. With Michael Capella's opponent soon out of the way, Michael would win a seat on city council, and with Craig's help, he would take over the mayor's seat, and then … that's when things would get more interesting. Tomorrow's events would only be the beginning.

"I'll talk to you again tomorrow," Craig said. He pressed the button to hang up and dialed another number. He listened impatiently as the phone rang a few times before the call was answered.

"This is Wolff."

"Wolff, we're ready to go. Is everything still on schedule there?"

"Everything is as planned, Mr. Craig," Wolff said. "The boy is ready."

"Excellent. You'll be well taken care of, and your family will be provided for."

"Thank you, Mr. Craig."

"And you're sure nothing will go wrong?"

"Absolutely not. We have a fail-safe device in place to ensure, in the event of a lapse on the part of the boy, that he can't possibly survive." Wolff paused. "However, I'm sure such an occurrence will not happen."

"I'm counting on it, Wolff."

"Don't worry, Mr. Craig."

Craig hung up the phone, flipped open the lid on his box of Stradivarius Churchill cigars, selected one, and clipped the end. He lit it and leaned back in his chair, enjoying the silky-smooth taste of the expensive stick. He watched as the smoke wafted upward and dissipated in the breeze of the lazy fan high above.

Tomorrow was going to be exciting. He could hardly wait.

CHAPTER 17

Tuesday, August 23rd, 5:18 p.m.

ANNIE HAD ARRANGED for Chrissy to watch Matty for an hour or two while she and Jake dropped by the mission.

Though they headed out in rush hour, traffic going into the heart of the city was manageable as more people traveled the opposite direction, eagerly leaving the city, on their way home after a long day at work.

Jake found a parking spot a half block from their destination. He pulled the Firebird to the curb and they stepped from the vehicle. They made their way down the bustling street and stopped in front of an ancient building.

Samaritan Street Mission had been faithfully serving the community from its humble location for well over a hundred years. With outreach to street youth, the elderly, and the homeless, the mission provided meals, beds, and spiritual aid, helping those most in need to turn their lives around.

A big sign on the front window welcomed everyone in. When Jake and Annie walked through the doors, they were greeted with a smiling welcome from an elderly man whose job it was to do just that. Make everyone welcome.

"This is an amazing place," Annie said as she swept the massive room with her eyes.

"Very impressive," Jake agreed.

Signs on the wall pointed to a variety of services: the youth center, the chapel, the food bank, and a large thrift store through double doors off to the right. To the back of the room, dozens of long tables were set up. Many enjoyed the free meals now being served in the cafeteria area stretching along the left wall.

A low hum from the diverse throng of people filled the air. Utensils clattered, men, women, and children talked and bustled about, and a shout or two could occasionally be heard above the murmur. In the background, the faint sound of music filtered through.

Annie turned back to the smiling greeter. "Can you tell me where we could find the manager, or the director?" She wasn't sure what the correct title would be.

The smile never left his face as he pointed toward the serving area. "That's her right there," he said. "The lady in the green blouse, serving the potatoes. Her name is Mrs. Pew."

"Thank you." Annie returned his smile.

As they made their way to the cafeteria, it seemed to Annie as though it was mandatory to wear a smile to volunteer here. As they approached the long food line, a dozen apron-clad servers beamed, grinned, and twinkled, dishing up plain, but wonderful-smelling food. People bustled in and out of the kitchen area behind the servers, bringing more food and replacing the emptying trays.

"She looks pretty busy right now," Jake said.

"Hmmm. I'm impressed," Annie said as she watched Mrs. Pew. "She runs this place and still finds time to serve food."

Mrs. Pew glanced their way and caught Annie's eye. She turned around and motioned to a man standing at the end of the counter, leaning against the wall, his arms folded, gazing around the room, perhaps acting as makeshift security. He unfolded his arms and came to Mrs. Pew when she beckoned. She spoke a few words to him and stepped back, allowing him to take her place behind the long row of food items.

Annie watched Mrs. Pew as she came from behind and approached them. She was a woman in her late thirties, plainly dressed, but with a look of refinement about her. She, too, was smiling as she said, "I'm Mrs. Pew. Welcome."

Annie caught her contagious smile and returned it, extending her hand. "Hi, I'm Annie Lincoln."

Mrs. Pew shook hands and said, "You don't look like you're here for a meal. May I help you with something?"

Annie glanced around the busy room. "Can we talk somewhere a little quieter?"

Mrs. Pew led them into a small office near the front of the room. "Have a seat," she said, waving toward a pair of chairs. She waited while they sat, and then took a seat opposite them.

Annie spoke. "I'm Annie Lincoln, and this is my husband, Jake. We're private investigators. We're here about Bobby Sullivan."

Mrs. Pew lost her smile as her face took on a doleful look. "Oh, such sad news."

"So, you've heard?" Jake asked.

"Yes, yes. Pastor Jackson told us. He's the pastor at the church where Bobby attended. He's here now, back in the youth room, no doubt. We're all very saddened to hear about Bobby. Such a good lad, and he got along so well with everyone."

Annie traded a glance with Jake and cleared her throat before saying, "We think his death may be related to another case we're working on."

"I'm happy to help in any way I can," Mrs. Pew said.

Jake said, "We're trying to determine a motive behind Bobby's death and so far have come up empty. It seems everyone we talk to liked Bobby and couldn't think of anyone who wanted to harm him."

"I'm afraid I can only tell you the same thing," Mrs. Pew said. "He was such a sweet young man. He was here every Tuesday and eager to help out. He never missed a week and there wasn't a job he wouldn't do." She took a deep breath and let it out as a sigh. "I can't imagine anyone would want to ... hurt Bobby."

"How long had he been helping out here?" Annie asked.

The woman frowned, thinking. "Perhaps a year. Maybe more."

"Did he ever mention anyone to you, or anything he did, outside of helping here?"

Mrs. Pew shook her head. "Other than church, helping here, and work, I got the feeling he liked to spend time at home with his aunt. He spoke very highly of her."

Annie smiled. "She spoke highly of him as well."

"That poor woman," Mrs. Pew said. "He was all she had left. She must be devastated."

"Yes, she certainly is."

"I must make a note to go around to see her. She's going to need some help and encouragement. And of course, Pastor Jackson will go and visit her as well."

"I'm sure she'll appreciate that," Annie said.

Jake said, "I know someone else who could use a little encouragement right now." He told her briefly about Cheryl Waters and her parents. He ended with, "I know you're busy, but perhaps someone—"

Mrs. Pew interrupted, "I'm never too busy for someone in need."

"I'm sure they would appreciate it," Annie added.

Mrs. Pew continued, "And we have a prison ministry as well. I'll make a note of Cheryl Waters's name, and she'll be sure to get a visit."

Jake allowed a moment to pass and then cleared his throat and asked, "Perhaps you can direct us to where we can find Pastor Jackson?"

Mrs. Pew twisted in her chair, waving over her shoulder in the direction of the far corner of the main room. "He'll either be in the chapel, or in the youth center."

"How'll we know him?"

Mrs. Pew chuckled. "He's big, and black. You can't miss him." She laughed again.

Jake smiled and dug a business card from his shirt pocket. "Please call us if you think of anything else that may be important."

Mrs. Pew took the card, glanced at it briefly, and tucked it into her apron pocket.

Jake turned to Annie. "If there's nothing else you can think of ..."

Annie shook her head and they stood. Mrs. Pew motioned toward the door, and followed them out.

"Thank you, Mrs. Pew," Annie said.

Jake bowed slightly. "Thank you, ma'am."

They watched as the busy woman went back to her place in the serving line before they headed toward the back of the room, past the tables of hungry eaters, and stopped in front of a door with a small sign, which read, "Youth Center."

Jake pushed the door open a few inches and they peeked inside. The room looked more like a gymnasium. A group of boys from a variety of ethnic backgrounds played basketball at one end of the court. It was a great place to keep inner-city youths off the streets and out of trouble.

At the near end of the gym, a handful of guys sat on benches, chatting and laughing.

Jake turned to Annie. "It looks like Pastor Jackson isn't in here. Let's try the chapel."

A sign pointed to the chapel at the far right of the main room. Jake followed Annie and they stepped quietly into the peaceful sanctuary. It was lined with a dozen or so rows of folding chairs, facing toward the front. A large cross hung on the wall at the back of a small stage, behind a portable podium.

In the front row, they saw Pastor Jackson. It had to be him. He looked just as Mrs. Pew described. He was black, and he was certainly big. He sat beside a young girl, his arm around her shoulder. Their heads were bowed and they appeared to be praying.

Jake and Annie slipped into chairs in the back row and waited.

In a couple of minutes, Pastor Jackson and the girl stood up. She appeared to be about sixteen years old. Barely to his shoulder, she gave the pastor a hug before turning toward the exit. She walked with her head down, glancing up briefly at the Lincolns. She was dressed in Gothic fashion with a long, flowing black dress, a black lacy shawl around her shoulders, black hair and fingernails, and a ring through her black-painted bottom lip. Annie smiled at her. The girl returned a fragile smile and hurried out.

They stood and moved into the aisle. The pastor noticed them and headed their way. "Welcome," he said, offering his hand. "I'm Pastor Jackson." He was every bit as tall as Jake, but perhaps a hundred pounds heavier.

They shook his hand. "We're Jake and Annie Lincoln," Jake said. "Can we talk to you a moment?"

"Sure can." A grin split the pastor's cheerful face. "Have a seat," he said as he flipped a couple of chairs around and motioned for them to sit. They sat and he dropped into another chair and faced them, leaning forward, his elbows on his knees. "What can I do for you?"

"We're private investigators," Jake said. "We'd like to talk to you about Bobby Sullivan."

The smile left the pastor's face as he sat back. He shook his head. "Tragic. Very tragic."

"We understand he attends your church, Richmond Baptist?" Annie asked.

"Yes, he does ... did, and he helps ... helped out here, as well."

"We talked to Mrs. Pew a few minutes ago," Annie explained. "She told us we could find you here. We suspect Bobby's death is related to another case we're working on, but we're running out of leads. We don't know if you can shed any light on it or not, but we wanted to meet you."

"A Detective Corning came to see me this afternoon at the church," Jackson began. "I told him all I knew, and I've been thinking about it ever since." He shook his head. "I can't think of anything new. Bobby attended Richmond Baptist faithfully. He got along with everybody, and when he was here ... same thing." He sighed. "So tragic."

Annie hadn't expected to learn anything new from Pastor Jackson. However, she had wanted to try to get a better understanding of Bobby's life. She really had no more questions for the pastor. She glanced at Jake. He, too, seemed to be unable to come up with anything else.

"Thank you for your time, Pastor." Annie dug a business card from her purse. "Just in case there's anything else," she said as she handed it to him.

The big man took the card and glanced at it. "Sorry I couldn't be of more help," he said.

Annie stood and offered her hand. "Thanks again," she said as she and Jake shook hands with the pastor. "You're doing great work here."

They left the chapel and made their way through the main room and out to the sidewalk. They walked in silence to the car, climbed in, and fastened their seat belts.

Annie sat quietly a moment, wondering if they were on the right track. The victim of the first murder was so unlike Bobby Sullivan. It seemed Bobby was more like Cheryl Waters in some ways, and had little in common with Charles Robinson. One victim was a real estate developer, and one pumped gas. Nothing was making sense about either of the two murders, but her instincts told her there was a connection. Both were confusing, and she knew they were missing something.

She glanced at Jake. He had started the engine and was leaning forward, staring through the windshield down the street toward the mission. "Remind me to put this place on our charity list," he said.

"We don't have a charity list."

"We do now."

CHAPTER 18

Tuesday, August 23rd, 7:50 p.m.

HANK HAD SPENT all day interviewing those who had known Bobby Sullivan and who might have information to help him find who had killed Bobby and why. He'd run out of leads, and though he'd been in constant touch with the medical examiner's office, they hadn't revealed anything else he could run with.

He returned to the station and leaned forward at his desk, leafing through the completed reports. The ME's findings on Bobby Sullivan were not a surprise. Forensics had gone over everything from the scene, and the complete forensic and lab reports were in. The observations he'd made at the crime scene proved to be correct.

He slipped the summary report on Bobby Sullivan from the stack of papers and reread it.

Report of Findings on the Death of Bobby Sullivan

Cause of death: *gunshot wound to the head.*
Manner of death: *homicide.*
Blood alcohol: *negative.*
Blood drug screens: *negative.*
Urine drug screens: *negative.*

My examination of the body of Bobby Sullivan revealed a gunshot wound to the head, with the entrance wound on the forehead, and the exit wound on the rear of the head. The trajectory of the bullet that went through Bobby Sullivan's head was front to back, and slightly upwards.

Bobby Sullivan also received a nonfatal gunshot wound to the left shoulder, four inches down from the top surface of the shoulder and three inches in from the armpit.

Trace particles of gunshot residue on the clothing of Bobby Sullivan suggested both shots had been fired from a distance of three to five feet.

In my opinion, Bobby Sullivan died of a gunshot wound to the head. Manner of death is homicide.

The bullet, ascertained to be of nine millimeters by the ballistics report, had been retrieved from the pavement below Bobby's head and was determined to have been fired from the gun that was found at the scene.

There were also details of a complete external examination of the body of Bobby Sullivan. There were no visible defensive wounds, and the findings revealed nothing unusual.

Hank leafed through the papers and pulled out the summary report on the killer.

Report of Findings on the Death of John Doe

Cause of death: *gunshot wound to the head.*

Manner of death: *suicide by a single, self-inflicted shot from a 9mm handgun.*

Blood alcohol: *negative.*

Blood drug screens: *negative.*

Urine drug screens: *11 ng/ml lysergic acid diethylamide detected.*

My examination of the body of John Doe revealed a contact gunshot wound to the head, with the entrance wound on the right side of the head, and the exit wound on the left side of the head. The trajectory of the bullet that went through John Doe's head was right to left and slightly upwards.

A muzzle stamp was imprinted on the skin surrounding the entrance wound. The muzzle stamp marks the position of the muzzle of the gun on or near John Doe's head at the time the gun was fired.

Gunshot residue found on the clothing and the right hand, and soot marks at the entrance of the wound, suggest the fatal wound had been self-inflicted.

In my opinion, John Doe died of a gunshot wound to the right temple. Manner of death is suicide.

An external examination of the killer had not revealed anything abnormal. The weapon was determined to be the same 9mm Glock found at the scene.

An internal autopsy had not been considered necessary on either victim and had not been performed.

Both reports were signed by Nancy Pietek, Deputy Medical Examiner.

The interesting thing was the presence of lysergic acid diethylamide, LSD, in the system of the killer. Certainly not a large amount, and probably not enough to have had any effect at the time of the shooting, but enough to show the unknown killer had taken LSD in the recent past.

The sketchy statement of the driver of the red Viper, Benjamin Butler, which had been attached to the reports, had been of little help.

Hank pulled forward the box of evidence gathered from the scene and tipped out its contents onto his desk. It contained a folder of shots the police photographer had taken, along with a Glock 9mm handgun and four shell casings. There were a few more items, including the recovered bullets, Bobby's wallet, a single key, and a few coins that had been in his pocket.

Hank sat back and scratched his head, staring intently at the evidence in front of him, trying to determine his next course of action. He spun his chair around and called to Callaway, a few feet away.

Callaway looked up from his monitor. "What is it, Hank?"

"Anything on our John Doe yet?"

Callaway shook his head. "Nothing. Fingerprints turned up nothing in the system. Facial recognition came up blank. His picture has been on the news reports, now nationwide, but nobody has called in to identify him yet."

Hank frowned.

Callaway shrugged and continued, "It may take a few days, Hank."

"Let me know the moment you get anything," Hank said and turned back to his desk. He gathered up the evidence and placed it back in the box, snapped open his briefcase, slipped the reports inside, and grabbed his cell phone from its holder. He selected a speed-dial number.

"Jake here."

"Jake, I wanted to see if you guys were home. I have the reports on Bobby Sullivan and want to run them by you."

"No problem. Come on over. We're out back."

"Be right there." Hank stabbed his phone off, tucked it away, picked up his briefcase, and strode from the precinct.

CHAPTER 19

JAKE DROPPED HIS iPhone onto the deck table and slouched back in his chair. "Hank's on his way," he said. "He has the reports on the Bobby Sullivan murder."

Annie was leaning against the railing, watching Matty and Kyle kick around a soccer ball in the backyard. She glanced at Jake. "Anything interesting?"

"He didn't say. I suppose if there was, he would've mentioned it."

Annie refilled her glass of lemonade from the icy pitcher and dropped into a deck chair across from Jake. She picked up a magazine from the table and leafed idly through it.

Jake sipped at his drink and glanced over toward Matty. With all of the problems he'd seen people immersed in lately, he felt fortunate his family was safe. Sure, they'd had a few harrowing times, but overall, he had nothing to complain about, and much to be thankful for.

Jake heard a shout from the backyard. It was Matty. "Hey, Uncle Hank." Jake spun his head around. Hank was coming across the backyard. He watched as Matty ran up to Hank.

"Hey, Matty," Hank said. He climbed the three steps to the deck, dropped into a chair, and set his briefcase beside him as Matty ran back to join Kyle again.

Annie tossed the magazine onto the table. "Do you want some lemonade, Hank?"

"Sure."

As Annie went into the house to get a glass, Jake asked Hank, "Anything interesting in the reports?"

Hank picked up his briefcase and set it in his lap. He clicked it open and withdrew a folder. "It's all here," he said. "The complete reports on both victims." He dropped the folder onto the table, closed his briefcase, and set it back down beside his chair. "It's pretty much what I expected, except for one very interesting bit of information."

Jake looked at Hank quizzically. "What's that?" he asked.

"The killer had lysergic acid diethylamide in his system."

"LSD," Annie said as she stepped from the house.

"Yup. LSD."

"I thought that went out with the sixties," Annie said as she set the cup on the table, filled it with lemonade, and handed it to Hank.

Hank laughed, took the drink, and sipped it. "Oh, it's still around, although it's not nearly as popular as the new designer drugs."

"So, the killer was high when he shot Bobby?" Jake asked.

"Not exactly," Hank replied. "There wasn't enough in his system at the time to have had any effect, but it did show he'd used it recently."

"How recently?"

"Can't tell for sure, probably in the last couple of days."

"Do you think that may've been a factor in the shooting?" Annie asked. "Frequent users may have long-lasting psychoses, such as schizophrenia or severe depression."

"But it doesn't usually lead to violence," Hank said.

"What about hallucinations?" Jake asked.

"During, yes, but not after the fact. And not one or two days later."

Annie sat forward. "Hank, I had a thought. Can you get a drug test done on Cheryl Waters?"

Hank grinned. "I'm ahead of you. I called Callaway on the way over and got him on it. If Cheryl will volunteer, the lab will do a test right away."

"And if she doesn't volunteer?" Jake asked.

Hank shrugged. "Then we'll need a warrant. But I think, given the circumstances, that shouldn't be a problem."

"I think she'll volunteer," Annie said. "And a positive result may answer a lot of questions."

"What questions?" Jake asked.

"Well, one question, really—whether or not the two murders are related."

Jake looked at Annie and cocked his head. "So, how do you know so much about LSD?"

Annie shrugged. "My mother mentioned it a couple of times. She was a real hippie, back in the sixties. That's how she met my father. They used to hang around Yorkville, the Canadian capital of the hippie movement. Not exactly Haight-Ashbury, but pretty close."

Jake frowned and grinned a crooked grin. "I never knew that about you."

"It's not exactly about me, and I never said I had a perfect family tree."

"Is that what happened to your mother? Why she's so batty?"

Annie gave Jake a playful slap on the arm. "Be nice," she said. "And anyway, my parents were never into drugs, just the hippie culture."

Hank laughed. "I didn't know there was a difference."

"Now you know," Annie said as she picked up the folder of reports. "What else is in here?"

"You're welcome to keep those," Hank said. "But everything else in there is as we suspected. A murder/suicide."

Annie browsed the folder a moment before looking up. "You still don't know the shooter's identity?"

"Not yet," Hank said. "We're working on it."

"We went to Samaritan Street Mission," Jake put in. "We talked to the lady who runs the place, Mrs. Pew, and we talked to Pastor Jackson."

"I talked to him as well," Hank said. "Did you find out anything I didn't?"

Jake shook his head. "We didn't get much from either of them, except that everyone liked Bobby."

"Everybody was agreeable on that point. Unfortunately, that's nothing to go on."

"What about Bobby's boss?" Annie asked.

"I talked to him as well. Bobby had been a faithful and hard worker. Always on time, and he had no complaints about him. And of course, like everyone else, he thought highly of Bobby."

"It's a real tragedy," Annie said.

Hank sighed. "It sure is." He took another sip of his lemonade and set the glass on the table. "I talked to his parole officer as well," he said.

"Let me guess," Jake cut in. "He liked Bobby a lot and thought highly of him."

Hank laughed. "Not really. He didn't have an opinion on Bobby. I guess he sees so many ex-cons he tries to separate his feelings from his job. All he told me is, Bobby showed up without fail every week, and on time. He said Bobby was adjusting well and seemed unlikely to be a repeat offender."

"How did he react to the news of Bobby's death?" Annie asked.

"He didn't react. He didn't shrug it off, but I got the feeling it didn't affect him in any way."

Annie closed the folder of reports and tossed it on the table. "The witness in the Viper, and the guy who discovered the body, had nothing to add either."

"What we're missing is the motive," Hank said. "We know exactly what happened; we just don't know why."

"Or who," Jake added.

"Yeah, or who. The identity of the killer might help us with the motive."

"So what's next?" Annie asked.

Hank shrugged. "I've been interviewing people and chasing down leads all day, and there's nothing left."

CHAPTER 20

Wednesday, August 24th, 11:12 a.m.

THE BOY COULDN'T have been much more than sixteen years old. Though it was a warm summer day, he wore a jacket, his hands tucked inside the pockets, as he made his way up the residential street.

He seemed unmindful of anything that went on around him. A car or two passed by, a couple of pedestrians wandered in the other direction across the street, a squirrel skittered up a tree nearby, all unseen by the lad who strode in a purposeful manner down the sidewalk of the middle-class neighborhood.

His thoughts were somewhat scattered. He knew his destination, and although his goal was firmly fixed in his mind, he wasn't exactly sure why Harold Garrison must die.

He knew Garrison was an evil man, of that there was no doubt, and he knew he'd been the one chosen to carry out this awful but necessary task.

The Wizard had spoken, and he was proud to have been selected from the small group of candidates to fulfill the mission. It was for the greater good and must be carried out as per the instructions he'd been given by those who knew best.

He'd been dropped off two blocks from his destination and had made his way through the community, following the map in his head, determined to bring his assignment, the death of Harold Garrison, to a successful conclusion.

It mattered not that he would have to sacrifice himself for the cause. The cause was good, and just, and necessary, and the will of the Wizard must be done.

His otherwise expressionless face took on a slight smile, a grim expression of satisfaction at the honor about to be his.

~*~

HAROLD GARRISON leaned forward and rested his elbows on the desk. His fingers were woven together, and he stared unseeing across the office, deep in thought.

The campaign was about to begin and he was wrapping up his final plans. The incumbent was down in the polls, and Garrison was sure he would win this election. There was no doubt about it, and he couldn't wait for the battle to begin.

Sure, it was only a seat on the city council, but he had drive, and it would surely lead to bigger and better things. The people in his ward had responded positively to his plans for the area. They wanted him, and he was proud to serve.

They would begin putting up the election signs in a day or two, and then the house-to-house canvassing would begin. There would be no campaign headquarters, other than his residence, but the brochures printed and stacked in the corner of his office welcomed anyone in the ward to contact him at any time.

He pushed his chair back from the desk, stood, and wandered from the office and into the kitchen. The house was always quiet this time of day. The kids were in school, and his wife, who taught third-grade English at Richmond Public, would be busy now, doing the job she loved so much.

He rinsed out his mug, drained the last cup of coffee from the carafe, and fixed up his steaming drink with a bit of cream and sugar.

His wife would be coming home for lunch, and they would have a quick sandwich together before she had to get back to her class, but right now his stomach was asking for food. He found the last leftover chocolate donut in the fridge and retrieved it from the box that had held half a dozen yesterday morning, found a plate in the cupboard, and sat at the kitchen table.

He started as the doorbell rang, breaking the quiet of the house. He dropped the donut, wiped his hands and mouth on a paper napkin, and took a quick swig of coffee before rising to his feet.

He hurried into the foyer and swung the front door open. He stared curiously at the young boy outside, wondering why he wasn't in school at this time of day.

"Are you Harold Garrison?" the boy asked.

Garrison nodded. "Yes, I am. May I help you with something?"

"Can I come in for a minute?"

Garrison stepped back and swung the door fully open, allowing the visitor to enter.

~*~

THE BOY CLIMBED the final step into the foyer and faced his intended victim. At the same time, he drew his right hand from his jacket pocket, clutching a gun, his finger already tightening on the trigger as he raised it in the direction of his target.

There was a blast, and a bullet spat from the gun and shattered a mirror on the wall of the foyer. Shards of glass sprinkled about the floor at his feet, but his quarry had eluded him, ducking in time to avoid the deadly fire.

The guy was fast. Too fast.

He spun to the left, corrected his aim, and trained the weapon toward Garrison, who stumbled and half-crawled into the front room.

The boy had been trained well, and his skill at hitting a bull's-eye was outstanding, but the second shot missed the fast-moving target and embedded itself in the hardwood floor.

This wasn't supposed to happen. The Wizard wouldn't be pleased if his carefully laid plans went amiss.

Garrison made it to his feet, and as the boy stepped into the front room and aimed again, his quarry spun out of sight through a doorway.

The assassin followed, the gun still poised and ready. He had him cornered now. He moved carefully to the doorway, his finger squeezing the trigger, ready to shoot as he stepped into the room.

He saw Garrison's head disappear, ducking behind a desk in what appeared to be an office. He moved carefully across the room, toward the desk, and then stepped around beside it. Garrison was crouched down, shielding himself behind the back of a chair.

The gun spat. One shot. Two. The cushy back of the leather chair, with its comfortable stuffing, proved to be no protection, as the deadly rounds pierced the barrier, bored through the skull of the victim, and ground to a stop, embedded in the hardwood floor.

As Garrison collapsed, his eyes glazed over and then took on the unseeing gaze of the newly dead.

The job was finished. It had been a success.

The killer smiled, pleased that justice had been done and his part in the great plan was finished.

The last thing the boy remembered was raising the pistol to his own head and hearing the resulting explosion as he squeezed the trigger.

He was unaware of his own body sinking to the floor as the shot echoed in the small room, and except for the trickle of blood that found a path between the cracks in the floorboards, all was quiet and still.

CHAPTER 21

Wednesday, August 24th, 12:01 p.m.

KIM GARRISON smiled as she shooed the last student from her classroom. Not that she was distressed, or annoyed in the least, by the youngsters she taught, but she was looking forward to a break. On the contrary, she wasn't averse to enjoying some of the antics of her students. She loved kids and was proud to be instrumental in helping guide them through their informative years.

She slipped her handbag from the bottom drawer of her desk, stood, and hurried from the classroom. She was thankful Richmond Public was only two blocks from home, and she could get there for a quick lunch with her husband and be back in plenty of time.

She left the school and stopped by a sandwich shop, conveniently located along her route. She picked up two thick submarines and hurried toward home.

As she neared the house, she dug her key from her handbag and stepped onto the pathway leading to the front door. She frowned as she saw the door open and, looking around the yard, she expected to see Harold. He wasn't around, however, and she climbed the steps to the door and stepped curiously inside.

"Harold?"

No answer.

She called a little louder, "Harold, are you here?"

Still no answer.

Perhaps he'd come outside and wandered around to the backyard for some reason.

She stepped inside the house, heard a grinding underneath her feet, and looked down at the shattered glass.

"Harold," she called again, more anxious. "Are you all right?"

She looked at the mirror on the foyer wall, cracked, broken into a spiderweb of pieces. She frowned. Something didn't seem right.

She hurried down a short hallway to the kitchen. A coffee cup was on the table, along with a half-finished donut. She tossed her handbag, and the bag of sandwiches, onto the table and stepped to the back door. She slid it open and peered onto the deck.

Harold wasn't outside.

Worried now, she went back through the kitchen to the office. She peeked inside the doorway, still calling Harold's name.

There was no answer, and the office appeared to be empty.

She ran upstairs and checked the bedrooms, and then down to the basement. Perhaps he was in the garage, looking for a box to gather up the broken glass, but her search came up empty, and she received no reply to her calls. Her husband was nowhere to be seen.

Unsure of what else to do, she went back to the kitchen table and sat.

She stared at his half-finished donut and touched the cup

of coffee. The drink was cold. Where could he be?

She jumped to her feet and reached across the table and grabbed her handbag, which she had tossed there earlier. She snapped it open, felt inside, and came up with her cell phone.

She hit speed dial one, Harold's number.

She heard it ring. Once. Twice. No answer. She let it ring as she stood and anxiously wandered from the kitchen to the front room.

It was then she heard a cell phone ringing, and the sound came not from her phone, but from his office.

She hurried to the office and stepped inside. She heard the ringing louder now, from across the room.

She eased toward the desk and gasped as she saw her husband, lying on the floor in an unnatural position. She thought at first he might have had a heart attack, but as she hurried around the desk, she stopped short and screamed when she saw a second body, the body of a young man, on the floor beside her husband.

When she saw the bullet wounds on her husband's face, and the stream of drying blood, she felt her legs grow weak. Her heart pounded, and she began to tremble. She felt faint and nearly stumbled as she crouched beside her husband's still form.

"Harold," she said anxiously, fearful.

She could tell he was dead, but she called his name again and shook him, hoping there was some mistake. He didn't respond to her hysterical plea, and his face was cold as she touched it with the tips of her fingers. Her tears came freely, falling on the face of the man she loved so much.

The cell phone went to voice mail, and her husband's voice came faintly from her phone. She barely heard it as she knelt, weeping and moaning his name, overcome with grief, unmindful of the dead boy who lay at her husband's feet.

Eventually her uncontrolled frenzy subsided, and she could think clearer. She straightened her back and turned her head toward the dead boy. She didn't recognize him. She saw the gun in his hand and, in confusion, staggered to her feet and dropped into a chair in front of the desk.

She leaned forward and mourned her husband, crying, bewildered, and afraid, her face in her hands.

In a few minutes she stopped weeping, sat back, and took a deep breath. In her confusion, she had dropped her cell phone beside her husband's body, so she retrieved it and dialed 9-1-1.

CHAPTER 22

Wednesday, August 24th, 12:31 p.m.

ALWAYS QUICK TO respond, the forensic unit was already at the Garrison house when Hank arrived. He pulled his Chevy up behind it, swung from the vehicle, and ducked under the yellow tape cordoning off the property. The forensics team, in their white coveralls, unloaded equipment from the van, streaming in and out of the house.

He made his way up the path to the front door. A uniform was leaning against the doorframe and greeted Hank as he climbed the steps.

"Another lovely day, Hank," the cop said, handing Hank a pair of booties.

"Yeah, beautiful," Hank replied as he slipped the shoe covers on and stepped inside the foyer. "Just beautiful."

An investigator was cleaning up some shards of glass inside the doorway and placing them in an evidence box. Hank stepped carefully around him and into the front room. Other investigators were busy conducting a rigorous examination. Hank spied lead crime scene investigator Rod Jameson and approached him.

"Afternoon, Hank," Jameson said.

Hank nodded hello. "Where's the victim?"

"Two of them," Jameson replied, waving toward the office. "In there."

Hank crossed the front room and stepped inside the office. Investigators were going over the room, fingerprinting and snapping photos. Hank saw the photographer across the room, on the other side of a desk. As he came closer, he saw the bodies on the floor. No matter how often he was called to scenes like this, he never got used to the sight, and was overcome by the senseless tragedy before him now.

He shook it off, stepped closer, and crouched beside the bodies. He saw the 9mm Glock in the hand of the young boy, the bullet wound in his temple, and the other victim beside him with two bullet wounds in his head.

It looked very much like another murder/suicide.

He sighed and checked the pockets of the boy, finding what he expected. Nothing. No identification of any kind.

He stood and turned to see the medical examiner, Nancy Pietek, come into the room. He greeted her with a nod.

"Hello, Hank. What have we here?"

Hank motioned toward the bodies. "Looks like a repeat of yesterday. Another murder/suicide."

Nancy approached the bodies, bending over and examining them a moment before standing again and turning to Hank. "An exact repeat," she said. "The wound on the boy's temple indicates he shot himself. I presume he killed our first victim and then himself."

Jameson came in the room and touched Hank's arm. "The victim's wife is in the kitchen if you want to talk to her."

Hank nodded. "I'll be right there. Was she a witness?"

Jameson shook his head. "No, she came home and found them here and called 9-1-1."

"I suppose there were no witnesses?"

"Nope. And their kids are still at school."

"Kids?"

"Two."

Two children, now fatherless. Hank sighed deeply. "I'd better go and see her now."

When Hank stepped into the kitchen he saw a female officer sitting at the table, talking softly to a woman who he knew must be Mrs. Garrison. Her eyes were red and she clutched a tissue in a trembling hand. The officer stood and left the room as Hank entered. He pulled back a chair beside the overwrought woman, sat down, and faced her.

"I'm Detective Hank Corning," he said, his voice gentle, soothing.

The woman turned in her chair and smiled weakly.

Sometimes Hank hated being a detective. His heart was breaking for this distraught woman, and for this broken family. His satisfaction came when they were able to track down the evil people who cared little for others and finally bring them to justice. That was the only thing that drove him on and allowed him to face this job day after day.

He touched the woman's hand. "I have a few questions, Mrs. Garrison. Is that all right?"

She nodded.

Hank cleared his throat. "Tell me about how you came to discover ..."

"I was at school ... I'm a teacher, and I came home to have lunch with my husband as I often do if he's at home. And when I came in, I saw the broken glass in the foyer. I searched for him, and finally found ..." She dropped her head, her shoulders hunched, and sobbed.

"The young man ... did you know him?"

She looked up and shook her head.

Hank remained quiet, observing her grief, and fought to squelch his rising anger. He had to separate his feelings from his job.

"My children," she said. "They're still at school."

"I'll send an officer to get them," Hank said and then added, "Maybe you'd better go with him."

"Yes," Mrs. Garrison said as she turned her head and blew her nose. Hank handed her another tissue from the box on the table. A bag from a sandwich shop down the street was on the table, along with a handbag Hank assumed was Mrs. Garrison's.

He asked her a few more questions, such as her husband's name, her name, and the names and ages of her children. He jotted the information in his notepad and tucked it into his pocket.

"We'll get your children now," he said as he pushed back his chair and stood. He went outside where a couple of the first responding officers lounged about near the front door. He arranged for one of them to take Mrs. Garrison to the school and retrieve her children.

The investigators waited until Mrs. Garrison was gone before carting a pair of loaded body bags to the waiting ambulances. The vehicles drove away, taking their burden to the city morgue.

Hank wandered back into the office. Nancy was talking to Jameson and turned toward Hank as he asked, "Can you tell me anything other than what we suspect?"

"It doesn't look like it, Hank. I'll let you know."

Hank nodded. He hoped she would find something. He needed anything that would give him a break in this puzzling case. Anything at all.

CHAPTER 23

Wednesday, August 24th, 1:54 p.m.

LISA KRUNK SAT BACK in the passenger's seat of the news van as it sped across town. They'd come from the latest crime scene and she was fuming because she hadn't been allowed access to the actual scene and the cops hadn't so much as given her the time of day.

She'd tried to corner Detective Corning on his way from the house, but he'd avoided her. All she had to show for her time was a few shots of the nonexistent action from outside the house.

She assumed this latest murder was related to the two recent ones, and had a suspicion the Lincolns were involved. She had to get a statement from someone which she could edit into the footage from the scene. At least she would have something.

As Don wheeled the van onto Carver Street, she smiled with satisfaction when she saw Annie's Ford Escort in the driveway. The garage door was up, and the Firebird was plainly visible, parked inside.

The Lincolns were at home.

She made it her business to know where people lived, what they drove, where they worked, and how they spent their time. It was necessary if she was going to be able to get the stories she needed.

Lisa pointed toward the curb, just before the driveway. "Pull over here."

Don touched the brakes and twisted the steering wheel, and the van pulled over and stopped.

"Let's go," Lisa snapped as she pushed the door open and stepped out.

Don popped open the driver's door, swung out from behind the wheel, and slid open the back door. He retrieved his camera and hoisted it onto his shoulder. He hurried to catch Lisa, who was already heading up the driveway toward the open garage.

Jake had the hood of the Firebird up and was fiddling around with something. He straightened his back and turned as Lisa reached the door of the garage.

"Jake Lincoln, I'm—"

Jake frowned. "Yes, I know who you are."

"Uh … I would like to ask you a few questions if I may?"

Jake pulled a rag from his back pocket and wiped his hands. He looked at the camera with its red light glowing, and then back at Lisa, and remained silent.

Lisa began, "Mr. Lincoln, as you know, there have been three murders in the last three days—"

"Three murders?"

Lisa smiled. She knew the Lincolns were pretty cozy with Detective Corning, and always seemed to be up on the latest news, but for once it appeared she had some information before Jake did. All she knew was what she'd heard on the police scanner, so she'd have to wing it.

"I just came from the scene of a double homicide," she said. "It appears to be related to the previous two. Can you tell me about that?"

Jake frowned as Lisa shoved the mike under his nose. "I am unaware of the details. Perhaps you should speak to the police about it."

"I spoke to the investigator in charge," Lisa lied, "but I was hoping you would have something to add."

Jake shrugged. "Nope."

Lisa hesitated. "What can you tell me about yesterday's murder of Bobby Sullivan? Are you investigating that case as well?"

"There's nothing new to add. Yes, we're working on it and so are the police. Again, maybe you should speak to them."

She wasn't getting anywhere. Time for a new approach. "Perhaps your wife, Annie, might have something to add?"

"I doubt it. She doesn't know any more than I do about this. And now, if there are no more questions, I have work to do."

"Thank you, Mr. Lincoln," Lisa said, faking a smile.

Jake grunted, stuffed the rag into his rear pocket, and turned back to the car.

Don aimed the camera toward Lisa. She said, "We will bring you breaking news as it happens. In an exclusive report, I'm Lisa Krunk for Channel 7 Action News." She motioned for Don to shut the camera down.

Lisa spun around and headed to the van, Don trailing behind. She wasn't satisfied, and couldn't understand why nobody wanted to talk to her.

~*~

JAKE TURNED AND watched Don and Lisa climb in the van and drive away. She was getting to be a severe pain in the neck.

He closed the hood of the Firebird and put away the tools he'd been using, shut the garage door, and went into the kitchen. After washing the grime from his hands, he went into the office where Annie was at the desk, poring over some paperwork. She looked up when he entered.

Jake dropped into the guest chair and folded his long legs under the seat. "I just got a nice visit from our good friend, Lisa Krunk."

"Oh?"

"According to her, there's been another murder."

Annie dropped the papers and sat back. "Did she give you any details?"

"Not really. Maybe you should call Hank."

Jake leaned forward, pulled his chair a little closer to the desk, and slipped his iPhone from his pocket. He set it between them, hit speed dial, and put it on speaker.

"Detective Hank Corning."

"Hank, it's Jake. What's this I hear about another murder?"

"Where'd you hear that?"

"Lisa Krunk."

Hank chuckled. "So she tracked you down, did she? I doubt if she had much information."

"Can you fill us in?" Jake asked.

"It looks like another murder/suicide. A guy by the name of Harold Garrison, killed by an unidentified boy, who then took his own life."

Jake and Annie exchanged a glance.

"Let me guess," Annie said. "The weapon was a nine-millimeter Glock?"

"Hi, Annie. Yup, you got it right."

"And no witnesses?"

"No witnesses," Hank said, adding, "I'll drop by and see you guys a little later. I've been making the rounds talking to friends and neighbors, and I have a few more calls to make."

"Okay, see you later." Jake clicked off the phone, slouched back, and whistled. "This is getting to be an epidemic." He motioned toward the papers on the desk. "Did you come up with any more ideas there?"

Annie shook her head. "No, but I'm working on it."

CHAPTER 24

Wednesday, August 24th, 2:45 p.m.

DAVID HAINES was tired of his father always harassing him about school, his grades, and studying. Confined in a classroom, or being suffocated in his room memorizing useless information from books, was not his thing. It bored him and made him feel like he was wasting his life doing the will of other people—doing what they wanted him to do instead of allowing him to pursue his own ambitions.

He realized his parents weren't all that bad, really. His father was a bit overbearing maybe, but at least they were still together. David knew of other kids who had only one parent, or none, or parents who fought all the time. Sure, they were okay as far as parents went, but they just didn't understand him. He had no desire to be a carbon copy of his father, tied to the same dreary job for as long as he could remember.

He needed more freedom than that. Why couldn't they understand?

He had lessened the agony of schooling by skipping classes whenever possible and hanging about on the streets. What he really wanted to do was get a job, make some money, and be independent. No more pencils, no more books ...

After all, he was sixteen now and was mature enough to make his own decisions.

He expertly maneuvered a carelessly discarded soda can into position and gave it a solid kick, sending it tinkling down the alley to land against an overflowing dumpster.

It wasn't that he was lazy; he actually wanted to make something of his life, but to do it his way. And his way didn't involve any stupid school or domineering teachers.

He was smart enough to know no one became a success overnight. Sure, he would have to work hard and put in his time, but he would struggle his way up until he was the master of his own destiny. What was wrong with that?

He just wasn't sure where to start.

Of course, he would have to explain everything to his parents. He knew they wouldn't see things his way, and if they kicked him out of the house, well, then, he could, and would, make his own way.

Across the alleyway, in the doorway of a deteriorating tenement, an unkempt man was leaning against the doorframe, his hands stuffed in his jacket pockets. David glanced at him briefly and kept on walking. He could tell a drug dealer a mile away, and even if he'd had the money, he wasn't interested in their wares.

He had tried drugs once, at the insistence of a so-called friend. It could've been cocaine, or maybe heroin; he didn't know much about drugs. It'd been okay, but he didn't like the fact that he wasn't in control of his senses, and he had no interest in trying it again.

A motorcycle roared behind him, making its way down the narrow alley. David flattened himself against the stained brick building to allow it to pass, and then wandered on, thinking and planning his future.

He had to have a plan. Perhaps he could find a job flipping burgers, or delivering pizza. He'd heard there was good money in that, maybe enough to find him a place of his own, and start him on the road to better things.

In the shelter of a doorway, a homeless man was huddled on a bed made of cardboard, covered with a filthy blanket. As David sauntered by, the bum sputtered and muttered, peering at him with one cautious eye, clutching his rags about himself as if protecting his domain from an unwelcome intruder.

David paid no mind to the vagrant except to wonder how a guy could get to be that way. He wondered if the aging man had at one time had plans and dreams like his own, and had somehow, somewhere lost his way. He felt a flash of pity for what seemed to be a life gone wrong, and was determined never to end up like that.

He wished he had a couple of bucks he could give to the guy, but all he had was coffee money, and he wanted a coffee badly.

One cup of coffee, a quick drink. He would enjoy it for sure, but then, when it was gone, it was gone.

David sighed and reached into his pocket and pulled out a couple of coins. All he had. He turned back and dropped the money onto the blanket beside the man. The hardened face of the bum seemed to soften somewhat as he looked up a moment, then snatched the coins, tucked his hands back under his tattered clothes, and continued with his persistent mumbling.

"Have a good day," David said as he turned away and continued down the thoroughfare.

He exited the cramped alleyway and stepped onto the crumbling sidewalk. The streets were narrow in this part of the city, the houses crammed together, disintegrating, and in much need of a repair job they would never see.

He didn't often make it to this area, but he'd been wandering around most of the day, discontented and frustrated with the way things were going for him, and had ended up here, still filled with hope for the future, yet surrounded by an ambience of despair and hopelessness.

He paused to watch as a shiny black Cadillac Escalade came down the street toward him. It seemed rather out of place in this bleak neighborhood, an area more used to beat-up cars and sluggish pedestrians than vehicles worth more than any of the houses in this forgotten community.

Shoving his hands into his pockets, David stood and watched curiously as the Escalade drew closer and pulled to a stop beside him, its engine purring, its darkened windows concealing whoever might be inside.

Perhaps they wanted directions. David stood and waited.

CHAPTER 25

Wednesday, August 24th, 2:45 p.m.

ANNIE HAD JOTTED down Harold Garrison's name when Hank had mentioned it on the phone. It was another murder/suicide, obviously related, and Annie wanted to find out more about Garrison.

Hank would surely have some valuable information from his interviews, but perhaps she could supplement it with a little online research.

Annie rolled her chair a little closer to the desk, tapped the space bar on the keyboard, and brought the iMac from its sleep. A web search for Harold Garrison brought up several possibilities.

The first result looked most likely to be the one she was after. It linked to a web site announcing Garrison's run for city council. She scrolled through pages outlining his platform and the hopes he had for his ward, as well as plans for the city in general.

It appeared Garrison was an insurance broker who now had political aspirations. She clicked on a link that brought her to the web site for Garrison Insurance. The company appeared to have been in business in east Richmond Hill for over sixty years, passed down to Harold Garrison from his father, and his grandfather before that.

Not a very threatening business, and not likely to create any enemies who would want him dead.

She browsed a bit more and, as expected, didn't find anything enlightening, just enough to give her an idea of who Harold Garrison was.

Jake came into the office and dropped into the guest chair. The chair groaned, but held. "Hank's on his way here," he said. "What've you been up to?"

"Doing a little research on Harold Garrison."

"Anything interesting?"

Annie filled him in on what she'd found online. "I also gave Bobby's aunt, Mrs. Mitchell, a call, to let her know what we've been looking into."

Jake jumped up as the doorbell rang. "There's Hank," he said as he left to answer the door.

Annie followed him into the living room, took a seat on the couch, tucked her legs up underneath herself, and faced the hallway. Hank came in, gave her a big smile, and dropped into the armchair while Jake slouched at the other end of the couch.

"It's been a busy day," Hank said.

"What'd you find out?" Annie asked.

"Not as much as I'd hoped, but I'm convinced all three murders are related. The same MO and the same type of weapon were used on all three occasions."

"But did you find anything else to link the victims?" Jake asked.

Hank shook his head. "That's the stumper. Until we can come up with a connection, and a motive, I'm baffled." He leaned forward. "There are a couple of other interesting tidbits, however. First of all, there are the guns."

"The nine-millimeter Glocks used for all three murders," Jake said. "Yes, we know."

"Not just that," Hank said. "But we have a definite connection. All three guns were from the same lot. Manufactured at the same time, according to the serial numbers, and so purchased together. I have a call in with the manufacturer to see where those guns were distributed. I didn't notice this at first, because the first two murders were initially treated as separate incidents, but when I started to put everything together, I took a closer look at the weapons, and that's when I discovered it."

Annie frowned. "But there's no connection between the victims and the killers."

"Not that I can find yet," Hank said. "But there has to be something we're missing. There's got to be a connection."

"All three killers were young," Jake said.

"That may be a start," Hank said. "However, two of the victims were older, and successful businessmen, while one was young and an ex-con. No connection with the victims I can see. I interviewed a lot of people. I can't find any business, church, or anything else they have in common." Hank leaned back and scratched his head. "I'm puzzled."

"You said there are other tidbits," Jake said. "What else did you find?"

"I got the blood results for Cheryl Waters. She volunteered, by the way. They came back positive for LSD, as well as trace amounts of scopolamine."

"Scopolamine?"

"Apparently, it can be dangerous if not administered properly. Scopolamine can render a victim unconscious, and in large doses it can cause respiratory failure and death. It's sometimes used criminally as a date rape drug, and has been known to be used as a truth drug because it can lower a person's inhibitions."

"And used in conjunction with LSD?" Annie asked.

"Who knows?" Hank said. "It sounds dangerous to me."

"So we can assume the third killer will show similar drugs in his blood," Jake said.

"We'll see. But I expect you're right."

Annie wrinkled her brow and looked at Hank. "So, since we have three seemingly unrelated victims, and three seemingly unrelated killers, there must be somebody, or something, out there who's orchestrating this."

"To me, it appears the three killers have one thing in common, besides their age," Jake said.

Hank glanced at Jake. "And what's that?"

"Two of them are unknown, suggesting they're either runaways or homeless. The third, Cheryl, almost fits into that category as well. She's not homeless, but she's transient. I believe her father called her 'flighty and irresponsible.'"

"You may have something there, Jake," Hank said. "But we're still lacking a motive."

"With similar drugs in their system, and similar MOs," Annie said, "it suggests to me the killers were all part of some type of organization."

Jake interrupted, "And the fact two of the three killed themselves shows they weren't in their right mind."

Hank said, "We can include Cheryl Waters in that as well. We know she wasn't in her right mind."

"So where does that leave us?" Annie asked.

Jake frowned. "Some kind of brainwashing?"

Hank pursed his lips. "It's starting to look like it," he said. "Or, at least, some kind of coercion."

CHAPTER 26

Wednesday, August 24th, 2:54 p.m.

THE REAR DOOR of the Cadillac Escalade slid open and David took a step forward. Two men in the rear seat looked his way and smiled.

"Excuse me." The nearest man turned in the seat. He was holding a map, poking at it with one finger. "Could you direct me to this street?"

David took another step, leaned in, and looked at the map. The location the man was pointing to was on the other side of the city.

Suddenly, the map whisked away, the man's hands shot forward, and David was seized by both arms and pulled off balance. He stumbled once, and before he could react, was dragged into the vehicle and something pulled over his head from behind. It felt like a cloth bag.

He struggled, his shouts muffled. "What are you doing?" He attempted to scream, but couldn't. The rear door slammed and he felt the vehicle surge forward.

He heard a zip as a plastic cable tie tightened about his wrists and held them securely. Strong hands at either side held his arms. He couldn't move.

"Where are you taking me?"

Silence.

He twisted in the seat and struggled to free his arms. The ties bit into his flesh and held on.

"Stay still. We're not going to hurt you."

The SUV picked up speed. The tires hummed as it traveled a short distance, and then he heard the click, click of the blinker. The vehicle swerved, and then the engine labored as it accelerated.

The musty smell of the bag in his nostrils impeded his breathing. He panicked, kicking his feet and continuing to struggle.

Where were they taking him? Who were these guys and what did they want with him?

"You must stay still."

He closed his eyes against the blackness and tried to relax. He was afraid and though he didn't know how to pray, he did his best. His panic subsided and he sat quietly, confused and bewildered.

They must have made a mistake. If this was a kidnapping, surely they must be confusing him with someone else. His parents had no money. If they wanted a ransom, he was doomed. He hoped it would be straightened out, but he wasn't so sure.

They drove for several minutes, making a variety of turns, speeding up, and slowing. Eventually, the vehicle came to a near stop and turned again, and he could feel the roughness of the road as the vehicle shook. They might be going down a driveway. A long driveway.

The Escalade slowed to a crawl and stopped, and the engine died. The doors hummed and he was yanked from the vehicle and dropped onto his feet. His captors continued to grip his arms.

"Walk," the same voice said, and he was pushed from behind.

He almost lost his balance a few times as they prodded him over rough ground. It felt like gravel under his feet.

A door creaked.

"Step up."

With his feet, he felt his way up three steps, then stumbled across a hard floor.

"Sit down," the voice said as someone pushed on his shoulders. He dropped into a hard chair.

The bag was whisked away and, for a moment, he was blinded by overhead lights. He squinted away the glare and peered around. He was in a small room, about the size of his own bedroom. The walls, ceiling, and floor were painted white, with no furniture in the room except a small bed against the far wall, the chair he was sitting on, and a toilet with a small sink above.

There were no windows in the room, but the fluorescent lights embedded in the ceiling lit the chamber with a dazzling glow.

One of his captors had left the room, the other still in front of him, eyeing him up and down.

David looked up, and his voice shook as he asked, "What do you want with me?"

"You'll be okay. Just relax."

"Please, please let me go," David pleaded, his lip trembling. "What are you going to do?"

"If you promise to stay still, I'll free your hands."

David nodded and didn't answer.

The man moved behind the chair. David heard a snap, like the sound of a switchblade popping, and the plastic ties sprang loose. He brought his arms forward and massaged his wrists.

"My parents have no money," David said. "If you're hoping for a ransom, there won't be much."

"You're not here for that reason." The man's voice was not unkind, but not pleasant either. "It'll all be explained to you later."

"My parents are expecting me home soon. When will you let me go?"

No answer.

The man avoided his eyes as David twisted in the chair and lifted his head. "Please let me go," he begged.

"Stand up."

David stood obediently.

"Go and sit on the bed."

David turned and trudged across the room to the bed. It was covered by a sheet with a single pillow at the top. He sat on the edge and watched as the man grabbed the chair and carried it from the room. The door breezed shut, and he heard the metallic sound of a bolt sliding in place, and then all was quiet.

He stared around the empty room, alone and terrified. Afraid for himself and afraid for his parents. They would undoubtedly be worried. Though he'd skipped school often, and basically done his own thing a lot, he never missed being home for supper. He looked at his watch. At least they hadn't taken that from him.

Eventually, he lay on the bed and stared at the stark white ceiling. He wanted to cry but held back. Surely this was all a mistake, and they would let him out of this place soon.

He felt hopeful, and then hopeless, and angry as he closed his eyes and attempted to pray again. He didn't know much about God, but he sure hoped He was listening right now.

CHAPTER 27

Thursday, August 25th, 7:30 a.m.

DETECTIVE HANK CORNING was being slowly consumed by this case. He'd had a sleepless night, with thoughts of the victims running through his mind.

He got up early and attempted to keep his emotions in check. He knew letting a case affect him personally was not a good thing for a cop, but he was angry. Angry at himself for not being able to come up with the solution, and angry at the senseless murders afflicting the city.

He felt numb, and as he took a quick shower and dressed, he ran the circumstances of the last few days through his mind. He thought about the three killers and their three victims. It all seemed so illogical and irrational. The death of another human being always affected him deeply, especially if that death was due to a cold-blooded and coldhearted choice of another.

He had a breakfast consisting of two pieces of toast with jam, then checked his service revolver, grabbed his briefcase, and left his humble apartment, heading for the precinct.

As he weaved his way in and around the morning rush hour traffic, he thought about the city he loved so much. He'd lived here all of his life, and it seemed to him things were getting worse. Richmond Hill's robbery/homicide division had always been small, and mostly he'd investigated robberies, as the few homicides rarely amounted to anything as mind-numbing as murder. The odd suicide, a fatal car accident, but barely a spattering of murder victims as long as he could remember.

Until recently.

It seemed like the city was changing. No, the world was changing, and he wasn't convinced it was for the better.

Hank pulled into the precinct parking lot, parked his Chevy in its usual spot, climbed wearily from the vehicle, and made his way around to the front of the building. As he came through the precinct doors and headed for his desk, he was stopped by Detective Callaway.

"This came in a couple of hours ago, Hank. I thought you might be interested. Could be related." Callaway handed Hank a sheet of paper, a police report. "A missing kid. 9-1-1 took the call and reported it."

Hank took the paper and glanced at it briefly.

"I know it hasn't been twenty-four hours yet," Callaway said with a shrug. "But still ..."

"Thanks, Callaway. I'll look into it. Right now, anything and everything could be important."

Hank turned and browsed the report as he crossed the precinct floor and sat at his desk. He leaned forward and studied the paper.

According to the report, a Mr. Haines had called and stated his son hadn't returned home from school the day before, and as of 6:00 am this morning, they still hadn't heard from him.

The boy was sixteen years old, and though he legally couldn't be forced to go home at that age, the report said he still lived with his parents and had never missed coming home every day, and he'd never been out all night before without his parents' knowledge of where he was.

He pulled his cell phone from its holder and called Jake.

It rang three times, and then he heard, "Jake here."

"Jake, we have a report of a missing boy. I'm going to interview his parents. Do you want to come?"

"A missing boy?"

Hank filled Jake in on the details that were in the report. "I can drop by there in a few minutes."

"Give me ten minutes and I'll be ready," Jake said.

"I'll be there in ten." Hank turned off his cell phone, tucked it away, snapped open his briefcase, and dropped the report inside.

"I'm going to see the missing boy's parents," he called to Callaway as he strode from the precinct.

~*~

JAKE SET HIS CELL phone on the kitchen table and looked at Annie. She'd paused her job of washing up the breakfast dishes and had turned to face him, a quizzical look on her face.

Matty was sitting at the side of the table, his feet pulled up under him, looking at something on the iPad. He seemed to sense something was up, and he set the tablet on the table and looked at his father.

Jake glanced at Annie. "There's a missing boy. Missing since yesterday."

Annie dried her hands on a towel, pulled back a chair, and sat. She waited for Jake to continue.

Jake looked at Matty, then back at Annie. "A sixteen-year-old boy. He didn't come home last night. Apparently, something he's never done before, and his parents are understandably worried."

Matty listened with wide eyes as Jake told Annie the details. He finished with, "Hank thinks it may be related. He called to see if I wanted to go with him to interview the boy's parents."

"What do you think happened to him, Dad?"

Jake turned to Matty. "We don't know. I hope he's all right, but the police need to look into it, just in case."

Annie looked worried. "I hope he'll just come home," she said and glanced at Matty a moment. "I know how his parents must be feeling."

"Perhaps you should come with us?" Jake asked.

Annie hesitated. "I would, but I don't want to overwhelm the parents." She looked at Matty again. "Perhaps I'll drive Matty and Kyle to school today."

Matty shot her a disapproving look. "Aw, Mom, we're okay. We always walk to school."

"Just for now, Matty. Just until—"

Jake interrupted. "Matty, your mother is right. Let her drive you to school for the next few days." They had drilled into him the importance of being careful, of using common sense, especially around people they didn't know. He wasn't as concerned as Annie, but still, you couldn't be too careful.

"All right, Mom." Matty closed the iPad cover and slid off the chair. "I have to get ready now." He paused a moment. "I hope the boy's okay," he said as he dashed from the room and headed upstairs.

Annie watched him leave and sighed. "I'm not being too overprotective, am I?"

"Not at all. Until this case is cleared up, I think we would be irresponsible not to take extra precautions."

Annie nodded and looked thoughtful.

Jake stood. "And now, I have to get ready. Hank's on his way."

CHAPTER 28

Thursday, August 25th, 8:23 a.m.

AS HANK PULLED the car to the curb in front of the Haines's residence, Jake eyed the small house. Located in an older part of the city, it was showing its age and was in need of a few critical repairs. The roof drooped slightly in the middle and the shingles were worn and buckling.

They climbed from the vehicle and walked up the crumbling concrete walk to the front door. Hank pressed the doorbell, and the door was opened a few moments later by a smallish man with lines of worry evident on his face.

"Are you the police?" he asked. He had a high-pitched voice, and as he spoke, he twiddled nervously with his fingers.

Hank nodded. They introduced themselves and then were led through the foyer to the front room. Mrs. Haines, a slight woman sitting in an armchair, watched as they took a seat on the couch. Anxiety showed on her face as she worked her hands in an agitated manner.

Mr. Haines dropped into a chair beside her and leaned forward. "Detective, as we told the woman on the phone this morning, David didn't come home last night, and we're very worried."

Hank slipped a notepad from his inner pocket, produced a pen, and flipped open the pad to an empty page. "We'll do our best to find your son, Mr. Haines. I'll need a few details first, such as names, et cetera."

Mr. Haines answered, "My name is Max, and this is my wife, Bev. David is our only child, and it's not like him to stay out all night. In fact, I don't believe he ever has before."

Hank jotted down the names before asking, "Do you know if he was at school yesterday?"

"I assume he was, but I can't be sure. He left here at eight thirty in the morning, as usual, and we haven't heard from him since. I know he does skip classes from time to time, but as of now, I can't get any information from the school yet. It's too early."

Hank looked at his watch. "I'll check on that a little later. What school does he go to?"

"Richmond Hill High School."

Hank scribbled in his notepad. "Does he have a cell phone?"

Mr. Haines shook his head. "No. That's not something we could afford to get for him. Money's a little tight lately."

"What about a job? Does he have a part-time job?"

"No. He spoke often of getting some kind of job after school and on the weekends, but he never did."

"And he's sixteen years old?"

"Yes. He turned sixteen last month."

Mrs. Haines voice was soft as she said, "David's not a bad boy, Detective. He's rather restless and perhaps naive about life at times, but overall he's a very good boy."

Hank nodded and forced a smile. "Does David have any close friends?"

Mr. Haines glanced at his wife a moment before replying,

"Not that I know of. David's a bit of a loner, really."

Mrs. Haines spoke. "I'm sure he knows some of the other kids at school, but he's never mentioned anyone in particular."

"What about a girlfriend?"

The woman shook her head. "I don't believe so. I'm sure he knows some of the girls at school, but there's no one serious as far as I know."

"Would you have a picture of him? Perhaps a school photo, or one that shows his face clearly?"

"Yes," Mrs. Haines said as she rose to her feet. She went to a bookcase on the wall and flipped through a photo album. She returned a few moments later and handed Hank a picture. Jake recognized the style as one of those posed shots with the fake scenery behind. It looked like a school photo. "This is a recent picture," she said.

Hank took the photo and examined it briefly. Jake glanced over at David's cheerful pose, a bit cocky maybe, with a crooked grin splitting his face.

Hank tucked the picture into his notepad. "We'll canvass the neighborhood and the area around the school. I'll talk to the people at the school as soon as possible and check with anyone who knows him and may have seen him yesterday."

Mrs. Haines was on the verge of tears. Her voice quivered as she spoke. "Please find my David, Detective."

"We'll do our best, ma'am."

Mr. Haines covered his wife's hand with his and gave it a gentle squeeze. He turned back to Hank. "Is there anything we can do?"

Hank pulled a card from his pocket, leaned forward, and handed it to Mr. Haines. "Give me a call if you think of anything else that might help. In the meantime, you can contact anyone who might know David. There's a possibility someone may have seen him yesterday."

Mr. Haines took the card and gave it a glance before tucking it into his shirt pocket. "We'll call everyone we know."

Hank glanced at Jake and nodded. As they stood, Hank said, "We'll get to work on this right away."

Mrs. Haines remained sitting as her husband followed them to the door.

"I'll be in touch," Hank said as they left the house.

They made their way back down the path and climbed in Hank's car.

Jake buckled his seat belt and glanced at Hank, who was leaning forward, his arms on the steering wheel, as he gazed through the car window toward the house.

"What do you think?" Jake asked.

Hank leaned back. "I don't know," he said. "I hope David turns up safe, but I have a bad feeling about this."

"Why's that?"

"For starters, I don't think he wandered off and never told anyone. He doesn't seem like that kind of kid, from the sense I get about him from his parents, and I don't think he has it tough at home."

Jake nodded. "Yeah, I get the same feeling."

"He's about the same age as the other killers," Hank added.

Jake sighed. "I sure hope you're wrong about what you're thinking."

"So do I," Hank said as he put the key in the ignition and brought the engine to life. "I'll drop you home and then head out to the school and see if I can find out anything."

CHAPTER 29

Thursday, August 25th, 8:45 a.m.

OLIVER CRAIG PULLED his BMW in front of the building, killed the engine, and stepped from the vehicle. He commended himself for his brilliant idea to turn this place into the nerve center of his operation.

It was far enough from the city that no one would likely wander here, but if anyone happened upon it, its innocent front would cover any suspicions there could be more to this place than seemed.

And anyway, the guard would keep trespassers away.

He pushed open the door to the building and stepped inside. As he passed the parked Escalade, his guard, a hired thug, stood, and Craig could see his hand tucked under his jacket, his fingers no doubt resting on the weapon concealed there, just in case.

The guard relaxed and sat back down when he saw Craig. He picked up a magazine he'd been reading and flipped it open. Craig assumed he was looking at the pictures. The goon didn't look like he could even read.

Craig crossed the room, pushed open a door, and went down a long hallway to the lab. It had been several days since he'd been here, but he knew it was in capable hands.

Wolff, who was pulled up at a desk studying some paperwork, looked up as he entered.

"Good morning, sir."

Craig didn't answer immediately. He glanced around the sterile laboratory before speaking to Wolff. "Everything seems to be running efficiently," he said.

Wolff pushed back his chair and looked up at Craig through round-rimmed glasses. His stooped shoulders were evidence of many years spent poring over research. He pushed back a wild wisp of gray hair and said, "Everything is going according to plan, sir."

"You'll be well rewarded, Wolff."

"The chance to carry on your father's research is reward enough. However, I do appreciate the financial side."

Craig dropped into a chair at the end of the desk and faced Wolff. "Our last operation went rather well. I have to commend you on your excellent work."

"Thank you, sir."

"Is Muller here?" Craig asked.

"He's with a patient at the moment. A young girl, who seems to be an excellent candidate. He thinks she's ready and is now putting her through some final testing."

"And what of the new acquisition?"

"He has a strong will, sir, but I believe he'll prove to be outstanding in time."

Craig dropped a hand on Wolff's shoulder. "Excellent. Excellent."

Wolff accepted the praise with a slight smile and a nod before speaking. "The entire process, from procurement of the subject to completion of the training, is being done in record time. I've never seen such exceptional results. We're making rapid progress." He waved a hand toward a row of binders overcrowding a shelf behind the desk. "All thanks to your father's research, of course."

"I couldn't do it without you, Wolff."

Wolff leaned forward and pulled a small stack of papers toward him. "I have a progress report here for you, sir." He licked the tip of his thumb, leafed through the papers, slipped one out, and handed it to Craig. "I think you'll be pleased."

"Thank you, Wolff," Craig said as he took the paper and glanced over it. He folded it, tucked it into his shirt pocket, and stood. "I'll think I'll have a look around."

On his way from the room, Craig stopped at a bench containing beakers, burners, tongs, clamps, and other equipment he didn't recognize. He leaned over, peered into a microscope, and saw a mass of small red objects. Waving like tails from each were black filaments. They dashed so rapidly his eye could hardly follow them. Craig had no idea what he was looking at.

Above the bench, a wall-mounted storage cabinet bulged with bottles and beakers, filled with chemicals, potions, and powders. All were a mystery to Craig.

He was fortunate Wolff knew exactly what he was doing, and fortunate to have found him. After he had discovered a path to power in his father's notes, and with Wolff to interpret them, his plans had begun to evolve.

He left the lab and went back to the hallway he had previously come through. A half dozen rooms, three on each side, led off the well-lit passageway in front of him.

Each door contained a sliding panel that would open a small peephole. Craig opened the panel on the first door and peered through the bulletproof glass. Against the far wall he saw a young boy, lying on his back on a small bed. His eyes were closed, possibly asleep. He shut the panel and looked at a label above the opening. In handwritten letters, he saw the name "Haines."

The next room was occupied as well, but was darkened. He knew total darkness for a period of time was one of the necessary steps to achieve the optimum results. Craig couldn't see anything through the panel, so he closed it again and moved on.

Across the hall, on another door, Craig saw the bolt lock was not secured. He looked through the peephole and saw Muller, sitting upright in a fold-up chair, his back to Craig. A girl was sitting on the bed facing him. He could hear the murmur of conversation but couldn't make out what was being said. This must be the girl Wolff had said was ready.

He had no immediate plans for her, but there were several possibilities at the moment. He would have to go over his strategy and see how best to proceed.

Of the three remaining rooms, only one was in use at the moment. It contained another boy who appeared to be in the latter stages of the process. His hands and feet were strapped to the bed and he was going through severe convulsions. His body contracted and relaxed rapidly as he shook in a violent manner. Occasionally, he heaved up as far as the straps would allow, and then dropped and continued to shake. His moans and intermittent shrieks filled the room.

All effects of the drugs, no doubt, combined with the necessary amounts of torture. Craig knew it was normal and nothing to be concerned about.

He closed the panel, spun around, and looked in at Wolff before leaving. He was bent over his desk again, no doubt checking and double-checking the procedures. He backtracked up the hallway, entered the garage, nodded to the guard, and left the building.

He'd seen enough to know everything was operating at peak efficiency.

CHAPTER 30

Thursday, August 25th, 10:22 a.m.

THE PRESS, AS WELL as the general public, had been demanding some resolution to the string of murders that had unsettled the city during the last few days. In an attempt to relieve the general unrest, Hank had arranged for a press conference at eleven o'clock.

Jake and Annie dropped by the precinct early, and as they entered the bustling main room, Annie could see Hank at his desk, probably going over notes of what he wanted to address at the conference.

Hank looked up and grinned as they approached his desk. "Grab a seat."

Jake dragged a couple of chairs closer and he and Annie sat.

"It looks like the vultures have started to gather," Jake said.

Hank leaned back in his chair and chuckled. "There hasn't been a lot of news for them to print lately. They're getting bored."

As well as the innocent victims in this string of murders, Annie was concerned about David Haines. "Hank, did you find out anything about David today?"

"Not a thing. He skipped school yesterday and no one has seen him around. Apparently, it's unusual for him to skip a whole day. Usually, when he skips out, it's just for the last class or two."

"So, I assume he didn't return home last night?"

Hank shook his head. "Nope. We still have some uniforms out patrolling the streets, but so far, no luck."

"What about the John Does?" Jake asked. "Any IDs on either of them yet?"

"Not a thing."

"And Cheryl Waters?" Annie asked.

"She'll be seeing a psychiatrist, as ordered by the court, and we hope to have a report on her in the next day or two. So far, she hasn't remembered anything." Hank leaned forward, picked up his notes, and shuffled them. "It's my hope the psychiatrist will help her remember something that'll give us a lead."

"A lead would be nice. It's frustrating when we have so little to go on," Annie said.

Jake leaned forward. "Hank, can you get me a couple of photos of the killers, as well as of David?"

Hank nodded and spun his chair around. He called across the room, "Callaway, bring me a couple sets of those photos." Hank turned back around. "You have an idea?"

"I may do a little canvassing on my own."

Hank shrugged. "It can't hurt." He looked up as Callaway approached the desk and handed him a manila envelope. "Here you go, Hank."

Hank took the envelope and handed it to Jake. "Here's a couple of packages the uniforms have. They contain photos of the killers as well as of David. There's a photo of Cheryl in there as well."

Jake peeked inside the envelope, then set it on the desk and leaned back. "I may show this around the mission as well. There's bound to be someone, somewhere who has seen him. Not everybody watches television or reads the newspaper, and the cops can't cover everywhere."

~*~

DAVID HAINES lay on the narrow bed and stared at the ceiling. He counted the white tiles above him for the thousandth time. He always got the same result, but it didn't matter. It kept his mind off his predicament and helped him keep his sanity.

According to his watch, he'd been confined for almost twenty hours, and no one had been to see him to give him any indication of why he was being held.

He knew for sure it wasn't ransom. If his abductors had checked out the small house they lived in, or the job his father had, which barely kept food in the fridge, they would know there was no money to be made. But what could be the reason?

He had held back his tears, and although he struggled with periods of fear, and then anger, he'd been able to sleep most of the night, regardless of the constant bright lights that lit the room.

He thought of his parents. Generally, they were good to him, and the upbraiding he got from his father on occasion seemed to be of little consequence. He would be overjoyed now to hear his father's voice.

And the hugs his mother gave him, the times he would push her away when she showed her affection; he would welcome that now. Thinking about her threatened to make him weep. He shook it off, swung from the bed, and paced the floor of the small white room.

He had given up hope of trying to escape; the concrete walls and the solid ceiling made sure of that. He had tested the thick metal door, but it was impossible to budge, secured from the outside. He had pounded it with his fists earlier, and shouted until his voice was hoarse, but it had been futile.

Right now, he wanted something to happen. Anything.

He kicked at the wall in frustration and only ended up hurting his toe. He cursed the wall and cursed his captors.

He was hungry, too. He hadn't eaten since yesterday morning, and that'd been a small breakfast. He wondered if perhaps their plan was to starve him to death.

Would that happen? Would anyone ever come to free him, or would he die here, all alone?

He panicked at the thought, and then fought it off and threw himself onto the bed. He lay there a moment before crawling to his feet and pacing some more.

He should be in school now, and as much as he hated being confined in a classroom, it was considerably better than this place.

He pummeled the door and yelled, "Let me out of here." His voice echoed in the small space, as if mocking him. He continued to pound until his fists were sore.

He felt a little better. But not much.

He went to the sink, filled the styrofoam cup with water, and took a long drink. At least the water was cold, but it didn't do much for his hunger.

He wiped his brow on his sleeve. He was a little warm, but not uncomfortable. The air was stifling and smelled sterile, but the small ceiling vent kept the room from becoming unbearable. He could hear the muffled hum of a fan, somewhere in the air duct, the only sound in the otherwise quiet room.

He was afraid, angry and frustrated, and wished someone would come through that door and tell him the joke was over, and he could go home.

Not likely.

He dropped to his knees, his head in his hands, and let the tears flow.

CHAPTER 31

Thursday, August 25th, 11:00 a.m.

THE WIDE STREET in front of Richmond Hill Police Station was clogged with news vans, cars, and the curious.

Yappy was directing traffic, and doing a remarkable job of it. The curious rubberneckers steered by as they craned their necks to get a hint of what was afoot.

Vehicles parked at arbitrary angles, further impeding the already congested flow of traffic.

Reporters ambled across the street, and some milled about in front of the podium being set up at the foot of the steps leading into the precinct. All carried cameras or notepads, recorders, and mikes, killing time until the main event.

The city wanted news, and the faithful gathered to hear the latest on the killing spree.

Lisa Krunk claimed her spot in front of the platform, Don dutifully at her side, his camera primed and ready.

The precinct doors burst open, and one by one a hush fell over the crowd. Reporters made a final scramble for position, their heads cocked upwards, pens, pencils, and recording devices poised.

Captain Diego and Hank were first out of the doors. They made their way down the steps and stood behind the podium.

Jake and Annie followed, but stayed back from the platform and to the side. A couple of uniforms positioned themselves at each end, like wooden soldiers, more for show than as security.

Hank looked around at the crowd of reporters. He recognized a lot of local faces, as well as several from Toronto news outlets. He took one step forward and placed his notes on the podium.

The bundle of microphones secured to the stand picked up his voice. "Welcome, and thanks for coming. My name is Detective Hank Corning." He motioned toward the captain. "And you all know Captain Alano Diego." The crowd murmured as Hank continued, "I'll make a brief statement, and then open it up for your questions."

The swarm waited.

"As you know, Richmond Hill has been hit with a string of murders in recent days. Three, to be exact. In all cases, the perpetrator has been apprehended. At this point, there seems to be little or no connection among the victims in all three incidents." Hank paused a moment. "However, we are making some progress in understanding the situation."

The crowd murmured.

"I want to assure the people of Richmond Hill there's no need to be concerned. We have no indication there'll be another murder, or that anyone is in imminent danger."

Hank had little else he could say. He was stumped, and with no obvious connection he could see, he couldn't honestly guarantee anyone's safety. However, he didn't want to alarm the people and cause undue panic throughout the city.

"Please use normal common sense until we have all the facts in. Don't go out alone at night, and if you're driving home alone, use caution. Keep your doors locked, both at home and when in your vehicles."

Hank paused and glanced at his notes. There was nothing else to say. He looked up. "I'll take your questions now."

Many voices spoke at once, like children trying to be heard.

Hank ignored them and pointed to a raised hand in the second row.

The selected newsman said, "Detective, we are aware, in the case of the first murder, the perpetrator claimed no knowledge of what she was doing. Is that still the case?"

Hank paused. "Yes. At this point, she still claims she was unaware of her actions."

"Does it not seem, then, the other two may have been unaware as well, considering they killed themselves?"

Hank weighed his answer. An affirmative answer could cause undue fear. He elected for vagueness. "We have no indication the other two were unaware of their actions." He selected another reporter, this time from a television station.

"Detective, you said the victims were unrelated, as far as you knew. But what about the killers? Did you find anything that connects them?"

Hank had to be careful with this answer as well. For now, he thought it best not to share the fact the guns were all from the same lot. "We've established a connection of sorts. All three perpetrators were young, and the MO, method of operation, was similar. We have other reasons to believe there's an underlying relationship in all three occurrences."

"What other reasons?"

"I'm not at liberty to say at this point." He pointed to Lisa Krunk, who was uncharacteristically biding her time, waiting patiently, her hand raised. "Yes, Lisa?"

"Detective Corning, I see the Lincolns are in your entourage. How are they involved in this case?"

Hank glanced at Jake and hesitated before turning back. He leaned into the mikes. "They are involved privately on behalf of one of the victims. We've worked successfully with them in the past, and they are privy to certain information. They are, however, still private citizens and have no authority to either speak or act on behalf of law enforcement."

Lisa stuck her sharp nose in the air. "So what, then, is their role?"

"Their role is partially on a consulting basis, as they have certain expertise, and in the interests of justice, we've elected to give them access to many of the facts of the case." Hank hesitated. "Now, if we can get back to the relevant discussion." He pointed at another raised hand.

"Is there any evidence of drug or alcohol use with the killers?"

Another touchy area. Hank thought quickly. "We don't have the complete lab results from all three victims and perpetrators yet, so any answer I would give you, at this point, would be premature."

"So you aren't denying it?"

"Let's wait for the lab results, shall we? And now, I thank you for your time. That's all for now." Hank turned from the podium and climbed up the steps toward the precinct doors, followed by the captain and the Lincolns.

The reporters remained unsatisfied, and they continued to call out questions. Questions Hank had no answers for. Answers he wanted to find more than anything.

And he was determined to get those answers.

CHAPTER 32

Thursday, August 25th, 11:30 a.m.

CHERYL WAS HAVING a hard time coping with the harsh environment at the women's detention center.

As someone who had always thought of herself as a gentle soul, and loving toward others, she found the level of animosity toward her, as well as the system in general, to be bewildering. But even more so, her being a murderer, and therefore rightfully confined to this place, was beyond her comprehension.

She lay on her side on the small bunk and glanced over at her cellmate, who was slouched on her cot, leafing through a magazine. The tough-looking woman had said her name was Bull, obviously a nickname, and not very feminine.

Bull noticed Cheryl's gaze. "You been havin' more nightmares, girl?" Her voice was husky, like sandpaper, but not unpleasant.

Cheryl shook her head. "Not today ... I'm afraid to go to sleep, though."

Bull sat forward and rested her tattooed arms on her knees. "Don't let it get you down, honey. We all have nightmares in this place. Just gotta learn to cope, that's all."

Cheryl nodded. She'd spoken a lot with Bull in the last

couple of days and realized the woman with the rough exterior wasn't as bad as she looked, and Cheryl was glad for her company.

"It'll get better. And once we get outta this place and get to a real prison, life ain't so bad. They take pretty good care of us." Bull grinned. She was missing a tooth in front, the rest stained and crooked. "TV, books and such, and the food ain't so bad either. And you get a job to do to keep busy. Keeps your mind from wandering so much. You'll see."

Cheryl shuddered. The thought of spending perhaps the rest of her life behind bars was more than she could bear, and she wondered how Bull could be so cheerful in her situation. "You've been in prison before?" she asked.

"Yup. Did four years awhile back. Made some friends. Knocked a few heads, and it weren't so bad."

"Why are you back again?" Cheryl couldn't imagine how anyone could face a possible prison sentence so lightly.

"Beat a guy up. He wouldn't open the cash register, so I helped him do it." She winked. "But I'm innocent, you know. It never happened." Bull laughed. "Least, that's what my mouthpiece says. Never admit nothin', 'cause you never know—you might get off."

"I don't think I'll get off," Cheryl said. "They saw me ... do it."

"Well, keep your chin up. You never know."

Cheryl nodded, but didn't feel as optimistic as her cellmate.

Bull looked thoughtful. "So, when do you see this shrink you were tellin' me 'bout?"

"Today ... soon." Cheryl was pleased the judge had ordered her to see a psychiatrist. She hoped he would be able to find the reason she could have performed such a despicable act.

"You lookin' forward to it?"

Cheryl nodded.

"I truly hope you get the answers you want, girl. You don't seem like such a bad sort, and not the kind as belongs in this place."

"You don't really belong here either, Bull. Don't you sometimes wish for a ... normal life?"

Bull laughed. "I'm 'fraid it's too late for me, girl. This is my destiny and I'm too old to change. Ain't no going back. My daddy was a con. He died four or five years ago. He said he didn't want me to end up like him, you know, but with my momma not around, and my daddy in jail half the time, well, I had to take care of myself. You know what I mean? Weren't nobody gonna do it for me." She sighed. "So, here I am."

"That's so sad," Cheryl said.

"Oh, I'm over the sad. Now it's just life for me."

A voice called, "Open sixteen."

Cheryl looked up from her bunk toward the sound of the voice. She heard a clunk, and then her cell door buzzed open and two guards entered.

"Stand up," one said, looking at Cheryl.

"Don't you move." The other held up a warning hand toward Bull.

Bull leaned back. "I ain't goin' nowhere."

Cheryl climbed from the cot and peered at the stone-faced guards.

"Turn around."

Cheryl felt cold metal as a pair of cuffs snapped onto one wrist, then the other. She was spun around and pushed in the direction of the door, each guard holding one of her arms.

"Good luck, girl," Bull said.

They marched her from the cell and the door clanged shut behind them. They prodded her into another room, a garage, where a paddy wagon was waiting. A side door in the van was open, and Cheryl was helped inside the small cubicle. She sat on the hard bench, and then the van shook as the door slammed. She was in a space about three feet square, and could only sit and wonder what was next.

She knew where she was going: to see the psychiatrist. But she thought he would've come to see her, and didn't know she would be taken in such an uncomfortable manner.

The cramped space smelled stale, and of old sweat, but she welcomed the change from the dreary cell where she'd spent most of the last three days.

She heard the rumble of the engine and a grinding of gears, and the vehicle jumped forward. The cuffs hurt her wrists, but Cheryl blocked out the discomfort and closed her eyes.

She heard the whine of the tires on asphalt, and felt the occasional jolt as the vehicle came to a stop, and then leaped forward again.

In a few minutes, the van came to its final stop and the engine died. She heard two doors slam, and then her cubicle was opened.

"Step down."

Her cuffed hands made it hard to keep her balance. She took a cautious step but stumbled, and a guard caught her arm and jerked her upright. "Be careful."

"Sorry. I ... I tripped."

As she was held by both arms and helped along, she took a glance around. They appeared to be in a lane, perhaps behind a mall, or a plaza. She was pushed toward a door in the brick building. Wherever they were going, it appeared they were taking the back way in.

Once inside, they moved down a long hallway, and then up a set of stairs and into a small lobby. A door straight ahead had a plaque on it. "Dr. William Lamb, Psychiatrist."

She was helped into the room and pushed into a chair. She caught her breath and looked up at a receptionist who was eyeing her warily.

"Dr. Lamb is expecting you. He'll see you now."

CHAPTER 33

Thursday, August 25th, 11:41 a.m.

LISA KRUNK PROWLED around in front of the precinct after the rest of the reporters had gone back to edit their stories.

Don was slouched on a bench, his head back and his eyes closed, his hands resting on the camera in his lap.

Lisa had hoped to be able to talk to Detective Corning, or the Lincolns, and was disappointed they hadn't come from the police station yet.

The traffic mess had subsided and vehicles flowed freely. Officer Spiegle's big job was done for the day. As Lisa saw him head back to the precinct, she stopped pacing and hustled to intercept him. "Come on, Don," she said, beckoning impatiently.

Don jumped up, tossed the camera onto his shoulder, red light glowing, and trudged after his boss.

Lisa cut Spiegle off at the bottom of the stairs. She gripped the microphone, white-knuckled and determined. "Officer Spiegle, I'm Lisa Krunk from Channel 7 Action News. I'd like to ask you a few questions if I may?"

Yappy looked at the microphone shoved in his face, and

then at the red light on the camera, and drew himself up, his chest puffed.

"Sure," he said, smiling for the camera.

Lisa had had some luck with Spiegle before, and was hoping he might have some tidbit of information she couldn't get anywhere else. There was a reason she was number one, often commanding the top story on the evening news—she was always willing to do what it took to get to the top.

"Officer, I understand your efforts are helping to crack this case, am I correct?"

He glanced back and forth from the red light to the mike, then back at Lisa. "Uh …"

"I was wondering why you didn't take part in the press conference?"

Yappy pushed up the brim of his cap and scratched his forehead. "I … uh. I had other important work to do," he said, settling his cap back in place.

"Of course. I realize you can't do more than your share."

The cop grinned and straightened his tie. "Yup."

She had finished massaging his ego. Now it was time to attack. "Detective Corning hinted there may have been some drug use among the killers. Can you tell the viewers what drugs were found to be in use?"

Yappy squinted at the red light. "There may have been some LSD involved … I think."

"In all three cases?"

He cocked his head. "I think so."

Lisa pushed on. "I understand the perpetrators were part of a conspiracy?"

"Um … I believe so."

Lisa loved this. Even though this dumb cop had no idea what he was talking about, she would be able to use it. She continued, "Are there others involved in the conspiracy? Perhaps more murders yet to take place?"

Yappy looked confused and thought a moment before answering, "We think so."

"So, should the citizens be afraid?"

He shuffled his feet and glanced around. "Well ... I guess it's something to be afraid of."

"What precautions should the people take?"

"Uh ... don't go outside, and don't answer the door until I ... uh, until we find out what's going on."

Lisa's wide mouth tightened into a triumphant smile. This was what she'd hoped to get. It made for good TV, a bit alarming perhaps, but alarming was good. Good for ratings.

She pressed on, "And what of the first killer, Cheryl Waters? Has she confessed yet?"

"Nope. Not yet."

Lisa glanced up. The Lincolns had exited the precinct and were coming down the steps, and she wanted to talk to them.

"Thank you, Officer Spiegle. You've been very helpful."

"Yup," he said. He turned to wave at Jake and Annie and then wandered around the side of the building.

Lisa caught Don's eye and motioned with her head toward the Lincolns. Don swung the camera their way and continued to film as Lisa wheeled around and hurried to intercept them at the bottom of the steps, her microphone in front, ready.

Don moved slightly to the left, his camera continuing to whir.

Lisa pushed the mike at Annie. "Annie Lincoln, you and your husband have been involved in some high-profile cases lately. I would like to ask you a couple of questions, if I may? Can you tell me a little bit about this one, and what leads you are investigating?"

The camera whirled.

Lisa smiled a thin, wide smirk.

Annie looked at the mike three inches from her nose and spoke without hesitation. "Detective Corning has released all the pertinent information. Any further investigations we, or the police, are doing, are strictly off the record until further notice."

The mike swung over to Jake. "What about the LSD found in the system of the killers?"

Jake and Annie exchanged a glance. "We have no comment," he said.

"Can you tell the viewers anything else?"

Annie leaned in. "I'm sorry, we have nothing else we can tell you. I'm sure Detective Corning will be releasing more information to you as the investigation continues."

Lisa tightened her thin lips in resolve, indignant and determined. The microphone was poked closer to Jake. "Can you tell me about the conspiracy?"

Jake frowned. "What conspiracy?"

Lisa felt smug. She raised her head, and her sharp nose sniffed. "The police believe there may be more murders planned. Do you know when, or where that may be?" Lisa waited and tapped her foot impatiently.

Annie leaned toward the mike, "We're unaware of any conspiracies. And now, we have no further comments. Please excuse us." Jake and Annie turned their backs and strode away in the direction Spiegle had gone.

Don followed as Lisa ran after them. "Just one more question," she called.

They ignored her.

Lisa stopped and frowned as she watched the Lincolns go. She'd always found it hard to get much from those two. She'd also tried the families of all the victims, and Cheryl Waters, and yet had been unable to secure an interview.

But she could make do with what she had for now. She turned to face the camera.

"We will bring you breaking news as it happens. In an exclusive report, I'm Lisa Krunk for Channel 7 Action News."

Don shut the camera off and lowered it.

"Come on, Don, let's go," Lisa said, spinning around and striding down the sidewalk toward the van.

CHAPTER 34

Thursday, August 25th, 12:05 p.m.

HANK LEANED FORWARD in the guest chair in front of Callaway's desk and rested his arms on the laminate top.

The cop looked up from his monitor and shook his head. "Still no ID on either of the John Does, Hank. I'm doing what I can, but we have no record of them in the system nationwide, and nobody has come forward to identify them."

Hank leaned back, folded his arms, and glanced around the precinct. There were more than enough cops hanging around here. If he had a bit more help, perhaps he could get a break. He stood and said, "Thanks, Callaway."

"Yup."

Hank crossed the precinct floor and tapped on Diego's open door. The top cop looked up from his paperwork.

"Can I see you a minute, Captain?"

Diego tossed his pen onto his desk, sat back, and motioned toward a chair. Hank dropped down and slouched back.

"What is it, Hank?"

"I need some more help. I need more uniforms on the streets. I can't do it all myself, and I haven't come up with any leads."

Diego wove his fingers together behind his head and worked a crick out of his neck. He eyed Hank closely a moment before speaking. "I haven't got any guys I can spare, Hank. You know that. I wish I could hire more cops, but the budget just won't allow it."

Hank motioned toward the precinct floor. "Look, Captain, we have a bunch of guys there, and a dozen more writing parking tickets on the streets. How about giving me some of them to help with a little canvassing?"

Diego shook his head. "Can't do it, Hank."

Hank stood and paced a moment, then turned suddenly, faced Diego and frowned. "Captain, the way I see it, it's a matter of priority. If we could spend a little less time chasing morality breakers and running after citizens who drive a little too fast, we might have the resources to catch some real criminals."

Diego shrugged a long shrug and took a deep breath. "I want to get to the bottom of this as badly as you do, but we need to feed the budget."

Hank sank back into the chair. The budget. It was always about the budget. "Can't you forget about money for a few days?" Hank raised his voice a notch in exasperation, "You were out there, at the press conference—you heard the questions—the people want some action on this. They don't care about the budget. You've got to be realistic. The police have a job to do, and that job is getting criminal scum off the streets."

Diego waved a hand in the air as he spoke, irritated at Hank's outburst. "Hank, we've had three shootings and have three perps. One is in jail, and two are in the morgue. What makes you think there are more out there, and if so, how is patrolling the streets going to help us?"

Hank closed his eyes, took a deep breath, and let it out in a slow stream. He leaned forward and frowned. "Because these shootings are all related. I know they are, and so do you. Something, or someone, is behind all of this, and the only chance of a lead right now is to find out who those two in the morgue are."

Diego picked up his pen and twiddled with it. He seemed to be thoughtful.

Hank continued, "And then, there's David Haines, who's missing."

"That's for Missing Persons to handle."

"It may be related. I have a feeling it is, and that's why I have the canvassers showing a picture of him around as well. If anyone saw him yesterday, I want to know about it."

Diego's brow wrinkled as he eyed Hank. "All right. I'll give you King. He can help you out on this."

Hank snorted in disgust. "King? Simon King?"

Diego shrugged. "I can spare him. There are two other detectives in the narcotics division. They can handle it for now, and King can partner with you on this one."

"I don't work with a partner, Captain, you know that."

"You can for now. King may be new, but he's all I can give you."

"I can't work with King," Hank said flatly. "Nobody can. There's a reason he was transferred here. Nobody in Toronto could get along with him either, so they dumped him here."

Diego laughed. "Not quite true, but if I know you, Hank, you can tame him."

Hank shook his head slowly and exhaled. "All right. You're the boss, but I don't answer to him, and if he gets in my way—"

Diego interrupted, "And I'll give you two more cops. Just

for a few days, and I hope to see some results by then."

"You'll get results, Captain."

"What are the Lincolns doing about this? Anything promising from them?"

Hank shrugged. "They're as stumped as I am right now, but Jake's going to hit the streets as well, and Annie's pretty smart. They may come up with something useful."

"Just make sure they don't get in the way. We can't be watching out for them as well."

"Come on, Captain, that's not fair. You know they've been a big help to us in the past. Sure, they may get paid to do what they do, but they genuinely care about catching the bad guys as much as we do. And half the time, they're helping people who didn't even hire them."

Diego sighed. "Yeah, you're right."

Hank crossed his arms. "So, where is King, and when do I get to team up with this idiot?"

Diego gave Hank a black look.

Hank's voice took on a sarcastic tone. "Sorry, Captain. I mean, when do I get to team up with the wonderful Detective King?"

"Just go easy on him, Hank. He's got some good qualities, and he's a good cop. You'll figure it out."

"Yeah, I'll figure it out," Hank said. "So, where is he?"

Diego shook his head. "I don't know where he is right now, but I'll bring him in and get this partnership started."

"I can't wait."

CHAPTER 35

Thursday, August 25th, 12:14 p.m.

THE 1986 PONTIAC FIREBIRD was speeding down Main Street, a few miles over the speed limit, but traffic was light, and Jake had a heavy foot.

Annie was used to his driving, having long ago given up trying to change the way he drove. He might break the occasional traffic law now and then, but he never took any unnecessary chances. Besides, she didn't want to be like her mother and try to change people who were okay the way they were, especially her husband.

Annie peered at Jake over her sunglasses. "I think Yappy's a bit of a problem. Lisa Krunk always manages to get something from him and he doesn't know how to keep quiet."

Jake nodded. "He's definitely a problem at times." He glanced at his wife. "Do you think it was him who told her about the LSD?"

Annie shrugged. "Maybe, but I don't know how he found out, because Hank didn't release that information, as far as I know."

"Word gets around. People talk. It may have come through the medical examiner's office, perhaps one of her assistants. It's hard to keep a secret."

Annie agreed. "Perhaps. Hopefully there's no harm done."

"Lisa always finds a way to cause harm," Jake said as he reached to his belt, freed his ringing iPhone, and touched the screen with his thumb. "Jake here."

"Detective Jake, how are things?"

"Sammy?"

"The one and only."

Jake laughed. "How's life on the streets?"

"Wonderful."

Annie reached over and poked Jake in the shoulder. "Give me the phone. You're driving."

Jake grinned at her and hit the speaker button. "Hold on, Sammy," he said, then handed the phone to Annie.

Sammy Fisher was an enigma with a big heart. Homeless by choice, he was an unusual but charming character, and she couldn't help liking him. They'd gotten acquainted with him recently when he'd helped to track down a fugitive.

Annie took the phone and held it up between her and Jake. "Hi, Sammy, it's Annie."

"Greetings, Detective Annie. How's my favorite lady private eye?"

Annie chucked. "I'm doing well, Sammy. Jake is trying to drive right now, so he gave me the phone. It's nice to hear from you."

"Nice to be heard." Annie heard a belly laugh come from the phone, and then, "I thought you might need my help again?"

Jake leaned over. "In what way?"

"I heard you were at the mission looking for some information. Thought I might be able to lend my expertise in some way. I have a lot of friends on the streets. Some of them have part-time jobs, but most of us are between jobs at the moment, and are at your disposal."

Jake gave Annie a thumbs-up and she nodded back. "As a matter of fact," she said into the phone, "we could use your help. We're looking for a missing boy and, so far, the police haven't found anyone who may have seen him."

"I know people who know people and can ask around. We may be homeless, but we're harmless, and still citizens of this fair city. Of course, there are a lot of nasties out here too, but I'm not talking about the criminal element. Most of the people I know are nicer folks than you might think," Sammy said, and then his voice turned serious. "How old is the boy?"

"He's sixteen years old," Annie said. "He skipped school yesterday and his parents are fairly certain he was wandering around the city. He hasn't been seen since yesterday morning."

"Just get me some pictures of him, and my colleagues and I'll get to work."

"How many pictures?" Jake asked.

"Fifty or so."

"Fifty?"

"Like I said, I know a lot of people. You've heard of six degrees of separation? Well, out here it's two degrees of separation, and they can cover this city like flies on a bag lady."

Annie laughed. "You got it. Fifty it is."

"They have nothing better to do, anyway," came over the line.

Jake grabbed Annie's arm and eased the phone a bit closer. "You still in the same place?"

"Yup. You remember where my castle is?"

Jake laughed. "I don't think I'll forget that." He put both hands back on the steering wheel and veered into the left lane to pass a slow-moving senior.

"Just tell me when you can be here, and I'll be at home waiting for you," Sammy said.

Annie glanced at Jake. "We can get some copies made right now." She jerked her thumb over her shoulder. "We just passed the copy shop."

"Give me an hour, maybe an hour and a half," Jake said into the phone.

"That's great. I have to go and dig up some lunch right now, and then before you know it, I'll be at home. I may be nappin' when you drop by, but just ring my doorbell and I'll have the butler show you in."

Jake burst out laughing. "I may wait outside. Don't know if I could fit into your castle."

"Are you calling from a pay phone?" Annie asked.

"Yup. Took my last quarter, so maybe you could lend me another one so I can call you back if we find out anything."

Jake laughed. "I'm sure I can spare that much."

"See you soon," Sammy said, and then the phone went silent.

Annie handed the iPhone back and Jake holstered it. He touched the brakes, glanced in his mirror, and then turned the wheel and made a U-turn. "We'll run to the copy shop now, and then I'll drop you home and go find Sammy." The engine roared and the tires spoke as he touched the gas.

Annie let go of her grip on the dash. "Why don't you get him a burner phone as well?" she suggested. "That way he can contact us any time he needs to."

"Good idea. There's a 7-Eleven a couple of blocks away. We can stop there later."

CHAPTER 36

Thursday, August 25th, 12:22 p.m.

THE DOOR TO Dr. Lamb's office yawned open and Cheryl was prodded inside. The doctor rose from his mahogany desk and stepped around to face her. His expensive suit perfectly fitted his tall body, a diamond pin holding his crimson tie in place.

Bug eyes stared down at her through dark-framed glasses resting on a long, straight nose. His mouth wore a hint of a smile, artificial, perhaps mocking her.

He looked at the guards. "Take the cuffs off."

One of Cheryl's escorts objected. "We can't."

"Take them off," Dr. Lamb repeated. "It's important she be comfortable. You may wait outside."

The guard wrinkled his brow, and then the cuffs rattled as he inserted a key and the restraints fell loose.

Cheryl rubbed her wrists. The metal had felt uncomfortable, and she was relieved to have them removed. She heard the door click behind her as the guards left the room.

Dr. Lamb extended his arm toward a padded leather chair. "Please sit down."

Cheryl sidled up to the chair and sat on the edge, her back straight, her hands in her lap.

Dr. Lamb dropped into a matching chair across from her, settled back, crossed his legs, and examined her. "Sit back," he said. "Please, try to relax." His voice was not unkind, but not exactly pleasant either. It reminded her of a history teacher she once had.

Cheryl adjusted her bright orange uniform and slid back, her arms stiffly in front of her, her feet pushed together. She couldn't relax.

He watched her awhile, his eyes boring into hers as if probing her mind, maybe staring into her very soul.

"Do you know why you're here?" he asked.

She nodded and remained silent.

"Why are you here?"

"To see what's wrong with me."

"What do you think is wrong with you?"

"I … I don't know." Her lip quivered.

Dr. Lamb thought a moment. "Do you know why you were arrested?"

Another nod. "Because I … I shot someone?" Her hands worked nervously.

"Yes. And we're here to find out why. Can you tell me why, Cheryl?"

She shook her head. "I … I don't remember."

He reached to a stand beside his chair and retrieved a notebook and pen. He placed the pad on his lap and settled back deeper into the chair, tapping the pen against his teeth, drilling into her with his eyes.

Finally he spoke. "You are here for a psychiatric assessment as well as a forensic assessment. One is to assess your state of mind, and the other, to establish whether you have the mental capacity to understand the charges against you, and to legally stand trial."

She nodded. "I volunteered."

"Because your lawyer told you to?"

Another nod.

He smiled slightly. "That's because he knew the judge would order it, and he may have thought volunteering in advance would look better to the judge." He cleared his throat. "But that won't make a difference. I have a job to do and I hope you'll help me. Is that fair?"

Nod.

"Try to relax, Cheryl. I'm not your enemy. We're not here to find guilt or innocence. Just the truth."

She tried to relax.

"It's important you be truthful, no matter what. Is that understood?"

Nod. "Yes."

"Very well." He flipped through the notepad and then stopped at a page and studied it. "I have already talked to your parents. They've given me some insights into you, your personality, and many of the events of your life." He glanced at her over his glasses, then back at the pad. He dropped it into his lap and clicked his pen.

She waited while he made a notation.

Finally he looked up, crossed his legs the other way, adjusted his pad, and cleared his throat.

"Now, tell me Cheryl, what makes you angry?"

Cheryl thought a moment. Lots of things made people angry. What did he want to hear? She said, "Injustice makes me angry. Racism, or people who look down on others because of race or social status."

He squinted through his glasses. "What about rich, or powerful people? Do you hate rich people?"

"No. I have nothing against rich people, only if their

money makes them snobs, or if they think they're better than the rest of us."

"And then, would you wish them harm, or maybe kill them?"

"No. Absolutely not. I would never kill ..." Her voice trailed off, and she bit her lip.

"Oh, but you did, Cheryl."

Was he trying to trick her somehow?

He looked down and scribbled something in his notepad and then looked up, twiddling his pen while he observed her.

She held his gaze for a few moments, then started to feel uncomfortable and dropped her head. She could feel his eyes, still watching her.

"Tell me about your nightmares," he said.

She looked up. "They seem so real, and always the same."

He waited.

"I am in a room, a white room, and all alone. Then, someone comes in. I can't see his face, but he's dressed like a doctor. You know, with those long white coats? And he sits down beside me, and then he says, 'I am the Wizard.'" She shuddered.

"Go on."

"Sometimes I feel pain. Extreme pain, like a thousand volts of electricity going through my body. Then I scream, and I wake up still screaming." Cheryl closed her eyes and took a deep breath. When she opened them again, he was writing something in his pad. She continued, "I ... I'm afraid to go to sleep."

Dr. Lamb looked at her and stroked his chin. "Cheryl ..." He hesitated, and then asked, "Were you ever sexually abused as a child?"

Cheryl frowned. "No, never."

"Not by an uncle perhaps, or a friend?"

She shook her head vigorously. "No."

The doctor looked at his pad, recrossed his legs, studied her face again, and then said, "Have you ever been in a personal relationship that was emotionally, physically, or sexually abusive?"

"No, not at all."

"Have you ever thought about injuring yourself or others?"

"No."

"Or recurrent thoughts of death, dying, or suicide?"

Again she shook her head.

The questions went on and on. Questions about her sex life, possible drug use, her fears, wishes, hopes, dreams … Cheryl felt violated by his probing and prodding as he scrutinized every area of her life.

By the time he was done and the guards led her out, she felt mentally and physically exhausted. She endured the trip back to her cell and welcomed the quiet where she could rest her troubled mind.

CHAPTER 37

Thursday, August 25th, 12:43 p.m.

DETECTIVE SIMON KING was not Hank's idea of a perfect partner. Hank hadn't worked with a steady partner for years, and wasn't looking forward to the captain's team-up.

He'd had a variety of partners when he was a beat cop, but after he'd made detective, he'd only had one. Someone he still looked up to, a mentor of sorts, from whom he'd learned a lot before the senior cop's retirement a few years ago.

Hank had been just fine on his own since then, and considering Hank's stellar record, Diego had cut him some slack.

But now, working with King, no matter for how short a time, was not going to be an ideal relationship. Diego seemed to think highly of this new cop, and he'd come here with a good recommendation, but Hank had heard talk around the station, and had serious doubts.

The talk was about payoffs and bribes, and perhaps even planting evidence. He would have to give him the benefit of the doubt, but this was Hank's case, and he wasn't going to let a crass young cop like King take over.

Detective King had returned to the precinct some time ago and was slouched at his desk, one foot resting on an open drawer, when Hank approached him.

"What do you make of it?" Hank asked as he settled into an empty chair and stretched his legs out under the desk.

King dropped his foot and looked up. He set down the open file folder he'd been browsing and motioned toward it. "Looks like a mess."

"Any thoughts?"

King shrugged. "I see they all had been taking some drugs. Drugs'll do that to you. They can make you crazy sometimes and do all kinds of nutty stuff, including killing people."

"Sure, maybe, but these killers weren't acting crazy. The murders were cold, likely premeditated. Doesn't that seem like more than a coincidence to you?"

"Dunno. There are such things as coincidences, you know."

Hank shook his head. "I don't think this one is."

King sat up and propped his elbows on the desk. "Homicide's just not my thing."

Hank was clearly disgusted. "But you're a cop," he said. "And whether it's drug dealers or murderers, the criminal mind is always the same. Self-centered thinking, with no regard for the property or lives of others."

"Maybe," King said. "Maybe."

"Look, forget about the philosophy of crime. What about the evidence?"

"There ain't none."

"That may be the point. The fact there's very little evidence is evidence in itself."

King frowned. "I don't get it."

"The MO is the same, with the perpetrators leaving very

little evidence, and the same type of people committing these murders. That's evidence of similarity."

King stared blankly for a few moments before finally grasping Hank's point, and he nodded slowly, a light dawning in his eyes. "Now what?" he asked.

"I was hoping you could answer that," Hank said. "Or at least, come up with some ideas. That's why Diego put you on this with me. I asked for some help, and he said you're a good cop."

What was wrong with this guy? Right now it didn't seem like King knew anything about police work. Then, it dawned on him: King hadn't read the reports.

Hank pointed to the folder. "You didn't read that, did you?"

"I browsed it."

King wasn't a stupid cop. He was just lazy.

Hank changed the subject. "You married?"

"Was once. Didn't work out. She left me for another guy." He drew himself up, raised his chin, and held his arms out at his sides. "Can you imagine any woman not wanting a piece of this?" He laughed at his own joke.

"I can't imagine," Hank said dryly and then asked, "Any kids?"

"Nah. The marriage didn't last long enough to produce any of those. Good thing, too."

Hank agreed. "Yeah, it's a good thing." He couldn't imagine King being much of a husband, let alone a father.

"Tell me about Toronto," Hank said. "Why were you transferred here?"

"You guys needed some more help up here. Narcotics crime is actually up in the suburbs, and down in the city, so I volunteered."

"And here you are."

"And here I am," King said, adding, "I'm much better on the streets. That's my element, dealing with the scumbags out there. Making them talk, things like that." He whacked his fist into the palm of his other hand and grinned. "You know what I mean?"

Hank shook his head and frowned. "That's not the way we do things here."

"Gets the job done. I get a lot of convictions. Ain't nobody can touch my record."

Hank looked at King a moment, at his stringy, unkempt hair, the three days' worth of growth on his face, and his sloppy clothes. And he smelled unwashed. He looked more like a drug dealer than a cop. Maybe that was how he fit into that line of work so well.

"You can keep the rough stuff for your drug dealers," Hank said. "This is a murder investigation, and our job is to ask questions, not beat up suspects and witnesses."

King shrugged. "Okay, then, I think we need to talk to the witnesses."

"I already did," Hank said, pointing to the folder, frustrated. "It's all in there."

"I'll take it home and look it over tonight."

Hank glowered at King. "It's early afternoon." His voice took on a sarcastic tone. "What do you suggest we do until you have had a chance to browse the evidence?"

King made a sweeping motion with his arm. "Lead on," he said.

Hank decided his partner was worse than having no partner at all. He sighed and looked at his watch. "I'm hoping to get the ME's report on the latest perp soon. There may be something in it that'll help."

"In the meantime?"

"In the meantime, I have some calls to make," Hank said as he stood and pointed to the reports on the desk. "And I suggest you study that."

Hank looked back over his shoulder as he went to his desk. Simon King had picked up the folder and was leafing through it.

Getting this case solved gave Hank another incentive. He couldn't wait to ditch this guy.

CHAPTER 38

Thursday, August 25th, 1:03 p.m.

DAVID HAINES was counting tiles again when he heard the lock on the door screech back. He sat up abruptly, hoping at last they'd come to let him out.

As the door swung open, he sprang to his feet, unsure whether to wait and see what was going on or, better still, try to run. But, he didn't know what was outside the door, and surely he would be caught before he got far.

When he saw a huge muscle-bound man step in and take up position beside the door, he reconsidered his plan. He would have to wait, but escape he would, determined they weren't going to keep him in this dreadful place.

He became aware of a faint squeaking, becoming increasingly louder, and then a stainless steel cart, pushed by a stooped man wearing a long lab coat, was wheeled in. The gray-haired man stopped halfway across the room, and the cart became silent.

"Please sit down," the man said.

David looked at the tray on the cart, and then at the thug. He wasn't sure what choice he had. He kept one eye on the door, hoping the goon would leave and he could make a dash for freedom. For now, all he could do was bide his time and hope for a chance. Just one chance. He sat uneasily on the edge of the bed and waited.

The man smiled. "That's better."

David dreaded the thought of what they might have planned for him. He stared up, wide-eyed, and then shrunk back as the man approached.

"I'm Dr. Wolff," the elderly man said. "I would like you to lie down, please."

David shuffled back further on the bed. "What are you going to do?" he asked, his voice trembling, his hands beginning to sweat.

"Lie down, please."

"No. Go away. What are you doing to me?" He looked around wildly, praying for a means of escape. He glanced at the door, at the thug, and then back at Wolff.

"You must lie down and relax, please," the madman said.

David thought a moment before finally succumbing. He dropped on his back and turned his head toward Wolff, then watched in horror as the peculiar man retrieved a pair of leather straps from a shelf on the cart.

"Put your arms by your side," Wolff said.

David crossed his arms in defiance and turned his head away. "No," he shouted. "I want to go home. You have no right to keep me here."

"Only for a short time, and then you can go. Don't you want to get this over with?"

David struggled to sit but Wolff held him back with one hand. Weak from lack of food, David fought in vain and was forced down.

"You'll go home soon enough," Wolff said as he turned his head and beckoned for the goon to help. David protested and fought as his arms were forced apart, and one at a time, were bound securely to metal bars on each side of the cot. He clenched his fists and fought against the leather straps, but couldn't budge his arms.

He kicked against his attackers as his feet were fastened securely to the end of the bed. He couldn't move his legs, only bend his knees slightly.

"Let me go," David shouted. "You can't do this." His struggles and shouts of protest went unheeded. He watched in horror as Wolff turned to the cart and spun back around, a surgical needle in his hand.

"Please lie still. This won't hurt, and it'll help you relax."

David didn't want to relax. Panic gripped him and he felt a sharp prick as the needle was inserted into his arm, just below his elbow. He tossed his head violently from side to side as the cool liquid was emptied into his bloodstream.

"Relax now," Wolff said as he removed the needle and dropped it onto the tray. He turned back and placed one hand on David's forehead a moment, then held his wrist, probably checking his pulse.

David vaguely saw a chair being set beside his bed, and the mad doctor sat and leaned forward. David's head was spinning, and as he gazed toward the ceiling, the bright lights were no longer white, but took on shades of red, green, blue, and yellow. They swirled around, dipping down and then up, and enveloped him in a rainbow of colors.

Colors he'd never seen before. He saw butterflies and birds forming, fractal flowers, neon stripes, trails, and tracers of various forms. He watched the swirling colors open-mouthed and speechless.

He felt a hand on his cheek and his head was turned. He forced himself to focus his gaze on the eyes now watching him. He blinked a few times and then stared, wide-eyed, as he looked into the universe. He could see the entire cosmos as it spiraled and spun, twisted and flowed. He beheld the sight before him in awe. He knew then what he was looking at.

He was looking into the face of God.

"Are ... are you God?" he asked as he stared at the face in wonder. A wise face, perfect, ever-changing, but always the same somehow.

God smiled. It was a beautiful smile, unlike any David had ever seen before. "No, I'm not God, but God has sent me."

"Who ... who are you?"

"I am the Wizard."

"The Wizard?"

The Wizard nodded. "You have been chosen. I am the Wizard, and I'm asking for your service."

David nodded violently. "Yes, yes."

The Wizard smiled again and placed his hand over David's eyes. "Sleep now," he said. "I'll return later."

David felt a keen sadness as the Wizard turned and retreated from sight. He looked again at the tiles on the ceiling. There were thousands of them now, no, millions, and they continued on and on for eternity.

David closed his eyes and thought about the universe, hoping the Wizard would soon return.

CHAPTER 39

Thursday, August 25th, 1:15 p.m.

CALLAWAY DROPPED a package on Hank's desk. The
ME's reports on the murder of Harold Garrison were in.

"Thanks, Callaway," Hank said as he leaned forward and
picked up the stuffed envelope. He dumped its contents onto
his desk.

The package contained the forensics reports as well as the
complete lab findings. The summary report was what he was
interested in. He flipped through the stack and pulled it free.

Report of Findings on the Death of Harold Garrison

Cause of death: *gunshot wound to the head.*
Manner of death: *homicide.*
Blood alcohol: *negative.*
Blood drug screens: *negative.*
Urine drug screens: *negative.*

*My examination of the body of Harold Garrison revealed two
gunshot wounds to the head.*

*Bullet A entered below the left eye, with the exit wound on the rear
of the head. The trajectory of the bullet was front to back, and slightly
downwards.*

186

Bullet B entered through the upper lip, with the exit wound on the rear of the head. The trajectory of the bullet was front to back, and slightly downwards.

There were no trace particles of gunshot residue on the clothing of Harold Garrison. However, residue on the chair suggests both shots were fired from a distance of three to five feet, the bullets first piercing the back of the chair before entering the skull of Harold Garrison.

In my opinion, Harold Garrison died of a gunshot wound to the head. Manner of death is homicide.

The bullets, buried in the floor of the office, had been retrieved and were determined by the ballistics report to be of nine millimeters. Further testing showed them to be from the gun found at the scene

A complete external examination of the body of Harold Garrison had also been done, finding no visible defensive wounds, and nothing unusual.

The summary report on the killer was similar to the one from the murderer of Bobby Sullivan.

Report of Findings on the Death of John Doe

Cause of death: *gunshot wound to the head.*

Manner of death: *suicide by a single, self-inflicted shot from a 9mm handgun.*

Blood alcohol: *negative.*

Blood drug screens: *trace amounts of scopolamine detected.*

Urine drug screens: *13 ng/ml lysergic acid diethylamide detected.*

My examination of the body of John Doe revealed a contact gunshot wound to the head, with the entrance wound on the right side of the head, and the exit wound on the left side of the head. The trajectory of the bullet was right to left and slightly upwards.

A muzzle stamp was imprinted on the skin surrounding the entrance wound. The muzzle stamp marks the position of the muzzle of the gun on or near John Doe's head at the time the gun was fired.

Gunshot residue found on the clothing and the right hand, and soot marks at the entrance of the wound, suggest the fatal wound had been self-inflicted.

In my opinion, John Doe died of a gunshot wound to the right temple. Manner of death is suicide.

The weapon was determined to be the same 9mm Glock found at the scene.

The bullet had been pulled from the wall of the office and the testing of the bodily fluid on the bullet revealed it to be the one that had killed John Doe.

An internal autopsy had not been considered necessary on either victim and had not been performed.

Both reports were signed by Nancy Pietek, Deputy Medical Examiner.

As Hank suspected, the lab found the presence of LSD, as well as scopolamine, in the system of the killer.

There was certainly no doubt now all three murders were connected.

Hank leafed through the stack of papers again. The autopsy report caught his eye. His mouth dropped open when he saw what it contained.

An external examination of the killer had found a microchip implant imbedded in the back of John Doe's skull near the amygdala.

Hank spun his chair and grabbed his mouse. He googled "amygdala" and found several pages explaining what the amygdala did. Apparently, in humans, the amygdalae perform primary roles in the formation and storage of memories associated with emotional events. It was all too technical for

Hank, but it had a lot to do with memory and emotion.

Hank sat back, the truth now hitting him full force.

Where was that chip? He wanted to see it.

He scooped up the phone and called the lab. He was notified they'd been doing some testing on it but were unable to ascertain its purpose.

"I want to see it," Hank said.

"I'll send it right up."

In a couple of minutes he was handed a small plastic bag stapled to a sheet of paper. He strained to see the tiny chip it contained, smaller than the head of a pin.

He grabbed the phone again and dialed a number. "Give me Nancy."

"Nancy Pietek?"

He got right to the subject. "Nancy, Hank here. Did you check John Doe number one to see if he had a chip in him as well?"

"I'm about to do that. I'll let you know."

He hung up, betting to himself she would find an identical chip.

Another phone call. This time to Jake.

When Jake answered on the second ring, Hank said, "Jake, we may have a breakthrough."

"Oh?"

"A microchip found in the head of our latest John Doe." Hank explained what he'd learned. He finished with, "I want to send it to Toronto for testing. Our lab doesn't know what it's all about."

"I take it you got the ME's reports?" Jake asked.

"Yes, they found LSD and scopolamine in John Doe. Nothing else surprising, except this chip." Hank peered at the tiny electronic device as he talked.

"Hopefully, they can track its source," Jake said.

"That's what I'm counting on." Hank paused and chuckled. "And there's more news. I have a new partner."

"A partner?"

"I asked Diego for some more help. He gave me two uniforms to help out on the streets and assigned Simon King as my partner."

Jake laughed. "I can't see you with a partner."

"Good thing it's only temporary."

"Speaking of the streets," Jake said, "I was talking to Sammy Fisher. You remember him? He wants to help, and asked for some photos. I'm about to look him up now."

"Sure, I remember him, and he's welcome to lend a hand. The more people we have out there the better."

"I'll let you know if anything turns up," Jake said.

They said goodbye and Hank hung up. He gathered up the reports and stuffed them into the envelope, and then strode across the precinct and dropped them in front of Simon King. King looked up. He was still going over the earlier file.

"Here's the reports on the latest murder. You can add this to the stack," Hank said.

King frowned, dragged the envelope closer and slipped it under the pile, then sighed and buried himself back in his studying.

Hank smiled and turned away.

CHAPTER 40

Thursday, August 25th, 1:30 p.m.

OLIVER CRAIG settled into his high-back easy chair, the one he'd won at a Christie's auction, and set his scotch on a stand beside the chair. It was his third drink today, and it made him feel powerful, invincible.

His plans were going extremely well. Wolff was proving to be a valuable, irreplaceable asset, and he rubbed his hands together, anticipating his next project. It would be a big step, executed soon, and Craig had faith its implementation would bring about sweeping effects. Soon the city would belong to him, and then ...

He reached to the stand and picked up the television remote and flicked on the TV, and the voice of the Channel 7 news anchor filled his massive office. The station was finishing a report on the increasing price of local real estate. Craig smiled smugly. News like that only made him richer, and becoming super-rich was what he strove for, lived for.

That, and power.

The anchor shuffled his papers and looked at the camera.

"And now, in an exclusive report on the murders of the last few days, here's Lisa Krunk."

Craig sat forward and watched with great interest as Lisa's unattractive face appeared on his screen.

"Thank you, Philip. I'm standing here in front of Richmond Hill Police Station where a press conference was held earlier today regarding the latest killings that have afflicted the city. The conference was held in response to my many demands, as I insisted the public be made aware of police proceedings in these affairs. My overwhelming pressure has amounted to what you see behind me now.

"The killings started this Monday, when President and CEO of Bonfield Development, Charles Robinson, was gunned down in his office. The gunman, or I should say woman, was immediately apprehended and remains in police custody. She has claimed no knowledge of her actions and has entered a plea of not guilty. We'll be anxiously watching her trial in the days and weeks to come.

"As reported by myself previously, the second victim was Bobby Sullivan, an ex-con. He was gunned down two days ago at Full Power Gas Bar where he worked. The killer then took his own life. From the people I talked to, Sullivan appeared to be a much-liked young man. There appears to be no motive for his murder. However, some have speculated it may have been a revenge killing. Sullivan had served five years in prison for an earlier crime and he may have made some enemies during that time.

"Given the frequency and manner of the murders, there seems to be some fear among the police that the killings could continue, and perhaps even escalate."

The scene cut to a detective behind a podium who was speaking. Craig recognized the cop as Detective Corning. He'd been present at all of the recent scenes Craig had orchestrated.

"Please use normal common sense until we have all the facts in. Don't go out alone at night, and if you're driving home alone, use

caution. Keep your doors locked, both at home, and when in your vehicles."

Then, the TV flashed and a picture came on of a dopey-looking cop, standing in front of the police station.

"I guess it's something to be afraid of. Don't go outside, and don't answer the door."

The scene zoomed in on a man and a woman standing near the group at the podium. They looked familiar to Craig, but he couldn't place them. Lisa spoke again.

"A reliable source has revealed to me that Lincoln Investigations, headed by Jake and Annie Lincoln, are heavily involved in this case. Apparently they are making some headway, but declined to comment."

The television flicked to a close-up shot of Jake standing beside Annie in front of the police precinct. Jake was frowning at the camera.

"We have no comment."

Then, the scene switched back to Corning.

"We've worked successfully with them in the past, and they're privy to certain information ... we've elected to give them access to many of the facts of the case."

Lisa came back on the screen. She was standing in front of a house Craig recognized. Yellow crime scene tape was wrapped around the property, police cars parked in front, and officers could be seen moving about, streaming to and from the house.

"As I reported yesterday, this is the house of Harold Garrison, the insurance broker turned politician. He was brutally murdered yesterday before the killer took his own life. He leaves behind a wife and two children who mourn his death.

"The murder of Harold Garrison is the third such murder in as many days, and there's some talk among the Lincolns as well as high-level police officials that there may be a conspiracy at play. However, officially, they declined to comment. Sources have confirmed those suspicions, however.

"To further complicate this already complicated case, yesterday, sixteen-year-old David Haines was reported missing. Sources fear his disappearance may be tied to these affairs in some way, although in exactly what manner remains uncertain. I'll be following his story, as well as reporting on further developments as they happen in these puzzling cases.

"Channel 7 urges the citizens of Richmond Hill to heed the words of Detective Corning and stay vigilant at all times.

"We will bring you breaking news as it happens. In an exclusive report, I'm Lisa Krunk for Channel 7 Action News."

Craig clicked off the television and stared at the blank screen. He'd heard of the Lincolns before. From what he understood, they'd cracked a few tough cases while working with the police.

And now they were involved in his affairs. Why didn't they mind their own business?

And then he grimly realized, this was their business—but now they meddled in his. Something had to be done about them before it was too late.

CHAPTER 41

Thursday, August 25th, 1:44 p.m.

JAKE KNEW EXACTLY where Sammy Fisher lived. He'd been there once before, and he chuckled to himself as he spun along Front Street, thinking about Sammy's little nest.

Sammy had once explained he preferred life in the suburbs rather than the inner city, because the quality of food to be found was much better here, the air was cleaner, the folks were nicer, and there was a much better class of homeless. He called himself a middle-class bum, not like the ones who inhabited the downtown core.

Buildings were sparse in this area, this close to the river, and as the Firebird approached the Richmond River overpass, Jake pulled to the side and stopped.

He grabbed the package of photos, jumped out, made his way to where the road touched the bridge, and swung over the low metal railing. The ground in front of him ran down at a steep angle to the riverbank. Richmond River flowed smoothly below, on its way through the city to Lake Ontario far beyond.

He climbed down a few feet and swung under the bridge. Right there, right where the bank ran up and touched the underside of the four-lane overpass, that was where Sammy's castle was located.

Jake pulled aside a concrete-colored canvas and revealed a dug-out space in front of him, maybe ten by ten feet wide and four feet high. The floor and walls had been carefully covered in boards, and a small metal stand contained a kettle as well as a few cans and jars of necessities. Sammy's other meager possessions were scattered about in a variety of places.

Jake heard a light snoring from the direction of a small cot pushed up against the far wall.

He whistled.

The man on the cot sprang up, coming to rest on one elbow. "That you, Detective Jake?"

Jake laughed. "Yeah, it's me, Sammy. Time to get up."

"Did you bring the pictures?"

Jake held up the package. "Right here."

"Time's a wastin'," Sammy said as he rolled off the cot, grabbed his tattered baseball cap from the floor beside him, and plopped it on. He kept his head low as he scooted across the floor. Jake moved back and Sammy popped out of the doorway.

He shook Jake's hand. "Let's go sit by the pool where we can talk."

Sammy dropped the flap, made sure it fell properly in place, and headed down the steep bank.

Jake followed him to the river's edge, where Sammy sank down onto a boulder. He motioned for Jake to sit. "Pull up a rock. Have a seat."

Jake sat on the edge of a craggy boulder and looked at Sammy. The epitome of a bum, he looked the part in his flapping sneakers, worn-out jeans, and bushy beard. Only his clear blue eyes, always smiling, revealed that this strange individual had an intelligent mind.

"Let's get to work," Sammy said, holding out his hand. "Let's see what you got there."

Jake handed him the package and Sammy peeked inside. "How many?"

"There are sixty of David there. I thought a few more wouldn't hurt. There're also sixty each of two unidentified people. Maybe somebody knows who they are." Jake pulled out a photo of David and handed it to Sammy. "Here's the missing boy."

Sammy took the 8x10, held it up in front of him and squinted. "Nice-looking boy. How long you say he's been gone?"

"Just one day. He was last seen yesterday morning before school. He never made it to class, so he must have been out wandering the town."

Sammy nodded. "Okay. These pictures oughta do it." He slipped the photo back into the package, set the bundle on the rock beside him, and looked back at Jake. "What do you know about this kid? He ever into drugs?"

Jake shrugged. "His parents don't seem to think so, but you know how it is. Parents are always the last to know, but I get the feeling this guy's pretty clean. Never been in any kind of trouble with the law, either."

Sammy nodded slowly, his beard bobbing up and down against his checkered shirt. "Just think it may be important to know a bit about him so we know where to look and who to ask."

"I got this for you, too," Jake said as he reached into his shirt pocket and pulled out a cell. "It's a burner phone."

"A what?"

"You really are out of touch, aren't you, Sammy? It's a cell phone you can throw away once the minutes are used up, or fill it up again with more time if you want." He held it out.

Sammy took the phone and studied it front and back.

"I got a hundred minutes," Jake said. "In case you need to call me. It's a lot easier than searching for a phone booth."

"How do you work this thing?"

Jake laughed and showed him how the phone worked. "I've put my cell number in there already."

"Amazing," Sammy said. "I knew cell phones were getting cheap these days, but I didn't know they were so cheap you could just throw them away when they were used up. Just like a wad of old gum."

Jake chuckled. "They're made in China. Stuff's cheap there."

Sammy was looking down the bank toward the river. "I already put the word out around town. Everybody knows somebody else they can get to help out. My people are ready to go soon as I get outta here."

Jake stood. "Then we better get going."

Sammy rose to his feet, stretched, and yawned. "I'm ready soon as I take a bath." He hopped down to the sandy edge of the river, knelt, dropped his cap beside him, and soaked his head. When he stood, water dripped from his face and beard. He shook it off and wiped his face on his cap before plopping it back on his head.

Jake watched in amusement. "Feel better?" he asked after Sammy had climbed up the bank.

"Feel like a million bucks. I'm primed and ready to go. If you give me a lift down to the park, I'll get this thing rolling."

CHAPTER 42

Thursday, August 25th, 2:00 p.m.

OLIVER CRAIG had come to a decision. The Lincolns were in the way and must be dealt with.

Immediately.

Maybe they weren't a present threat, but now that he'd come so far, he couldn't allow a chance of them getting in the way of his ultimate objective.

He leaned forward in his chair, dropped his freshly lit Cuban in the ashtray, picked up the phone, and dialed a number. Muller answered almost immediately.

"Muller, is the girl ready?"

"She's all set to go, ready and waiting your commands."

"I'm very concerned about Lincoln Investigations. We have to do something about them this afternoon. Can that be accomplished?"

"That should be no problem. The girl has proven herself to be exceptional in many ways, perhaps the best I've seen, and she's eager to be assigned a mission."

Craig watched the smoke twirl up above his desk. Muller and Wolff were doing a great job, thanks to their prior experience and, of course, his father's notes.

Muller interrupted his thoughts. "How do you want to proceed, Mr. Craig?"

Craig tucked the phone between his shoulder and ear and sat back. He stroked his chin, formulating a plan of action. Finally, he said, "If both targets can be eliminated at the same time, that would be ideal. However, at least one of them must be removed."

"Just one, sir?"

"The way I see it, if it's not possible to eliminate both, the other will be distracted and won't be a threat anymore. But if they are, we can deal with it at that time."

"I'll get Wolff to give the girl her instructions. Do you want the same end result? No survivors?"

Craig hated the idea of spending so much time conditioning the candidates, and then using them up. If there was a way they could be reused, it would save time and resources. However, he elected for the safer plan, one that would ensure their own protection. "We must," he said. "We can't take a chance of her getting captured and endangering our plans. No survivors."

"Yes, Mr. Craig. I'll get it done right away."

"Oh, and Muller?"

"Yes."

"Besides the girl and the new boy, do we have any other candidates?"

"There are two others in various stages of completion, but nothing available at this time. It may be a matter of a few more days."

"Good. I have plans for them soon." He gave Muller a few instructions on how the afternoon's events were to occur and then hung up the phone. He knew between Muller and

Wolff, they would get the job done. And now he had other things to do while he waited for the good news that their objective had been completed.

Thursday, August 25th, 4:23 p.m.

THE GIRL WAS excited, and honored to be included in the Wizard's plans. She was ready to go, and she listened intently as the Wizard repeated the instructions the final time.

What was required of her was simple, the reasons were clear, and the mission would be accomplished precisely as the Wizard had instructed.

"Go now," the Wizard said. "And be thankful to have been chosen."

The girl nodded slightly and rose to her feet. "Thank you for this honor." She adjusted the handbag over her shoulder and waited.

The Wizard went ahead and opened the door, and she followed him down a corridor. He stopped before another door, hesitated a moment, his hand on the handle, and turned to face her.

"Is everything all right, Wizard?" she asked.

"Yes, yes." He sighed, then turned back to the door and opened it.

The exit led into a garage where a black Cadillac Escalade was waiting, the engine running, the back door open. A man stood by the vehicle and motioned for her to get into the backseat. She climbed in and the door clicked shut behind her.

The driver stepped into the front seat, and then a narrow door in the wall of the building hummed upwards, and the vehicle eased through.

The girl slipped the handbag from her shoulder, reached inside, and removed a gun.

She checked the familiar semiautomatic compact pistol she'd been provided with. Wolff had given her a lot of practice time, and she was more than competent in its use. The magazine of the 9mm Glock contained fifteen rounds. She didn't expect to need all the ammunition; they were just a safeguard. She assumed five would be enough.

Two for each target, and one for herself.

If the second target was unavailable, three rounds would be sufficient.

She fought to curb her excitement. Enthusiasm was fine, but being overly eager could compromise her mission. That would never do. She must remain calm and carry out the operation without hesitation.

She'd studied the map of the area and memorized the street names. She had an exact picture of the outside of the house in her mind. She would recognize the targets anywhere, thanks to photos she'd been shown, and was certain nothing could go wrong.

The Escalade pulled to the curb and stopped. She surveyed the street and, seeing no pedestrians or vehicles in this quiet area, she opened the door, stepped out onto the sidewalk, and closed the door behind her.

The Escalade eased away. She watched it drive out of sight, then turned and strolled the other way.

Not too fast. Not too slow. Don't attract attention.

She took a left at the next intersection and continued on for a couple of minutes before recognizing the house that was her final destination. There was a Ford Escort parked in the driveway. She'd expected that.

She'd been told there might be a Firebird as well. There

wasn't. Perhaps there would only be a single target.

The house appeared to be quiet, and no one was around as she strode up the walkway to the front door. She peeked through the small window, but didn't see anyone. She adjusted her handbag and reached inside. Her hand tightened around the grip of the pistol, one finger caressing the trigger.

With her other hand, she reached out and rang the doorbell.

CHAPTER 43

Thursday, August 25th, 4:25 p.m.

AFTER JAKE HAD dropped Annie home, she'd spent the last couple of hours going over her notes, struggling to come up with something to shed some light on this puzzle. Matty had come home from school an hour or so ago and was next door, playing with Kyle, so the house was quiet, allowing her to concentrate.

But she was getting nowhere, and was frustrated.

She tossed her pen down onto her desk, slid the chair back, and stretched. She wandered into the kitchen and started a fresh pot of coffee, hoping a break would clear her mind before she attacked the problem again.

While the coffee brewed, she sat at the table and leafed idly through a magazine, not seeing anything on the pages, her mind continually drifting back to the baffling question: why were people being killed, and what was behind it all?

Soon, the smell of fresh coffee filled the room and she fixed herself a cup. She dropped into a chair, and as she raised the steaming drink to her lips, the doorbell rang. She took a quick sip, set the cup down, and went to see who was calling.

She peeked through the small window in the front door. It was a young girl, perhaps sixteen or so.

She swung the door open and smiled at the visitor.

The visitor didn't smile back.

Annie noticed the girl's hand in her bag, perhaps pulling out some advertising material, or a pamphlet of some kind, but when she stared into the caller's cold eyes, her intuition kicked in.

Something was terribly wrong.

She took a cautious step back as her eyes moved to the handbag. She saw a glint of metal, and then the barrel of a gun as a weapon was withdrawn. The girl stepped into the foyer and leveled the pistol.

Annie reacted on instinct and jumped to her left, momentarily shielded by the door, and then scrambled up the steps toward the second floor.

A shot exploded behind her. Missed. Another shot. The bullet splintered the wooden step in front of her.

With a final leap, she fell onto the top landing. She heard the assassin on the steps behind as she stumbled to her feet and raced for the master bedroom.

She slammed the door and leaned against it. The door had no lock, and she had no time to set up a barricade.

Her eyes frantically swept the room, searching for a weapon, anything to defend herself with. She saw nothing.

Footsteps sounded outside the door, and then she heard a low squeak as the knob turned. She braced her feet and forced her weight against the door. It shook as the killer attempted to push it open. But it held. For now.

The gun erupted again. A hole appeared above the doorknob and a bullet smacked into the floor by her feet, bringing with it the faint odor of gunpowder.

She wasn't safe here. The killer was attempting to shoot her way in.

Annie looked to her left. The master bathroom was her only hope. It had a lock, but it wouldn't hold long, and she would be cornered. The door behind her crashed open as she raced to the bathroom. She slammed the door, locked it, and swung around.

The window.

It was small, and a long drop to the grass, but she had no choice. It was her only chance to get out alive.

She leaped to the window as the door splintered behind her. A shot had weakened the latch and the lock was almost free. She had but a moment to spare.

She released the window bolt, pushed up, and then hoisted herself into a crouch on the small window ledge.

Wood snapped as the door strained. The assassin was coming through.

She carefully twisted around and hung by the ledge with her fingers. She looked at the ground, a long way down. She took a breath, pushed out with her feet and let go.

She hit the ground, her legs bent, and she rolled as she landed. She lay still a moment. Her left leg was sore but okay, and her shoulder was bruised where she rolled, but she was otherwise uninjured.

She saw the girl appear in the window as she scrambled to her feet and took a glance up. She dashed around the corner of the house, out of the line of fire.

She had to get to a phone.

She dared not go back into the house for her cell. She made a snap decision and jumped the small hedge dividing their house from Chrissy's. She heard Matty and Kyle playing in the backyard. She couldn't endanger them, so she raced to the front of the house and banged frantically on the door.

In a few seconds it popped open, and Chrissy stared at her, wide-eyed. "Whatever is the problem, Annie?"

Annie rushed into the house. "Quickly. Shut the door and lock it. I need your phone," she said as she ran to the kitchen.

Looking bewildered, Chrissy locked the door and followed Annie.

"Bring the boys in. Hurry," Annie said as she scooped up the phone and dialed 9-1-1.

CHAPTER 44

Thursday, August 25th, 4:39 p.m.

A SWARM OF police cars screamed to a standstill in front of the Lincoln residence. The officers, well trained in active-shooter situations, leaped from the vehicles and surrounded the building.

Annie watched through Chrissy's window as officers eased through the front door, guns drawn and ready. They would be checking room to room, and would expertly apprehend the shooter if she were still there.

A few minutes later, as officers wandered from the house, their guns relaxed or holstered, Annie could tell the fugitive hadn't been found. It was certain she'd disappeared when Annie had fled.

Annie had called Jake immediately after notifying the police, and he was on his way home.

Hank and King had just pulled up and were talking to the officers who'd searched the house. Annie knew the next step would be to put out an APB to try to locate the girl. They would need a description.

She turned to Chrissy standing beside her, still wide-eyed. "I need to go over there. Please keep the boys inside until it's safe."

Chrissy nodded. "I'll make sure they stay upstairs." She followed Annie to the front door.

"And lock the door behind me," Annie said as she slipped outside. She heard the bolt slide in place behind her.

She stood on the stoop a moment and looked down at her still trembling hands. She'd thought she wouldn't have been so afraid, but she'd found out the hard way, having a gun pointed at you, and perhaps being one moment away from being shot, was a terrifying experience.

She shook it off and headed down the steps. Hank noticed her when she reached the edge of the property and came across the lawn to greet her. "Are you all right?" he asked.

Annie nodded uncertainly. "I'm okay, just a bit of a sore leg from landing on it." She detailed the entire story as Hank jotted notes in his pad.

"What did the girl look like?"

"About sixteen. Maybe five foot two or so. Reddish-blond hair. She was wearing blue jeans and a white t-shirt."

Hank scribbled the information down and then asked, "Are you sure you don't want to go to the hospital to get that leg looked at? You may have broken something."

Annie rubbed her leg. "It'll be all right. It's feeling better already and I'm sure nothing's broken."

"Okay," Hank said.

Annie turned as she heard a familiar roar. The Firebird swung into the driveway and Jake jumped out. He raced across the lawn to Annie and wrapped his arms around her, drawing her close. He looked down at her. "You okay?"

She offered him a weak smile and nodded. "I'm fine."

Simon King wandered over. Hank turned and shoved the notepad at him. "Here's a description of the girl. Call it in right away."

King frowned and took the pad. Without a word, he turned back and headed toward Hank's Chevy.

Jake watched King leave. "That your new partner?" he asked.

Hank glanced at King. "Temporary partner," he corrected. "Detective Simon King."

"And you didn't feel the need to introduce us?"

Hank grunted. "Like I said, he's temporary."

"You don't sound too happy about it," Annie said.

Hank shrugged and changed the subject. "Annie, you couldn't describe the gun the girl had, could you?"

"I ... I don't know much about guns." Annie chuckled. "It was black, but I didn't stick around long enough to take a good look."

Hank nodded. "Of course," he said. "Did the girl say anything to you?"

"Nothing. But the look in her eyes said it all. A cold, hard look, like a killer."

"She can't be far away," Jake said. "Let's hope they apprehend her."

Hank glanced toward the house. "The forensic unit will be here momentarily. They may be in the house awhile, though. Do you have a place to go?"

"I'm sure Chrissy will take us in for now," Annie replied.

Hank nodded. "It may not be safe to go home until we get the girl."

"Do you think she'll be back?" Jake asked.

"She seemed intent on killing Annie," Hank said. "She may be back. In the meantime, I'll make sure a pair of officers watch Chrissy's house, just in case."

Annie had noticed a van pull up to the curb in front of their house. It had the familiar Channel 7 logo on the side. "It looks like Lisa Krunk is here," she said. "She's the last person I want to talk to right now."

Hank and Jake glanced toward the street. "You two go on back to Chrissy's," Hank said. "I'll take care of her."

Annie and Jake hurried into Chrissy's house. Chrissy greeted them at the door. "Now, are you two going to tell me what this is all about?" she asked as they came inside.

"We're not exactly sure," Annie said.

"It has to do with a case we're working on," Jake added. "Where are the boys?"

"They're fine. They're upstairs." Chrissy went into the front room and sat on the couch.

A light tapping was heard on the front door, and then, "Hello?" It was Hank.

Jake turned and swung the door open and Hank stepped inside. "I gave Lisa a quick statement," he said as he followed Jake into the front room and dropped onto the other end of the couch while Jake and Annie sat in the loveseat.

Hank turned and grinned at Chrissy. "Sorry about invading your house like this, Chrissy."

"It's okay. That's what friends are for, but ... I wish you would tell me what this all means."

"We're unsure right now," Hank said. "But I believe it's related to the murders that have been taking place lately."

Chrissy caught her breath and leaned forward. "Are we in any danger here?"

Hank shook his head. "A couple of officers will be parked outside to watch the house until the girl is apprehended. We have other officers combing the streets and canvassing the houses right now. They'll check out anyone matching the girl's description." He turned to Jake. "Any luck today?"

"Not yet. Sammy is on it with a gang of people he knows. He's more confident than I am."

Chrissy's head moved back and forth from Jake to Hank as they talked.

"I got some interesting information from Nancy," Hank said. "She checked the body of our second killer, the one who murdered Bobby Sullivan, and found an identical chip to the one inside the latest John Doe."

Annie spoke. "I'm betting when you catch this girl, she'll have one too."

Hank's phone buzzed. He pulled it from its holster and in a moment swung it toward Annie. "Is this the girl?" he asked.

Annie looked at the puzzled girl on the screen and shook her head. "No, that's not her."

Hank texted back a reply and then asked, "Annie, do you have your cell with you?"

"No, it's in the house. I couldn't get to it."

"I have mine," Jake said.

Hank nodded. "I'll have them send any more pictures of possible suspects to your phone, so Annie can take a look at them. Finding this girl is our prime concern right now. She could be the solution to stopping this madness."

Hank made a call and arranged with the officer in charge of the search, then stood and said, "I'd better get back out there. Be sure to stay in the house for now. I can only assume you're still a target, and we don't want to take any chances."

CHAPTER 45

Thursday, August 25th, 5:59 p.m.

OLIVER CRAIG reached to a stand beside his easy chair, retrieved the remote control, and flicked on the television. The announcer's rich voice filled his den, proclaiming the upcoming news.

Craig never missed the news. It was his way of keeping his finger on the pulse of the city, his city. Or at least, it soon would be, if everything continued according to plan.

The familiar Channel 7 logo flashed on the screen and the anchor announced the top story. Craig leaned forward with great interest, sipping a bourbon, as the face of Lisa Krunk appeared. She was standing on the sidewalk in a residential neighborhood. Police officers milled in the background, some carrying rifles or pistols, now relaxed and at their side. Patrol cars with flashing lights parked in awkward angles at the curb.

Craig smiled grimly. It looked like another coup for him. The girl had succeeded in her mission, and now he could feel the momentum building. He was one step closer. He could taste it, smell it, feel the power as it filled him and propelled him on. He took another sip of his drink and relaxed deeper into the chair.

"I'm standing in front of the home of private investigators Jake and Annie Lincoln, where just a few moments ago, a shooter invaded the home. Several shots were reported fired but the intended victim managed to escape unharmed."

Craig choked on his drink and managed to sputter a string of curses. Something had gone terribly wrong.

"The unknown assailant, described as being a teenage girl, has not yet been apprehended. Police have organized an intensive manhunt for the would-be killer and they expect to make an arrest shortly.

"According to informed sources, the target of the assassin was Annie Lincoln. Viewers will recall my previous reports on the recent murders in Richmond Hill, and it's suspected this latest attempt is related. The Lincolns have been deeply involved in that, and it's my belief this is a desperate attempt to remove them from the investigation.

"I spoke briefly to Detective Hank Corning, the detective in charge of this situation. As most of you remember, Detective Corning has been investigating the prior murders we've seen, and his record has been impeccable as long as I've known him."

Craig was livid, his face contorted into an angry frown. Had he underestimated the Lincolns, or had the girl failed him somehow? He leaned forward in his seat and listened to the rest of the bad news as the scene cut to a close-up of a familiar face. Detective Corning looked straight at the camera.

"I want to tell the citizens there's no immediate cause for alarm. Police will be doing a door-to-door canvass of this area in Richmond Hill. This is not a random targeting and there's no indication anyone else is in any danger, but if you live in this area, please exercise caution and stay in your homes. Don't answer the door for anyone except the police until the shooter is apprehended."

The camera panned, showing a shot of the scene, the street, and the police cars, their lights still flashing. Lisa Krunk appeared to be mocking Craig when her face reappeared.

"Channel 7 will keep you informed of any breaking developments by special bulletins until the danger has passed. In an exclusive report, I'm Lisa Krunk for Channel 7 Action News."

Craig jumped to his feet and turned off the TV. He tossed the remote aside and reached for his cell phone. He hit speed dial and paced impatiently until he heard Wolff's voice on the line.

Craig screamed into the phone, "Wolff, what happened?"

There was silence from the other end, and then, "What … what is it, sir?"

"The girl, you fool. She failed in her mission."

No response for a moment, and then, "She failed, sir?"

"Yes. The target got away. What happened?"

"I … I don't know, sir. I …"

Craig took a deep breath and tried to cool himself down. This could jeopardize everything. He had to think clearly.

"Wolff, can you find her?" He spoke more calmly now.

"Yes, we should be able to pinpoint her exact location. Do you want me to send the boys to bring her in?"

"Yes, yes. Bring her in immediately. And, Wolff … ?"

"Yes, sir?"

"Tell them if they can't bring her in safely, they must deal with the situation."

"Deal with it how?"

"Eliminate her. She must not be exposed to any police interrogation."

"I believe she would remain loyal if … if that were to happen."

"We can't take that chance. Bring her in or get rid of her. Those are our only safe options."

Wolff protested, "Sir, as you recall, the first girl was captured and, as far as we know, she has remained loyal. I believe they have been conditioned properly, leaving no element of danger in such a situation."

"The first girl may be loyal so far, but we have no guarantee she'll remain that way. It's definitely a real problem, and I can't afford another error." Craig paused a moment before continuing, "Now, do as I say. We have no choice."

Wolff sighed. "Yes, sir. I'll get them on it right away."

"Let me know exactly how things are going." Craig hung up the phone and tossed it onto the chair.

What a mess. How could this have happened? The girl had a lot of practice with a handgun and was a good shooter, as well as familiar with a knife.

For a moment, Craig felt a wave of fear, and then desperation. They hadn't planned for a situation like this. In fact, he'd never expected anything like this could happen. But if all turned out well, perhaps they should slow down, let his plans take a little longer to be accomplished, and do more testing of the candidates before assigning them their missions.

He dropped back into his chair and hoped he would come out of this unharmed.

CHAPTER 46

Thursday, August 25th, 6:10 p.m.

FROM THE UPPER-FLOOR window, the girl had watched her target race across the back lawn to the house next door.

She hadn't been given instructions on how to proceed should she fail in her attempt. She only knew the operation was still active, the prey was on the loose, and she must succeed. Those were her orders. That was her plan.

She'd been shown pictures of both targets and given their names. She'd memorized the information and was determined not to disappoint the Wizard.

After she'd dropped from the back window, her first instinct was to pursue the target. But Annie Lincoln would be on her guard. It would be better to let things cool, and then proceed.

She'd noticed a couple of boys in the backyard of the house where the quarry had entered. Someone had appeared at the back door almost immediately and called them in. They weren't her target, and it was better they were out of the way.

After skirting around behind the Lincoln house, and then to the property behind the house where Annie Lincoln was, she had lain in wait, patiently, under cover of a row of thick bushes that bordered the property, for what she calculated to be well over an hour.

She needed to be sure the police had cleared away from the rear of the house, and all was quiet, before she proceeded with her assignment. She must not fail.

She checked her weapon. She'd used four rounds. Still plenty left, and she was thankful the Wizard had been wise enough to load the weapon fully. She checked for her knife, attached in a sheath at her ankle. The backup weapon was still there.

She listened intently but heard nothing to cause alarm. The backyards of both houses were clear, and as she scrutinized the dwelling in front of her, no one could be seen moving about.

Time to move.

She scrambled forward, out of the bushes, and stood to her feet, the gun in her right hand. She kept low as she dashed across the lawn and crouched in front of a basement window. She assumed the doors would be locked. This was her only way in. She peeked cautiously through the window. The room was darkened and no one was about.

Removing the knife from its sleeve, she balanced it a moment on one finger, then flicked it around and forced the razor-sharp edge into the space between the upper and lower panes. She worked several minutes before finally hearing a satisfying click, and the clasp was free.

She carefully tucked the knife away and eased up on the lower frame of the window. It was tight, but she managed to work it loose. It groaned and squealed as she raised it completely.

She paused and looked around, listened a moment, and then swung through the window, feet first, and landed with an easy drop to the concrete floor below.

She turned and surveyed the dim room. A washer and dryer. Some stuff on a row of shelving, and a door beyond.

She crossed the small room, twisted the knob, and eased the door open a couple of inches. She listened, then swung the door enough to glide through.

She was in a larger room—the rest of the basement. It was dark as well, but she could make out a set of steps that led upwards. She skirted around some exercise equipment, avoided a pile of boxes, and stopped at the bottom of the stairs. The stairwell was dark, and she would have to be careful.

With one hand on the railing, the other clutching the pistol, she took the first step. She'd expected the stairs to squeak and was pleased when all was quiet. She couldn't afford to warn the target. There would be no likelihood of a third chance should she fail this time. The Wizard would not be pleased and she would be devastated. The thought was unbearable. She must succeed, at all costs.

She took the second step carefully, her foot feeling the way in front. The wooden step made no sound.

More confident now, she climbed upward, testing each step before resting her full weight. Twelve steps up, she gently touched the door at the top and felt for the knob.

Her hand rested on a handle, a lever. She pushed it down carefully. It made a slight squeal. She waited, then pushed again, and the door clicked. The latch was free. One inch. Two. The door swung away and she listened.

She could hear the faint sound of voices, but couldn't tell from which direction they came. She peeked through the crack. The doorway led into a short hall. She saw a kitchen to her left, but couldn't get a view in the other direction.

She eased the door fully open and stepped into the

hallway. To the right of her was the front door of the house. She saw an archway that led to another room. That must be the living room, and that was where the voices were coming from, a little louder now, though she still couldn't make out what they were saying. She could hear a man's voice. Jake Lincoln must have come. Perfect. She would have her choice of targets.

She made a quick decision and moved to the left, toward the kitchen. She needed to be sure she had the right target, and she would wait until one of them presented themselves.

She ducked into the kitchen and stood around the corner, out of sight of the hallway. She waited several minutes and was finally rewarded.

Someone was coming up the hallway.

She raised the gun, ready to fire the moment her quarry appeared. The footsteps drew closer and her target stepped into the kitchen. She pulled back on the trigger, and then hesitated as an unfamiliar face stared at her, mouth wide.

This was not her target. She'd been given no instructions on what to do in such a case.

She dropped the pistol to her side as the woman screamed.

CHAPTER 47

Thursday, August 25th, 6:21 p.m.

JAKE HEARD the scream and jumped to his feet. It was Chrissy, and it sounded like she was terrified.

Annie looked toward the sound, in shock, unable to move for a moment, and then stood and exchanged a look with Jake. Her mouth was open, her eyes wide, holding her breath.

"Stay back," Jake whispered as he moved to the doorway and stepped into the hall. Chrissy was backing slowly from the kitchen, her hands raised above her shoulders. She turned when Jake asked, "What is it, Chrissy?"

Then a girl stepped into view, a pistol raised.

"Chrissy. Get down." Jake dove, grabbed Chrissy's arm, and whipped her toward him. They hit the floor and rolled into the living room as the gun exploded.

He dragged Chrissy to her feet. As Annie dove behind the couch, he prodded Chrissy in the same direction. She stumbled forward, fell, and then scrambled on all fours and disappeared behind the couch with Annie.

Jake spun around. There was no room for him to hide with the girls, and if the killer came into the room shooting, the couch would offer no protection.

He had to draw fire his way. He had to become the target.

Without getting himself killed.

He couldn't take the chance to dash across the hall and upstairs. The boys were up there, anyway. Not a smart move.

The closest thing at hand was the coffee table. A potted plant went flying as he swept up the table with one hand. He gripped it and waited.

The assassin didn't appear. He assumed she would be creeping up the hallway and would be on them in a second.

He listened carefully and heard a whisper of running shoes on the ceramic floor.

He moved to the doorway, swung the table blindly around the corner with all his might, and let go. It whipped up the hallway. He heard it clatter, and then a moan.

He'd hit his target, but he still couldn't see her.

He poked his head around the corner and took in the scene with a quick glance. The table had connected. The girl was on her knees, her head down. The table lay on its side in front of her, but she still gripped the gun.

This might be his only chance.

He dove into the hallway and made a flying leap into the table. The force knocked the girl on her back as the gun went spinning toward the kitchen.

He dove for the weapon and retrieved it, then stood and tucked it behind his belt.

The girl was stunned. She moved her head from side to side and moaned. She must have hit it when she fell, and now she was no longer a threat.

He stood and scrutinized her. She was just a young girl, and like the rest of the young killers, she didn't look the part.

"Annie. Chrissy," he called. "It's safe now."

The girls stepped cautiously into the hallway and peered at the downed assassin.

Chrissy hugged herself, her body trembling. Annie didn't seem much better than her friend, but she put her arm around Chrissy to calm her.

Jake stood, hands on his hips, looking at the girl. "Now, this is why we need to carry a gun. The bad guys do, and we can't."

He looked up as he heard a frantic banging on the front door. A cop peeked through the small window. "Are you all right in there?"

Annie turned, unlocked the door, and opened it. "We're all right now," she said.

A young cop stepped in, with a second one, a little older, crowding in behind him. They looked in amazement at the girl on the floor. "We heard a shot," the young one said.

Jake patted the pistol in his belt. "She tried to kill us. I got the gun."

"You better give me that." The officer pointed to the weapon and held out his hand.

Jake sighed and reluctantly slipped it from his belt. "It's all yours," he said as he handed it over.

"It's evidence," the cop said.

"Yeah, it's evidence," Jake said dryly. "Evidence that almost got us killed."

"Is that a nine-millimeter Glock?" Annie asked.

The cop looked at her with surprise. "You really know your guns."

"Yeah, she knows her guns," Jake said, winking at Annie.

The girl moaned and opened her eyes. She struggled to her knees and looked up, first at Annie, then at the cops, and then at Jake behind her. She was trapped and wouldn't be going anywhere.

As she stood, the older cop reached behind his back and

retrieved a pair of handcuffs. The killer didn't struggle as the cop stepped forward and expertly snapped them on her wrists.

Jake heard a low whistle and looked up. Matty and Kyle had come down the stairs a few steps and were peeking through the bannister.

"Who's she?" Kyle asked, wide-eyed.

"Dad," Matty said. "Did you catch another killer?"

Jake grinned. "Looks like it."

Chrissy hustled the boys back upstairs. "I'll stay up here with them awhile until you get this cleared away."

The older cop frisked the girl and retrieved the knife, and then the officers, one on each arm, walked the girl out the door and locked her in the backseat of the cruiser.

Annie put her arms around Jake and looked up at him. "You may have saved our lives."

Jake laughed and kissed her. "I can't say as much for the coffee table."

He carried the bruised and wobbling table into the living room, set the plant back in place, and retrieved his cell phone from its holder. "I'd better call Hank," he said to Annie. "Then, we'll need to go down to the station and give our statement. I'll fix that busted table later."

"And as soon as forensics is done at our place," Annie said, "they can come over here."

Jake laughed. "They're earning their paycheck today."

CHAPTER 48

Thursday, August 25th, 7:40 p.m.

JAKE PARKED THE Firebird behind Richmond Hill Police Station, and he and Annie hurried up the steps and inside.

Hank saw them approaching and came to meet them as they crossed the creaking hardwood floor. He looked a little worried. "I'm glad you guys are all right." He punched Jake on the shoulder and gave Annie a quick squeeze. "I should've had the officers stay inside the house."

"It turned out okay," Annie said. "Who could've known the girl would be that brazen, with all those officers around?"

"I should've."

Jake changed the subject. "Where's the girl now?"

"She's in the interview room. King and I are about to see what we can get from her. You can watch through the glass if you want, and I can get your statements later."

"Sounds good," Jake said.

Hank turned and beckoned to King. The detective sauntered over and Hank finally introduced them.

"So, you're the guy who brought down a vicious killer," King said as he shook Jake's hand.

As Jake shrugged, Annie thought King sounded a little sarcastic. Annie smiled to herself. He was probably jealous.

"This way," Hank said, and the Lincolns followed him, King coming behind, to a doorway at the back of the precinct. It opened into a short hallway and led to another door.

They entered a small room containing only a couple of chairs. The far wall consisted largely of a two-way mirror showing a room beyond. Hank waved toward the mirror. "You can watch from here," he said as he and King went through a small door into the adjoining room.

Annie peered through the glass into the interview room. It was a small area, brightly lit, with barren, blank walls. The girl sat on the far side of a metal table, facing the mirror, her hands cuffed to a ring on the table.

The girl paid no attention as the detectives entered the room. Hank sat at the table and faced her while King leaned against the side wall and crossed his arms.

Hank leaned forward, rested his elbows on the table, and cupped his hands under his chin. He studied the girl a moment before asking, "What's your name?"

She glared at him, emotionless, cold, as if not seeing him. She gave no answer.

Hank leaned back. "Why'd you try to kill the Lincolns?"

No answer.

"You're in a lot of trouble, but no one was hurt. It may not be so bad for you if you can tell us about it now."

The girl glared.

Detective King stepped in and slammed his fist on the table. He leaned in, his face a few inches from hers. "You need to talk. Now. Do you understand?"

The girl moved her eyes and stared at King, unflinching.

"Just because you're a girl," he shouted, "doesn't mean we can't make you talk."

"Detective," Hank said as he gripped King's arm. "Relax a moment."

King straightened his back, threw his hands in the air, and resumed his position against the wall.

Annie looked at Jake. "Good cop, bad cop."

"Looks like it." Jake chuckled. "But I think they're being their natural selves."

"She's not going to talk," Annie said. "I know it. No matter how much King yells and screams, or how nice Hank is to her, she won't talk."

Jake shrugged. "You may be right."

"She's like the rest of them. For whatever reason, their objective is more important than themselves."

Hank was leaning forward again. His voice was soft, almost pleading, "Will you at least give us your name? That's all we want right now."

No answer.

Hank sighed. "You're going to be charged with attempted murder unless you help us. Is that what you want? You'll be locked up for a long, long time."

The girl dropped her head. Was she breaking?

The cuffs rattled as she adjusted her hands. Her head came up, but she avoided Hank's eyes and stared at the mirror, straight at Annie. The cold stare made Annie shudder. Could the girl see her?

Anne stepped to one side. The killer's eyes didn't move, and Annie breathed again. Of course the girl couldn't see her.

King stood up straight. "Let her cool behind bars awhile. Once she gets a taste of this place, she'll talk."

Hank looked up at King. Was he considering his suggestion? Annie couldn't see his face. Perhaps he was warning King with his eyes to be quiet.

Hank turned back to the girl. "You wouldn't want to be locked up, would you?"

King said, "Let's lock her up."

"It's not a nice place to be," Hank said.

Still no response from the prisoner.

Hank leaned back, sighed, and observed the girl for a few moments. Finally, he said, "Lock her up."

King grinned and swung open the door, brushing past Annie and Jake and through the outer door. He returned a minute later with an officer who uncuffed the girl from the table and prodded her through the door.

Annie watched the officer lead the would-be killer out. Somehow she felt sorry for the girl, but angry and uneasy at the same time. She was more determined than ever to get to the heart of this case.

Hank followed King from the interview room, dropped into a chair, and looked at Jake. He shook his head slowly. "We have to find out who this girl is."

"I'll get Callaway on it," King said, "but I doubt if she'll be in the system either."

"Maybe not," Hank said, "but we'll add her photo to the package and see if our cops on the street come up with something."

"I'm betting she has a chip in her," Annie said.

"Maybe," Hank said. "It'll be too dangerous to remove, but we'll get her checked out."

"There will be," Annie said.

"Speaking of chips," Jake said, "have you sent the first one to Toronto yet?"

Hank nodded. "I sent it this afternoon. I hope to hear back soon."

"But you have another one, right?"

Hank squinted at Jake. "Yeah?"

"Can I borrow it?"

"It's evidence."

"I know."

"And you want me to lend it to you?"

"Yup."

Hank looked at King, who shrugged and said, "Why not? Can't hurt."

"Okay, then. I'll get it for you." He frowned and looked at his watch. "I have to get it from evidence, but it's too late for today. I'll get it first thing in the morning." He paused. "But it's not really something I should be doing."

"I know."

Hank laughed.

"I won't tell anybody," Jake said.

CHAPTER 49

Thursday, August 25th, 8:06 p.m.

OLIVER CRAIG leaned forward at his desk and held his head in his hands. The bad news he'd received regarding the girl was causing him undue stress and he felt a headache coming on.

The smoke that wafted up from the Cuban and smothered his desk wasn't helping his head either. He butted it out and rubbed his aching temples. He hadn't heard back from Wolff regarding the girl's whereabouts and assumed she hadn't been picked up yet.

He dug in his desk drawer and found a bottle of ibuprofen, popped the cap, and downed three capsules with the help of a long gulp of bourbon.

He didn't want to be disturbed right now, and as he heard the tapping on the door of his office, he sighed and sat back.

"What is it?" he called.

The door swung inward, and his father's nurse eased into the room. She approached the desk, a somber look on her face.

"It's your father, sir," she said.

"Yes, yes. What about him?"

"He's gone, sir."

Craig cocked his head. "Gone? Gone where?"

"He's passed on, sir."

Craig's mouth dropped open a moment, and then he said, "Dead?"

"Yes, sir."

Craig stared at the nurse, not seeing her, and then let his gaze wander across the room. His eye rested on a portrait of his father on the far wall. Dead. His father was dead.

He blinked and looked back at the nurse. "Thank you. You can go now."

His mind felt numb. It was a shock, to be sure, and he'd expected it any time, but now that the old man was finally gone, he struggled to understand how he felt.

He rose to his feet. Perhaps he should go see his father.

As he entered the large foyer, the doctor was just adjusting his overcoat, ready to leave.

The doctor turned as Craig approached. "Hello, Mr. Craig."

Craig nodded and was silent.

"Do you want me to take care of your father's body?" the doctor asked.

Craig nodded. "Yes, yes."

"I can get someone to make the arrangements, unless you prefer to do that yourself."

Craig looked toward the hallway leading to the old man's room. He was silent a moment and then spoke abruptly. "Yes, yes. Please do that, doctor."

The doctor nodded. "I'll take care of it for you. Good night, sir," he said, closing the door quietly behind him as he left.

Craig turned his gaze back to the hallway a moment, then strode across the foyer and down the darkened corridor. He stopped in front of the door, took a deep breath, and stepped inside the old man's room.

The nurse, in the chair by the window, looked up as he entered. He averted his eyes from the deathbed and spoke to her. "The doctor will find someone to make arrangements."

"I'll stay with him until then, sir."

Craig turned, dropped into the chair beside his father's body, and looked at the man he'd barely known. He didn't appear much different than he had earlier. Still the same paper-white skin, with pale, tight lips, his eyes closed, but now in death.

He thought a moment about the afterlife. Was there really such a thing, and if so, did his father deserve to be in a better place? He brushed off the idea and decided it wasn't worth worrying about now. He had a long time to go before he would be his father's age. Perhaps he would consider it then. No use clogging up his life now with thoughts of a God he'd never considered before.

No, he had too much to accomplish.

He stood abruptly, left the room, and strode back to his office.

He should let Wolff know. It would be the decent thing to do. Wolff had worked under his father's guidance many years ago and thought a lot of the old man.

Wolff answered the phone on the first ring.

Craig got straight to the point. "Wolff, my father has passed on."

There was silence.

"Wolff, are you there?"

"Yes, sir."

"It happened just a few minutes ago."

"I ... I'm very sorry to hear it, sir."

Craig sighed. "We've been expecting it for a long time."

"Yes, I know, but ..."

"He would want us to continue his work."

"Yes, sir. Your father was a great man and it's an honor to have known him. He ... he was like a father to me."

"We'll have time to mourn later," Craig said. "But for now, we have more important things to be concerned with."

"Yes, sir."

"The girl. What about the girl?"

"It appears she has been captured."

Craig swore. "Captured?"

"By the police. We traced her and found her location to be the police precinct."

Craig rose from his desk and paced. This was a bad turn of events. Too many things were going wrong with his carefully laid plans, and he had no idea what to do about it.

"I believe she'll be loyal to us, sir," Wolff said. "It's certainly a problem, but not one we can't overcome."

"I hope you're right, Wolff, and I assume the mission was aborted?"

"I haven't heard for sure, but when we first started the trace, her initial location was near the Lincoln home. She may have tried to continue, and perhaps she succeeded before being captured. Our boys reported police action near the neighbor's house, where the target may have gone, but they couldn't safely get close enough to see what was occurring."

"So we've no idea if the mission failed or succeeded?"

"I only know the girl survived."

Craig terminated the call and sank into his chair. Had he underestimated the Lincolns? If so, they were even more of a threat than he'd anticipated. He was at a loss in how to deal with the situation, but determined to carry on.

Though Wolff's idealistic worldview didn't coincide with his own quest for power, the doctor was his best asset, and as long as Wolff believed their goal was the same, Craig could use him to the fullest, and he would eventually triumph.

Now that his father was gone, nothing had changed. He'd already had control of his father's assets, and had substantial funds of his own.

It wasn't more money he needed. It was the power he hoped to attain, and that was what he couldn't let slip from his grasp.

CHAPTER 50

Thursday, August 25th, 9:22 p.m.

FORENSICS HAD FINISHED with the Lincoln house and Jake was lounging on the couch in the living room, flicking through the TV channels, when his iPhone rang.

He looked at the caller ID. It was the number from the burner phone he'd given Sammy Fisher.

"Hi, Sammy. Tell me some good news."

"Greetings, Detective Jake. I do have some news, but it's not all good."

"Oh?"

"One of my associates talked to a guy who saw the boy. Apparently, a scumbag drug dealer saw him earlier in the day."

Jake swung his feet to the floor, sat up, and leaned forward. "Where was that?"

"Downtown, just off Auburn Street. That's a rough part of town there, you know."

Jake scrambled to his feet and scrounged in a side table for a pen and something to write on. He came up with an envelope and scribbled the street name down. "What time was that?"

"Early afternoon, yesterday. He didn't know the exact time."

"Did he talk to him, or see where he came from, or went to?"

"Yeah, he sure did. He saw David get into a vehicle. He wasn't so close, but he swore David was abducted. He said it sure didn't look like he'd gotten into the car on his own."

Jake paced, listening intently and thinking. So, David was kidnapped. That was what they'd suspected, only now it was confirmed. He didn't think the drug dealer would have a reason to make the story up. But who had abducted David?

"I may want to talk to the dealer," Jake said. "How can I find him?"

"He hangs around the alleyways there, looking for customers. He's got long, stringy hair and wears a black leather jacket and baseball cap. I don't know his name and I'm sure he wouldn't give that anyway. But he may not be so interested in talking to anybody who looks like a cop."

"You think I look like a cop?"

Sammy's laugh came over the line. "Maybe not."

Jake chuckled and asked, "I suppose the guy didn't get the license plate of the vehicle?"

"Nope, but he said it was an Escalade. He said he knew what it was because he lifted one once."

"What color?"

Sammy sighed. "They didn't get that."

"Did he see who was in the vehicle?" Jake asked as he scribbled on the envelope.

"When they opened the door he saw at least one guy in the backseat, maybe two. He couldn't see anything else because the vehicle had tinted windows."

"Excellent work, Sammy."

"My people are still out there. Someone else may know something. It's not likely, but they have nothing better to do, so why not keep them busy?"

"It all helps," Jake said.

"And there's something else I need to tell you."

"Yeah?"

"We couldn't find out anything on the other two kids, the unidentified ones, but it appears there may be a few people missing in the area lately. Homeless, but younger ones. It may be just rumors, or maybe they're paranoid now, but some of my associates have noticed that a few kids who used to hang around the usual areas haven't been seen for a while."

"Any specific names?"

"Hard to tell. It's more of a feeling than actual fact. You get a feel for certain things when you live in the open air. A lot of familiar faces but you don't always know their names or anything about them."

"It seems to fit, Sammy. Most of the killers have been unidentified. They may be some of the ones who are missing, because so far, nobody seems to know who they are."

"It's a mean world, Jake."

"Yes, it sure can be."

And a lot of cruel people. Jake desperately wanted to get to the bottom of this, and they might finally have a good lead. He had to call Hank and let him know.

"Sammy, let me get on this right away. I appreciate your help and I'll talk to you later. Maybe I'll drop by soon."

They hung up and Jake dialed Hank.

"Detective Hank Corning."

"I have something for you," Jake said and then told Hank the information he'd gotten from Sammy.

"I'll get Callaway to look into it first thing in the morning, but there are a lot of Escalades around."

"Yeah, but with tinted windows?"

"Most of them seem to have tinted windows, and I'm not even sure we would have that information," Hank said. "But let me see what I can come up with and I'll get back to you tomorrow."

"And don't forget to bring me that chip."

"I won't forget."

CHAPTER 51

Thursday, August 25th, 10:22 p.m.

DAVID HAINES WAS waiting. He had a plan. A desperate plan, to be sure, but it was all he could think of.

He'd awoken a couple of hours ago, his mind a little fuzzy. He vaguely remembered Wolff had come into the room, probably several hours ago, strapped him to the bed, and injected him with something. He couldn't recall much after that.

Strange thoughts floated through his mind. Something to do with a wizard, or a wolf, or God, he wasn't sure; it was all very hazy. Maybe it'd been a dream, but if so, it had been a very strange dream.

Wolff had freed him from the straps and brought some food an hour ago. It wasn't much. A few dry crackers on a paper plate with an apple for dessert. He'd washed it down with a cup of lukewarm water from the tap.

But Wolff had said he'd be back soon, and David waited. He paced his cell, patiently biding his time.

He heard a scraping sound as the bolt on the door was drawn and the madman stepped into the room. David sat on the edge of the bed as the door slammed and Wolff approached.

"How do you feel?" the doctor asked.

"Okay."

Wolff stopped a yard away, tucked his hands into the pockets of his long white coat, and stood silently, observing the boy.

Now!

David had little strength, weakened from the sparse amount of food the last day or so, but he had determination. He dove forward, his right shoulder slamming into Wolff's midriff, knocking the wind from his captor with a whoosh, and Wolff went down. The desperate boy grabbed a lock of sparse gray hair and slammed the back of the mad doctor's head against the concrete floor.

Once. Wolff groaned. Twice. Three times.

Wolff lay still, out cold, but breathing. The boy didn't want to hurt anyone, but he had no choice. He needed out of this crazy place.

He sprang up and dashed to the door, pulled it open, and peeked out. He saw a hallway, running in either direction, lined with several doors similar to the one he'd been locked behind.

The hall was empty, so he stepped out, uncertain what to do next. He hadn't planned beyond the point of getting free of his cell, with no idea what he would find.

To the left, the corridor ended at a concrete wall. A dead end. To the right, past several doors, was a larger room, brightly lit. The panel on the door of the next cell was pulled open and he peeked inside. Another doctor, one he hadn't seen before, was sitting in a fold-up chair. He appeared to be talking to a boy who lay quietly on a cot. Another prisoner, like himself.

He stepped back, tiptoed toward the large room, and

peered inside. It was a laboratory of some kind, the walls lined with cabinets, desks, and benches, with all manner of equipment David couldn't identify.

He stopped to listen. No one was there, so he stepped uneasily into the room. He glanced toward a door on the far wall. Would it take him outside and away from this madhouse? It appeared to be his only way out.

He hurried to the door and eased it open a few inches. It led into a garage with a black Escalade parked inside. The same one they had used to grab him.

In horror, he saw the monster of a man sitting in a chair on the other side of the room, beyond the vehicle. It was the thug who'd helped strap him to the bed. A mean-looking pistol was fastened in a holster under his arm. His head had drooped down and his eyes were closed, a magazine threatening to fall from his lap.

Was he asleep?

He eased the door open enough to slip through, carefully shut it, and crouched down. He took a chance and raised his head. The ugly goon hadn't moved. Keeping low, he crept forward and peeked into the vehicle. The keys weren't in the ignition.

He glanced at the huge garage door in front. He couldn't possibly find a way to get it open and jump through in time. That was out of the question, and the only other door to freedom lay beyond the thug.

The brute grunted and David ducked. He heard a loud yawn, and then the rustle of the magazine as it hit the floor.

He looked around desperately for a means of escape, frantically trying to come up with an idea. Wolff would wake up before long, and he would be trapped between a crazy doctor and a vicious brute.

He thought of rolling under the vehicle to hide. There was plenty of space, but from the guard's sitting position, he would be seen.

His heart was thumping, his mouth was dry, and he was terrified, but he had an idea.

He scanned the floor for something to throw and draw the guard's attention. The floor was clean, but he had a better idea.

He lay horizontally beside the vehicle, opened his hand, and slapped the side door full force with the palm of his hand.

"Who's there?" the thug called in a gravelly voice. David twisted his head, peeked under the vehicle, and saw him stand.

Again, louder, and meaner, "Who's there?"

As the feet moved his way, David rolled quietly under the vehicle. The thug had reached the back and was coming around, but David had now slithered silently to the other side. He rolled free and crouched.

This would be his only chance.

The goon was on the opposite side of the Escalade as David crept to the exit. He twisted the knob and pulled the heavy door open.

The guard looked up. "Stop."

David dashed into the dark. He was outside, but the goon would be at his heels.

"Stop or I'll shoot you."

David darted across the gravel toward a row of trees, far beyond. He was weak and he stumbled and fell. He rolled to his feet and staggered on, exhausted, his breath labored.

He heard a horrible laugh from the thug, close behind.

He wasn't going to make it.

He didn't make it.

He felt an iron grip on his shoulder and was yanked to a stop. His feet kicked up gravel as powerful arms lifted him and hugged him like a vise.

Struggling and helpless, he was carried back to his prison, the monster chuckling in his ear all the way.

CHAPTER 52

Friday, August 26th, 8:12 a.m.

JUST AS HANK had promised, he arrived at the Lincoln home bright and early.

Annie watched from the kitchen as Matty swung the front door open. "Hey, Uncle Hank. Catch any bad guys lately?" he asked, giving Hank the usual fist bump.

Hank laughed. "Not today," he said. "But I'm working on it."

Annie poked her head through the basement doorway and called to Jake, who was doing his daily workout. "Hank's here."

"I'll be up in a minute."

Matty scrambled upstairs to prepare for school while Hank wandered into the kitchen and sat at the table. Annie fixed him a cup of coffee and set it in front of him.

He pulled a plastic bag from his jacket pocket and handed it to Annie. "Here's the chip you wanted to borrow. The other one seems to be exactly the same. Oh, and I'll need it back when you're done."

Annie squinted at the bag's contents. "It's tiny."

The basement door popped open and Jake stepped into the room. He'd built up a sweat and was wiping his forehead

244

with a towel. He peered at the bag Annie was holding. "So, that's it, huh?"

Hank shrugged. "That's it. I hope to hear back from Toronto on the other one sometime today. It might be a GPS tracker, but our lab doesn't have any expertise in that area."

Annie smiled. "We do."

"Good luck with it," Hank said and took a gulp of his coffee. "Can't stay long. King is out in the car. We're going to see if we can round up that drug dealer. If we can get the color of the Escalade, we'll have more to go on."

"That'll save me trying to look him up," Jake said.

"Did Callaway find anything on the car?" Annie asked.

"A list a mile long. We'll go over it and see if anything stands out, but it's a slim lead until we get the color."

Jake broke in. "How about lending us your pistol, Hank?"

Hank chuckled. "Can't do that. I don't mind bending the law once in a while, but not that much."

"Just thought I'd ask. Anyway, I'll call you later. I need a shower," he said as he dropped the towel over his shoulder and left the kitchen.

Hank finished his drink with two more gulps, stood up, and headed for the front door. "Thanks for the coffee," he called over his shoulder as he left.

Matty wandered back into the kitchen a few minutes later, grabbed his lunch, and kissed his mother.

"I'm off to school, Mom."

"No, you're not. We're driving you again today. You can go and get Kyle and then come back here. Your father will be ready any minute, and then we'll go."

"Aw, Mom," Matty said, and he went out the back door.

Annie cleaned up the kitchen while waiting for Jake to get ready. In a few minutes he came down. Matty and Kyle were back, and they were ready to leave.

They drove two blocks, dropped the boys at school and, a few minutes later, they screeched to a stop in front of a row of townhouses.

They stepped from the vehicle, squeezed past a banged-up Hyundai, and ran up the steps of number 633. The door opened as they approached it.

"Come on in, my friends. Annie, I haven't seen you in a while."

"Hi, Jeremiah," Annie said as she stepped inside.

He approached her, half-bowed, and kissed her hand.

"Hey, Geekly," Jake said, holding out his hand.

"I'll just shake yours."

Jeremiah Everest was appropriately nicknamed Geekly for obvious reasons. He looked the part, with hair down over his ears, a thin, stringy goatee, and glasses only a true geek would wear.

He and Jake had been friends for a long time, and his expertise had been useful to their investigations several times in the past.

Jake slapped him on the back and followed him into the living room.

Annie couldn't tell if it was a living room, an office, or a computer parts warehouse.

The walls were lined with makeshift shelving containing computers, printers, and a variety of other electronic stuff. Dials and meters adorned other equipment.

Off to the side, within easy reach of his chair, were a tower and a shelf stuffed with DVDs, drives, mice, and cables.

A small television and an easy chair in one corner of the room were all that gave any indication of a life outside of microchips.

A desk in the corner sported a pair of monitors, a keyboard, and a mouse. Geekly slid over a pair of extra chairs and dropped into his own. "Have a seat. Let's see what you have there."

They sat and Jake slipped out the bag and handed it to his friend. Geekly held it up to the light and squinted at the chip. He swung around, found a magnifying glass under a stack of paper, held it up, and squinted some more.

"Yeah, I'd say it's a GPS transmitter. Maybe. I'll have to do some tests."

"Can you do it now?" Jake asked.

Geekly tilted his chair and combed his hair back with his fingers. "May take a while."

Jake and Annie exchanged a look. "We'll call you," Annie said.

"How about I'll call you?" Geekly said, pushing his glasses up on his nose. "I may have to consult with a friend on this one. He's got more equipment for this sort of thing than I do."

"Can you see him right away?" Jake asked.

"Yup. I already called him yesterday, straight after you phoned. He's expecting me. We'll get this thing figured out, no problem."

Jake stood. "We need it ASAP."

"Don't worry. I'm on it. Now get out of here and let me do my job."

CHAPTER 53

Friday, August 26th, 9:14 a.m.

THE TEAM OF Hank Corning and Simon King approached Auburn Street and circled the block for the third time.

It was a decrepit part of the city, narrow streets, squat two-story tenements, dark alleys, and steaming sewers. A row of government-subsidized housing held a mix of the lazy, the lonely, and the leeches, many preying on others, some struggling to live, most surviving honestly and hoping for better days.

Hank turned down Auburn again, and from the passenger's seat, King scrutinized the few who trod the dusty, littered streets. None yet fitted the description of the drug dealer they were searching for.

"I think we're chasing a bum lead," King said. "How can you trust the word of someone who lives on the street and probably never worked a day in his life?"

Hank shot King a frown. "Just relax, will you? We'll find him. You worked narcotics, so you know he has to show up eventually or he's out of business."

King pointed down an alleyway to his right. "That could be a crack house."

Hank slowed and peered at the ravaged building, long

since neglected, with broken windows and graffiti-clad walls.

"There he is," King said. "Keep moving. Pull over up there."

Hank steered to the curb past the alleyway and King jumped out. He shut the door and said through the open window, "Drive around to the next street and come down the alley from the other end. I'll come at him from here, and if he tries to run, he'll be trapped."

Hank nodded and touched the gas. He circled the block, pulled over, and jumped out. As he entered the alley, he saw King step into view at the other end.

He closed the gap, avoiding overflowing dumpsters, a skittering rat or two, broken bottles, and rusty tin cans.

The quarry turned his head toward Hank and watched a moment, then spun the other way, but stopped short when he saw King. He turned back and dashed into the building.

Hank and King scrambled to the doorway. Hank kicked the half-open door and it sprang inward, threatening to fall from its hinges. They could hear the target ahead, running up a flight of stairs.

"Police. Stop."

The man paid no mind.

They charged inside, Hank first, King behind, the taste of foul air in their mouth. Hank withdrew his gun, held it ready, and moved cautiously up the steps. King drew his weapon and followed.

The sound of running feet thumped the floorboards above.

At the top of the stairs, a hallway led to several rooms. Hank caught sight of a leather jacket disappearing through a doorway down the hall. The door slammed, but Hank's jackboot splintered it open.

Their prey scrambled through a window in the room, trying to get to a fire escape. His cap fell to the floor as he attempted to twist around. Too late. Hank caught a handful of jacket and heaved the frightened man in.

He landed on the floor, panting. "I didn't do nothin'. What do you want?" His voice quivered as he whined.

King trained his gun on the squirming man. "We want to talk to you. Stand up."

The man lay still. "What're you going to do? Let me go."

Hank slipped his pistol back into its holder and turned to King. "Put your gun away."

King holstered his weapon, bent down, and gripped the suspect by the jacket with both hands. He yanked him to his feet, slammed him against the wall, and held him. The terrified man's feet dangled inches off the floor.

"We want to talk to you," King said.

"What about? I ain't got nothin' on me."

King freed one hand and reached into the pocket of the man's jacket. He pulled out a handful of small, neatly wrapped packages. "What's this?" he asked, tossing the packets over his shoulder. They fluttered to the floor.

The dealer looked down at his scattered wares. "That ain't mine."

King laughed. "Whose is it?"

A shrug, fear in his eyes, and then, "What do you want?"

Hank put his hand on King's shoulder. "Let him loose. He's not going anywhere."

The man brought his hands up chest high and tried to look honest. "He's right. I'm not going anywhere. I swear."

King released his grip on the jacket and stood back. The dealer's feet reached for the floor, and then he stumbled, tottered, and fell back against the wall, but managed to stay upright.

"What's your name?" Hank asked.

The hood straightened the collar of his jacket and looked sheepish. "John."

"Last name?"

He thought a moment. "Jones."

Hank laughed. "Well, John Jones, we want to ask you about what you saw yesterday."

"And you won't run me in?"

King looked at Hank and then moved in, his face a few inches away from the villain. He glared. "I oughta run you in just for being an idiot."

"Take it easy, King," Hank said. King stepped back and the dealer watched in horror as the cop stomped a couple of his precious baggies into the floor.

"We won't run you in, Mr. Jones," Hank said. "If you tell us about the boy you saw abducted yesterday."

The man lifted his eyes. "What boy?"

Hank sighed and waved toward King. "Do you want this guy to ask you next time, or would you sooner I did?"

The dope peddler looked at King, and then back at Hank. "All right. I seen him."

"What did you see?"

"The kid was in the alley. I never seen him before and he just walked past and out to the street."

"And?"

"And this car pulls up and he got in. But I think they pulled him in. Kidnapped him, maybe."

"What kind of car?"

"It was an Escalade. Black."

"You're sure it was black? Not dark blue?"

"It was black for sure. I swear, it was—"

King interrupted with, "What else did you see?"

"Nothin'. It just drove away."

"How many guys?"

"Two … I think. Plus the driver."

"Did you recognize them?"

"Nope. I swear, I never seen none of them before."

King leaned in, his fist clenched. "If you're lying to us I know where to find you."

The man raised his hands as if to protect himself from a blow. "Why would I lie? That's what I saw."

"He's telling the truth," Hank said.

"Can I go now?"

Hank stood back and waved toward the door. "Go."

King stepped aside and the pusher crouched down and scrambled to gather up his scattered merchandise. King's boot caught him heavily in the shoulder and sent the dealer tumbling to his back. He glared up at the cop. "What'd you do that for?"

"Leave that and get out of here." King pointed to the door.

The dealer looked at his packets on the floor, and then stumbled to his feet, grabbed his cap, and limped from the room, holding his bruised shoulder.

King folded his arms and watched him leave. "I may come back for that lowlife later."

Hank looked at King. "You can if you want, but wait until you get back into narcotics. Right now, you're a homicide cop, and we have a lead to follow."

CHAPTER 54

Friday, August 26th, 9:22 a.m.

WOLFF STRAIGHTENED his back and pushed his chair away from the desk. The boy had seemed to be making progress but had caught him completely by surprise the evening before.

He went into the adjoining washroom and checked the bandage on the back of his head. He no longer needed it. The bleeding had stopped now, but his head was still sore. He decided to be more careful.

He didn't really blame the boy. He was obviously frightened and desperate, and like a caged animal, had done what he could to escape.

Wolff was satisfied with the overall results they were achieving. The conditioning of the candidates was going well, though he wasn't pleased with losing them when their mission had been completed. He still firmly believed in the cause, but all this killing was not to his liking. Sure, the targets deserved it, but there was no reason the assassins should be eliminated.

In a way, they were just victims of circumstances, but now with the tracker, he hoped they could bring them in when the job was completed, and only eliminate them if necessary.

That would be more efficient and would allow him the proper amount of time to assure each candidate was at peak conditioning.

He thought back to the period, decades ago, when he'd been working on the official project with his mentor, Oliver Craig, Sr. They hadn't had the same technology at the time, and once the mission was begun, it was impossible to track progress, and often things didn't go as planned.

Thanks to new technology, combined with his own research and Mr. Craig's personal notes that had survived the project, he was seeing vast improvements in the whole process, and he had perfected the methodology.

He didn't really enjoy the first stages of the procedure. The kids were frightened and, at times, Wolff felt some compassion toward them, especially during the periods when the various forms of torture were necessary. However, he was convinced it was for the best and would benefit society as a whole.

The later stages however, were what he enjoyed most. Watching as he shaped them into what was needed, and then, when they were fully formed, he felt like he'd created something wonderful. It made him feel like a wizard, not just in name for the sake of conditioning, but in reality.

He went back to the laboratory and looked at the vast array of equipment amassed since this current project had been founded. He was adept in the use of everything he saw before him, and though he knew he might not be long for this world, he was pleased Craig in his wisdom had found another who would carry on his work.

Muller was young but showed definite promise, and his dedication to the cause reminded him of himself in his younger years.

Yes, Muller would be the future of the project, and their efforts would continue through him.

He was startled by the phone ringing. He hurried to his desk and picked it up.

It was Mr. Craig.

"Wolff, the girl failed in her second attempt."

"I'm not happy to hear that, sir."

He heard Craig sigh over the line. "Neither am I."

"Are you convinced the Lincolns are a threat?" Wolff asked.

"I am. We must try again."

"We have no more candidates ready, sir."

Craig swore. "How long?"

"The new boy has a lot of spirit and may take longer than anticipated, and the other two are still in the middle of the process. Fortunately, there has been a dramatic decrease in the time necessary since the first girl. She was more of a learning process for us, and we have made great strides since her. However, it may be a few days before I can safely offer you the next perfected candidate."

There was silence. Finally Craig said, "Then we must wait." He swore again.

"Sir?"

"Yes, what is it, Wolff?"

"I know you have insisted in the past that after each mission the candidate should eliminate themselves, but I think that will soon be no longer necessary."

"It's too dangerous, Wolff."

Wolff hesitated. "I have been working on a kill chip, sir."

"A kill chip?"

"Yes. Combining it with the transmitter will allow us to trigger it remotely in the event of a capture. This would eliminate any danger which could result."

"Why have you not implemented it yet?"

"It's not ready, sir. Laboratory tests on mice have been successful. However, there have been a few failures. I still need to do more testing."

"How long until it's ready?"

"I can't say, sir. Perhaps a week or two. A month at the most. In the last three candidates, as a test, we've successfully implanted the GPS transmitter next to the amygdala, where the new device will eventually go to function properly."

"Excellent work, Wolff."

"Thank you, sir."

Craig sighed. "So now we must wait for more candidates before we proceed with our plans."

"Yes. However, that may give things a chance to cool off."

"Yes, I suppose you're right. At any rate, it wouldn't hurt to send the boys out to search for another acquisition."

"Yes, sir. I'll send them later today."

"Keep me posted, Wolff."

"I will, sir."

Wolff hung up the phone. He couldn't understand why Mr. Craig was in such a hurry. The cause had been alive for decades, and perhaps in one form or another for hundreds of years. It certainly wouldn't be fully accomplished in his lifetime, and not in Mr. Craig's lifetime either.

But, like his father, Mr. Craig was one of the elite, and knew what was best.

CHAPTER 55

Friday, August 26th, 10:44 a.m.

JAKE PACED THE living room floor, thinking about the case, eagerly waiting for Geekly to get back to him.

He'd picked up his cell a couple of times, but changed his mind. He knew his friend would call as soon as he came up with something.

Annie was in the office doing some vital research for a client; nothing she couldn't take care of in a few minutes online, and she wanted to get it out of the way.

The Escalade was the best lead they had at the moment, and Jake was impatient. He grabbed his iPhone and speed-dialed Hank.

"Detective Hank Corning."

"Hank, did you have any luck finding that guy?"

Sounds of traffic came over the line. "Sure did." A car honked and King swore.

"What'd you get from him? Did you get the color of the vehicle?" Jake asked.

"It's black. The Escalade is black. I've already called Callaway and he'll have a list for me when I get back to the station." Hank paused. "What are you planning on doing with the information?"

"We may do a little research on our own."

"What kind of research?"

"Not sure yet," Jake said. "Did he have anything else?"

"No. Nothing at all."

"You think he's telling the truth?"

"I think so. King's not so sure."

"Why would he lie?" Jake asked.

"That's what I said. Anyway, King did a number on him and he was too afraid to lie."

Jake heard King laugh and then say, "That little weasel had it coming."

"Let me know if Callaway's list turns up anything," Jake said, then terminated the call. They had something at least, not much, but more than they had a while ago.

He tucked his phone away, wandered into the office, and dropped into the guest chair. Annie looked up at him.

"The Escalade is black," he said and then filled her in on the rest of the conversation.

"They couldn't make it easy for us, could they?" Annie said. "Black is the most common color for Escalades. Why couldn't it be yellow or something?"

Jake chuckled. "The bad guys always like black. Black cars, black hats, and black deeds."

"To match their black hearts."

The office phone rang and Annie put it on speaker.

It was Geekly.

"I have something for you. This is definitely a GPS transmitter."

Jake leaned forward and gave Annie a thumbs-up. He spoke into the phone. "Excellent work, but why didn't the police lab come up with that?"

"It's rather sophisticated and different than usual. A GPS

transmitter normally transmits at regular intervals and sends the position of the device. This device transmits infrequently, presumably to extend battery life. The police lab likely didn't allow for a long enough testing period, or perhaps don't have the right equipment."

"And you do?"

"My friend does."

Annie asked, "So, it's emitting a signal, but can you tell where the signal is being picked up from?"

"My friend was able to locate approximately where the GPS receiver is located. I didn't think it was possible, but he's a whiz at this kind of stuff."

"Spare me the technical details," Jake said. "Just tell me where the receiver is."

"Northeast of the city. He couldn't track it down any closer, but likely less than a couple of miles from the outskirts."

"That's a lot of territory."

"It's a lot of territory, but a lot of it is farmland with only a few roads in the area."

Annie had turned back to the computer. Jake glanced over. She was doing something with MapQuest. She had the satellite view up and was leaned in, peering at the monitor.

"Anything else you can tell us?" Jake asked Geekly.

"That's all there is."

"Thanks, buddy. I owe you one."

"You owe me a lot more than one."

Jake laughed. "Someday I'll return the favor."

"I'll wait. Talk to you later."

Jake pushed the "Hang Up" icon and looked back at Annie. "I should let Hank know about this."

She nodded, and Jake called Hank's number.

"This is Detective Hank Corning. Leave a message."

Jake detailed what Geekly had found and ended with, "We may drive out there and take a look around." He dropped the phone back in its cradle.

Annie hit a final key and sat back. In a few seconds, the printer hummed and pages eased out into the tray.

"I'm printing the satellite view of the area, as well as a road map."

"It looks like we're going on a trip," Jake said.

"We are."

CHAPTER 56

Friday, August 26th, 11:13 a.m.

AS JAKE DROVE, Annie used a fluorescent green highlighter and marked places of interest on the satellite map. There was beginning to be a lot of green circles.

"There are too many possibilities here," she said. "It would take all day just to drive past them all, and much longer to check them out thoroughly."

Jake was taking frequent glances at the map, moving his eyes from the road and back again. "The way I see it, there are only two main roads leading from the city to that part of the countryside."

Annie looked at Jake. "What are you getting at?"

Jake reached over and pointed to the map. "See that road there, coming from the city?" He moved his finger. "And that one there?"

"Yes."

Jake put his hand on the steering wheel and turned his eyes to the road. "If the Escalade comes into the city, it would have to use either of those two roads to go there and come back again."

Annie understood. "You think we should stake out those two roads?"

Jake pulled over to the side and stopped. "That's what I'm saying. Let's see the road map."

Annie handed it to him and he studied it. "Let's just say, for the sake of argument, they go to the Auburn Street area again. There are too many streets for us to cover, but when they return, I'm betting they would take Valleydale Sideroad." He pointed to the map and traced the route with his finger. "To here at least."

Annie said, "And after that, there are a lot of possibilities."

"Right." He touched a spot on the map. "But if we stake out here somewhere, we'll see them if they're out today."

"You think that's a possibility?" Annie asked.

"I think it's more than a possibility. I think it's a probability they come into the city every day."

"Then let's do it."

Jake pulled the Firebird back onto the road. "We should've brought your car. Mine's too easy to identify if they see us."

"Then let's make sure they don't see us."

They drove several minutes before reaching the area Jake had indicated on the map. He drove slowly, looking for a place to park where they could watch the road and not be seen from passing vehicles.

Annie pointed to a lane on the right, which led back to a farmhouse far beyond, the entranceway partially hidden by a row of trees. "Stop there."

"Looks good." Jake pulled beyond the lane, backed in, and stopped. From their vantage point, they could see the road between the branches of the trees, just enough to make out oncoming vehicles.

They sat and waited.

And waited.

Annie had brought some sandwiches and bottles of water. They had polished off the meal some time ago, and Jake had stretched back, his eyes closed.

Annie had climbed from the vehicle and was sitting on the grass, carefully watching the road. Several cars had passed, a few SUVs, but no black Escalade yet.

She was beginning to think they were on the wrong track when she saw an SUV coming up the road, and it looked like an Escalade. Black. She squinted. With tinted windows.

She watched as it came closer, and then she hopped up and opened the door of the Firebird. "Finally, there it is," she said.

Jake was startled from his nap and sat forward. He glanced toward the oncoming vehicle, started the car, and grinned at Annie as she jumped in. "Let's hope that's it."

"Should I call Hank?"

"It's just a black Escalade. There's no guarantee it's the right one."

"Maybe. Maybe not," Annie said, more sure than Jake they had the right vehicle. They were in farm country, and farmers would be unlikely to own that type of vehicle. They would be more apt to use pickup trucks. Why would an Escalade be traveling side roads?

"Whatever you think," Jake said. "It won't hurt to let him know where we are."

Annie slipped out her cell phone and hit speed dial. "No signal," she said. "They need to get more towers out here."

"We'll try again later."

They watched as the vehicle drove by, and then Jake touched the gas and eased onto the road. He stayed back far enough so, if the Firebird was seen by the driver, it wouldn't be recognized.

After several minutes, the Escalade turned onto a side road. Jake hung back, barely keeping the SUV in sight as it kicked up clouds of dust. Jake followed the dust as the vehicle made a couple of turns.

And then, the Escalade disappeared around a curve.

Jake touched the gas and sped up. When they rounded the curve, the SUV was gone.

"He's pulled off somewhere," Annie said, glancing around.

They saw a farmhouse with a modern barn off to their left. Across the road was another house, this one with an old barn and a pond in front. Up further was another group of buildings.

Jake pulled to the side of the road while Annie flipped open the glove compartment and dug out a pair of binoculars. She scanned the properties around them, looking for signs of the Escalade.

"I don't see it," she said.

"It's got to be at one of these three properties." Jake pointed to a narrow service lane leading into a field. "I'll back in there and we can have a look around." He turned the steering wheel, kicked up gravel, spun around, and backed into the lane. The vehicle was hidden from view of the houses, behind a thick row of pine trees, which separated the two properties.

They climbed from the vehicle and Annie glanced around. She pointed to the house with the old barn. "That one has a pickup truck parked in front." She waved toward the group of buildings further up the road. "I can make out a couple of cars on that property." She turned to the house with the modern barn. "But none there. We should try that one first."

"And what if there's somebody home?" Jake asked.

Annie thought a moment. "Tell them we're looking for directions."

"Then, where's our vehicle?"

"Good point. Maybe tell them our car broke down and we want to use their phone."

Jake nodded. "That works for me."

They went up the long driveway toward the house. There was a garage attached to the dwelling at one end. Annie scrutinized the front windows of the house and saw no signs of life, so she scooted over to the far side of the garage and peeked through a small window. There was lots of junk, but no vehicle inside.

She joined Jake. "The garage is empty. This doesn't appear to be the right place."

Jake looked at the front of the dwelling. "And I haven't seen anyone moving around inside."

Annie climbed the steps to the front door and rang the bell. There was no answer after the third attempt. She looked at Jake and shook her head.

Jake circled the house toward the backyard and Annie followed. No one was there either, so she climbed the back porch. The inner door was open and she called through the screen door, "Hello?"

No answer.

She tested the door; it was unlocked. She looked back at Jake and he shrugged. She wasn't sure whether to go in or not. It didn't appear to be the correct house, but she swung the door open and stepped into the kitchen. She called again, "Hello?"

Still no answer.

She went through the kitchen and into a hallway leading to the front room. There was a door to the right. She pulled it open and peered down a set of wooden stairs into the darkness below. A musty smell stung her nose. She closed the door and peeked into the sparsely furnished living room.

Nothing looked unusual, although the house appeared dusty and unused. She went back to the kitchen and opened the fridge. There were fresh vegetables in the crisper and the contents of a carton of milk didn't smell sour.

She returned to join Jake. "Nothing out of place, but somebody lives here and they're not home."

"Wrong house," Jake said. "Let's try the one up the road further."

They walked to the road and toward the car. Jake stopped. "I want to go back and look in the barn, just in case."

Annie turned around. "You go ahead. I'll take another look at the maps and wait for you in the car."

CHAPTER 57

Friday, August 26th, 1:47 p.m.

AS JAKE APPROACHED the barn, he stopped and looked around. It struck him as odd that the vast fields surrounding the property weren't cultivated, and there were no signs any type of grain or corn, crops common to the area, had been planted either this year or last.

The barn itself appeared to have been built within the last few years. It was a sprawling building, with a round, wooden roof, supported by solid, windowless concrete walls.

The near end of the structure was mainly one large wooden door, an access door beside it, with a small window at each end.

Jake moved to the closest window and peeked inside.

A black Escalade.

He stepped back quickly. This was the place, but was this the vehicle that had been seen when David was abducted?

Only one way to find out.

He crept to the window again and took a longer look. By the dim lighting inside, he could see the area where the vehicle was parked was walled off from the rest of the building. The large room had enough space for two or three vehicles, but the Escalade was the only one inside. Another door led deeper into the building's interior.

A set of shelving on the far wall contained neat rows of white boxes. A workbench held more boxes, tools, and large bottles of water.

No one had been inside the house, so the driver of the vehicle could be inside this building somewhere. He had to get inside and take a look around.

He tested the access door. Locked.

He circled the building completely. There were no more windows or doors; this was the only way in. He peered through the window again, then stepped back quickly. The door leading into the rest of the building was opening. He chanced another look. A man, possibly the driver, was coming his way, and he was huge.

Jake stepped back and moved around the corner of the building, where he waited. He heard a metallic grind as the outer door creaked, and then footsteps on gravel and the door slammed.

He breathed cautiously and waited. He could hear the man's feet on gravel as he shuffled about, just around the corner. There was a faint metallic click, and then the smell of a freshly lit cigarette as smoke wafted past.

Jake eased forward and peeked around the corner. This might be his best chance and he had to do something now.

He stepped around the corner and pounced, bore the brute to the ground, and straddled him. He punched the ugly face twice before being thrown off onto the sharp gravel. The stones bit into his arm as he twisted and sprang to his feet.

The monster growled like a hungry bear as he spun to a crouch and leaped forward. He clamped Jake around the legs and they both went down again.

The goon was on top, snarling, one hand reaching for the gun strapped to his chest, the other around Jake's neck. He had the gun free, but Jake swung a massive fist and knocked it from the man's grasp. It spun across the gravel. As the goon leaped for it, Jake's boot caught him full in the chest. Breath shot from the thug with a whoosh as he was sent sprawling onto his back. Jake rolled toward the weapon, wrapped his hand around it, and sprang to his feet, the gun in his hand.

He'd never owned a gun and didn't know how to use one in the way it was intended. As the brute growled and reached for him with powerful arms, Jake swung his fist back, the butt end of the weapon catching the thug on the side of his head. The brute groaned as a second swing knocked him to the ground, out cold.

Jake tucked the gun behind his belt and looked at the man. He wasn't as tough as he looked, and he would be unconscious awhile.

He opened the door to the building and dragged the thug inside. He dug in the cartons on the shelves and came up with a box of medical equipment. Two lab coats were folded neatly inside. With the help of a sharp metal corner of the shelf, he was able to tear one of them into strips, and he bound the goon's arms and legs securely.

He tested the restraints. The thug was strong, but they should hold.

He tied a double strip of cloth around the man's ugly mouth, making sure he could breathe properly, and then dragged him over to the workbench and rolled him underneath. He wouldn't be seen there if anyone else came around.

He peeked through the tinted glass into the back of the Escalade. It was empty. In the front seat, the keys were in the ignition, but it was empty as well.

He turned his attention to the inner door. It was unlocked. He withdrew the weapon from his waist, studied it a moment, and then eased the door open.

There was a long hallway in front of him, several rooms leading off at each side, and a large room at the end, dead ahead.

He listened a moment, then stepped inside and eased the door closed behind him. He crept up the hall, the weapon in his hand, toward the brightly lit room. Something hummed, machinery of some kind, enough to cover any noise his feet made as he inched forward.

He heard the sound of breathing behind him, then felt a massive blow on the back of his head. His sight blurred and his thoughts faded as he crumpled to the floor.

CHAPTER 58

Friday, August 26th, 2:02 p.m.

ANNIE LOOKED at her watch. Jake had been gone for fifteen minutes and he should've been back by now.

She stepped from the Firebird and moved to the tree line where she could see the barn. She couldn't see Jake and wondered if he'd gone inside, and if so, what was taking him so long.

Her heart stopped as she was startled by a blackbird that squawked in the tree above her head and then fluttered and soared away, screaming as it went.

She laughed uneasily and, as her heart took on its normal rhythm, she considered going to the building, but decided to give it a few more minutes. Jake was probably inside looking around, or perhaps out of sight behind the barn.

She went back to the car, got the maps, and sat on the grass studying them. She wanted to take a look at the other nearby properties. She could drive there herself, but thought it better to wait for Jake to return.

She grabbed the binoculars and zoomed in on the buildings up the road. The vehicles she'd seen earlier hadn't moved, and not a soul was in sight.

Across the road, all remained the same as before.

She trained the lenses toward the barn where Jake had gone. She could see the large wooden door, with the small door beside it.

She lowered the binoculars and went back to the car, beginning to feel uneasy.

She would wait, but not much longer.

~*~

AS JAKE'S SENSES began to return, he felt a pounding in the back of his head. He lay on a hard surface; a concrete floor, perhaps.

As his vision sharpened, he rolled onto his back and attempted to clear his mind. He'd been slugged from behind.

He heard a laugh and swung his head in the direction of the sound.

A goon, a different one, leaned against the wall, leering at him. He had a pistol in his hand, trained his way.

"Lay still."

Jake turned his head and examined his predicament. He was in a white room, lying on the floor. There was a small cot pushed against the wall near him. The goon was by an open door that led into the hallway.

He took a chance and struggled to a sitting position.

The man was smaller than the one he'd tied up earlier, but Jake was too far away to attempt anything, and unlike himself, the goon looked adept with the weapon clenched in his fist.

"Welcome back," the thug said and laughed again.

Jake only glared.

The man's smile turned to a frown. "What are you doing here?"

"I'm selling vacuum cleaners."

"And I'm Santa Claus. Now tell me what you want, or ..." The goon leveled the gun. "Bang, bang."

Jake stood slowly to his feet. "I'm looking for David Haines."

"Never heard of him. Now, sit back down." He waved the gun and Jake sat down on the cot and leaned back.

"Stay there." The man grinned and reached into his jacket, removing a wallet. "Here's your wallet, Jake Lincoln." He tossed it at Jake.

Jake caught the wallet.

"Where's your wife?"

"She didn't come with me."

"Maybe I'll check around outside anyway. You must have got here somehow, and when I find your car, hopefully she's there too."

Jake continued to glare and didn't answer.

The thug smiled. "The boss is coming over. I'm sure he'll be happy to meet you."

"Who's the boss?"

"You'll find out." The goon laughed. "And before we're done with you, you'll be worshipping at his feet."

The man turned, left the room, and pulled the door closed behind him. Jake heard a grating sound as a bolt lock slid shut.

He raced to the door but it was securely locked. As he

shook it, the metal barrier rattled on its hinges but remained solid.

He felt the back of his head. There was a lump, but the aching had subsided.

Annie was in danger and he had to get out of here somehow.

CHAPTER 59

Friday, August 26th, 2:12 p.m.

ANNIE JUMPED from the vehicle. She had to find out what was keeping Jake. He'd been gone too long, and she was worried he may be in danger.

She ducked under a low-hanging branch, went to the tree line, and stopped short. Someone was coming from the barn, and though she couldn't see clearly from this distance, she could tell it wasn't Jake.

She crouched down and squinted to see better as the man stood and glanced in all directions, as if looking for someone, and then headed to the road.

She had an uneasy feeling something was wrong. Where was Jake? If he was in danger, and she was discovered, they could both be in big trouble.

She scrambled past the Firebird, and then, keeping low, she scurried deeper down the lane, hidden by the row of trees, until she was parallel to the rear of the barn.

She stopped behind a sprawling pine, peered around, and saw the man, still ambling toward the road, his back to her.

The barn was fifty feet away, but she could make it. It was the only choice she had.

Keeping one eye on the man, she dashed across the open field and then, unseen, to the back of the building. He'd made it to the road and was peering left and right. The Firebird wasn't visible from where he stood, but she knew he would discover it eventually.

She dashed along the back of the barn and circled to the far side. There were no windows in the building, and as she moved forward, she kept an eye on the road, fearful the man might return.

She peeked around the front corner. He was moving toward the row of pines, and their vehicle. It was still out of sight, but he would see it soon. She had to hurry.

She eased forward and peered in a small window beside the entrance door.

A black Escalade. They had the right place.

She saw no one in the garage, so she tested the door and found it unlocked. Jake must be inside.

She turned and glanced toward the road. The man was out of sight, so she eased the door open, stepped inside, circled the vehicle, and crept across the room to another door that led into the main part of the building. She inched the door open and peered down a hallway. She could see a series of closed doors leading off both sides, and the main room of the building at the end of the hall.

Where was Jake?

Swinging the door open carefully, she stepped into the hallway. The door clicked behind her as she eased it shut. She spun around. The only way out of this place lay behind, and only the unknown lay ahead. What had they gotten themselves into?

She shook off her fear, took a couple of deep breaths, and tiptoed to the first room on her right. There was a sliding panel on the door, and her heart jumped when she saw a handwritten label above the panel.

David Haines was here.

She started to tremble. This was certainly the right place, a dangerous, crazy place, and only her thoughts of Jake kept her from turning back.

She slid the panel and peered through the small viewing window. A cot stood against the far wall, and a boy lay on it, his knees bent, with his hands behind his head. He faced the door, and she recognized him from his picture. It was David.

The bolt scraped as she pulled it back. She eased the door open and stepped inside.

David sat up abruptly as his mouth dropped open, his eyes wide. He stood and watched her curiously as she approached. "Who are you?"

She shushed him with a finger to her lips, and whispered, "Shhhh. I'm here to help you. My name is Annie."

He whispered back, "Can you get me out of here?"

"I'll try."

He frowned at her. "Are you alone?"

Annie nodded. "I'm alone, but I think my husband is in here somewhere."

He looked at her doubtfully. "There are at least four of them. Two monsters and two doctors."

"One of the monsters is outside. I saw him earlier, and he'll be back soon, so we have to hurry."

He looked her up and down. "You don't look like you could handle them. Do you have a gun?"

She shook her head. "No gun, but they don't know I'm here." She slipped her cell phone from her back pocket and worked it frantically. "No signal," she said as she moved to the door. "I need to find my husband and then get outside and call the police."

She opened the door a couple of inches and peered into the hallway, straight into the startled eyes of a man in a long white coat. Annie jumped back as he sprang forward and pushed the door.

"It's Muller," David whispered.

She backed up against the wall as the doctor took a step into the room.

"Who are you?" he demanded.

Annie remained silent and wished she'd brought a tire iron with her.

David had moved to the side of the room, his back to the wall. In her peripheral vision, she saw him push off the wall and spring forward. He tackled the doctor, forcing both of them to their knees.

Annie didn't hesitate. She moved in to help David, who had been thrown backwards, his arms pinned underneath, struggling against the larger man on top. She gritted her teeth and aimed the heel of her running shoe at Muller's head. The blow stunned him, long enough to allow David to free his arms and help Annie force the man to his back.

With the look of a maniac in his eyes, David straddled Muller and pounded his captor's face, over and over. The doctor's breath rasped, and blood spewed from his nose and mouth as he fought to breathe, until finally he stopped struggling and lay still.

Annie reached out, clenched the furious boy's shoulder, and spoke sharply. "David. That's enough."

David took one last blow, then sat back and looked up. He panted, his breath coming in short, quick gasps.

"It's over, David."

The boy stood and looked at his hands, spattered with blood. "He deserved it," he said as he gazed on the ruined face of the doctor.

"I'm sure he did, but we'll lock him in here and go."

David looked at her and nodded.

CHAPTER 60

Friday, August 26th, 2:37 p.m.

JAKE HAD BEEN trying to loosen the hinges on his cell door.

He had been able to twist loose a piece of iron bar from the cot and was using it to work at the metal pins that held the door securely, but at this rate, it would take him hours to get free.

He didn't have hours to waste. Annie was in danger and he was desperate to get to her.

He stepped back to the side of the door, out of sight, when he heard the viewing panel slide back, and then a faint voice came through the glass. "Nobody in here."

It was Annie.

He spun back to the door and looked through the panel, straight into Annie's eyes. He tossed the metal bar aside as the bolt was slid and the door swung open. She dashed forward and wrapped herself around him as he smothered her in his arms, planting kisses on her hair.

She looked up at him. "Are you okay?"

He grinned at her. "I am now."

Annie pulled loose and motioned toward David, who had stepped into the room. "This is David Haines."

Jake recognized the boy from the photo. He nodded at David and asked, "Do you know your way around here?"

David shook his head. "I haven't been outside of my cell until now."

"Then let's go," Jake said as he moved to the doorway. He peeked into the hall. "All clear. Stay behind me."

Jake led the way, and they moved cautiously into the passageway. He spun toward the door leading to the garage as he heard a metallic scrape, and the door began to open.

He turned and motioned with his arm, and he and David flattened against the wall. Annie dashed back into the open cell, out of sight.

The thug appeared and stopped short when he saw the intruders. With a low growl he wrenched his pistol from its holster across his chest and leveled it.

The goon's small eyes became smaller. "Don't move," he said as his mouth twisted into a cruel smile.

Jake and David raised their arms. They were a few feet away, and Jake calculated his chances. They didn't look good.

The villain waved his gun toward the open cell and advanced a couple of steps. "Get back in there, both of you."

David dashed back into the room. Jake stood still and scrutinized the goon, his flat ears, his square head, and a scarred face, which looked like it had been punched one too many times. Maybe not so bright, but he looked like he could use a gun.

"Get in there," the goon repeated.

Jake took a backwards step into the cell.

The man eased forward and gestured with the weapon. "Back up."

Jake retreated into the room and stopped beside David, his back to the wall.

"Shut the door," the goon ordered.

Jake stood still.

The goon frowned, forced his small brain to make a decision, and then took a step and reached for the door handle.

"Don't you want my gun?" Jake asked.

The man paused and glared.

"It's in my belt, behind my back."

The goon advanced one step. "Turn around."

Jake turned toward the wall and raised his arms, his palms against the concrete. The man stepped forward and frowned. "I don't see it."

Annie stepped from behind the door and swung the iron bar. The goon wobbled on his feet, and his gun arm dropped to his side. His eyes rolled, and he crumpled to the floor, out cold and harmless.

David dove forward and wrenched the pistol from the thug's hand. His eyes were on fire and his hands trembled as he stood, raised the weapon, and pointed it at the fallen thug.

Jake touched the boy's arm. "It's okay, David. He's not going to hurt anyone now."

David dropped his arm, glared at the thug a moment, and then stuffed the pistol in his waistband. He raised his eyes toward Jake and nodded.

"We need to get out of here. Now," Annie whispered.

Jake nodded at her, then asked David, "How many people are in this place?"

"I think there are four altogether, but Annie and I locked up one of the doctors."

Jake nodded. "And I tied up a goon in the garage, so that makes one left."

"Dr. Wolff," David whispered.

Jake wondered if he should try to catch the doctor or leave and call the police. He thought it better to leave. "Let's get out of here."

"You're not going anywhere," a voice said.

Jake spun around. An elderly man in a long white lab coat stood in the doorway. He gripped a pistol with both hands, his head hunched forward, the butt of the gun clenched to his chest below his chin. Jake saw panic in the doctor's wild eyes. A dangerous thing to see when faced with a man carrying a loaded weapon.

"Dr. Wolff," David said.

Wolff twisted his head toward David, then back at Jake. "Come out of there. Put your hands up," he said in a frenzied voice as he backed into the hallway.

The three captives obeyed and Jake stepped out first. "Don't shoot," he said. "We just want to get out of here, and then we'll leave you alone."

"No, no. You can't leave now," Wolff said as he backed up toward the exit door and freed one hand from the gun. He pointed a shaky finger toward the lab. "Go that way."

They moved down the hallway to the laboratory as Wolff followed, a few steps behind.

Jake looked around at the collection of equipment, electronics, and chemicals; it looked like a serious operation. A Bunsen burner spat flame into the air beside racks of test tubes and rows of beakers. Wolff must have been doing some kind of experiment when he was interrupted.

"Over to the far wall," Wolff said. "Sit on the floor."

They obeyed, and the elderly doctor followed and stopped across the room opposite them.

"What ... what are you going to do with us?" David asked.

The man was silent as he glared at the boy. Finally, he spoke. "I'll have to call Mr. Craig. He'll know what to do."

CHAPTER 61

Friday, August 26th, 2:49 p.m.

ANNIE SAT AGAINST the wall and watched as Wolff edged to the desk and picked up the telephone receiver.

Keeping his eyes on his captors, the doctor dialed a number, the gun trembling in his right hand.

"Mr. Craig," he said into the phone. "I've captured the Lincolns. I ... I don't know what to do with them."

He listened intently for a moment and then carefully hung up the phone. "Mr. Craig is already on his way here. I have to lock you in one of the rooms until he arrives."

David sprang to his feet, reached to his waist, and removed the pistol he had stashed there. "No," he shouted as he raised the weapon and pointed it at Wolff. "I'm not going back in there."

Wolff swung his pistol toward David. His voice shook as he talked. "Put the gun down, David."

Annie took a sharp breath, and her eyes darted back and forth between the doctor and the frightened boy. With two nervous people, both pointing a gun at each other, something could go terribly wrong.

"I won't go back there," David repeated. "I've had enough torture from you."

The doctor spoke soothingly. "I'm your friend, remember?"

"No, you're not."

"I am the Wizard. Do as I say."

David frowned and bit his lip, and then lowered the gun a few inches. Jake stood and reached out carefully. "Give me the gun, David."

The boy shook his head violently and raised the pistol in Jake's direction. "Stay back."

Annie realized that by invoking the name of the Wizard, the mad doctor was appealing to some kind of conditioning he must have put David through. Annie spoke sharply. "David, the Wizard is not your friend."

David looked at Annie, then at the Wizard. His lip trembled, and he tightened his grip on the gun.

"You must do as I say, David," the Wizard said, and then raised his voice. "I am the Wizard. Put the gun down."

David dropped the weapon and sank to his knees, his head in his hands.

Annie saw her chance.

She dove for the gun, retrieved it, and spun to a crouch. She wrapped her hand around the grip and aimed it at the Wizard. As Wolff swung his gun toward her, she saw his finger tighten on the trigger.

She closed her eyes and fired. The shot was deafening, and echoed through the confined space.

Wolff screamed, panic in his voice. "You shot me." The pistol slipped from his grasp as he sank to his knees. He grabbed his reddening arm and tried to stop the flow of blood. "You shot me," he screamed again.

Jake lunged for the fallen pistol and recovered it.

Annie's hold on her weapon loosened, her nerves shattered. "You'll be fine. You only got hit in the arm."

Wolff sank into a chair and held his wound. He looked at Annie and swallowed, his face going slack, a flicker of fear in his eyes.

Jake tucked his pistol away, moved forward, put his arm around Annie's shoulder, and grinned at her. "Nice shootin', honey."

She handed him the pistol. "Here, take this thing."

He laughed and took the weapon. "There's nothing to worry about. That little mouse can't do anything now."

"You watch him and I'll call the police."

Jake found a first aid kit and wrapped Wolff's arm to stop the bleeding, then dropped into a seat. He kept an eye on the vanquished doctor while Annie went to the desk and called 9-1-1.

"It'll take them a few minutes to get here," she said as she dropped into the chair. She thumbed through the papers on the desk, and then brought down a few of the note binders from the shelf above.

"Mr. Craig will be here very soon," Wolff said. "He'll know what to do."

"We're ready for him," Jake said as he brandished the pistol.

Annie spun her chair around. She waved a paper at Jake. "You know who this Craig guy is?"

"Who?" Jake asked.

"Just as I originally thought. He's Oliver Craig, the owner of Sheridan Construction." She looked at Wolff. "Is that why he had Charles Robinson killed? Because he was bidding on some property against him?"

Wolff shrugged. "It was all for the best."

Annie glared at him. "And what about Bobby Sullivan? Why was he killed?"

Wolff glared back defiantly. "He was a rapist. The girl's father is a good friend of Mr. Craig's. He was doing his friend a favor by ridding the world of the scumbag who raped his daughter."

"And you think that's justified?" Jake asked.

"Mr. Craig thought so. I must agree."

"Why must you agree?"

"Because he's from the bloodline of the elite."

Jake frowned. "The elite?"

Wolf sighed. "Of course. It goes back many, many generations. His father before him was one of the few." He paused. "The few who are destined to rule the masses."

"How do you fit into all of this? Are you one of the elite?"

Wolff shook his head adamantly. "No, no. I was fortunate enough to be able to work with Mr. Craig's father on the government project, many years ago."

Jake and Annie exchanged a glance. "The government project?" Annie frowned.

"Yes, back in the 1950s and 1960s. When the project was abandoned, Mr. Craig Senior kept his own extensive notes on the project. When Mr. Craig inherited his father's research, it made mention of me, so Mr. Craig, fortunately, looked me up. I was excited to get back on the project after so many years."

Annie leaned forward. "Are you talking about MK-Ultra?"

"Yes, yes. That's what it was called then, but that was just an offshoot of the struggle that has gone on forever."

"The elite against the rest of us?"

"Not against us. For us. The goal of the elite is to make the world a better place for everyone."

Jake laughed. "That sounds like communism, or fascism, to me."

"Not at all. Some people call it elitism. Call it what you want, it's for the best." Wolff continued in a defiant voice. "There are others out there, and they will eventually prevail."

Jake shrugged. "If they do, you won't be there to help."

Wolff shook his head. "It doesn't matter. I would gladly give my life for the cause."

Annie spun her head and listened intently. She could hear the door down the hall opening. "Craig's here," she whispered.

CHAPTER 62

JAKE STOOD, whipped across the room, and nudged Wolff's forehead with the muzzle of the pistol. "Don't say a word."

Wolff stiffened, and resignation showed in his frightened eyes as he peered upwards. Jake held the weapon in place until the newcomer's footsteps sounded outside the room, then pointed it toward the doorway and waited.

Craig's hands shot up by instinct as he stepped in the room, and then he froze, his mouth open and speechless.

"Come on in," Jake said, waving the gun.

Craig looked at Wolff, at Annie, at David, and then back at Jake.

Jake kicked a chair over to land beside Wolff. "Sit down."

Craig moved to the chair, sat down uneasily, and frowned at Wolff. "How did this happen? Why didn't you lock them up when I told you to?"

"I'm sorry, sir, but they shot me."

"Where are the guards? Where's Muller?"

"I ... I don't know, sir."

Jake said, "We've taken care of them. They won't be bothering us anymore, and neither will you once the police get here."

Craig glared up at Jake, murder in his eyes. "How did you find us?"

"Quite easily. We followed the signal of your trackers."

Craig scowled and spun his head toward Wolff. "You said it was safe."

Wolff was silent.

"This is quite an organization you have here, or should I say, had here," Jake said.

Annie turned in her chair and faced the villains, papers in her hand. "You've ruined a lot of lives."

Craig gave her a black look.

"Wolff already filled us in on your plans." Annie waved the papers in the air. "And I see you've documented everything very carefully."

"I'm sure the police will be grateful for that," Jake said.

Annie's voice took on a disgusted tone as she continued. "You used all these kids, and had them kill in cold blood in your lust for power."

"And what about the innocent victims?" Jake added.

"They weren't innocent," Craig shouted, and looked toward the hallway as if expecting one of the thugs to rescue him. No one did, and he turned back and looked frantically around the room.

"The rest of your underlings are safely locked up," Jake said.

Annie looked at Craig and pointed at David. "What did he ever do to you?"

Craig shrugged.

Jake put the pistol to Craig's temple, leaned in, and gritted his teeth, their faces inches apart. "Did you even know the names of the kids you used? All those innocent lives you destroyed for your own selfish purposes?"

Craig didn't answer and moved back uneasily as Jake withdrew the weapon, straightened his back, and looked in disgust at the two lowlifes.

Jake looked at his watch. The police would be here soon, and it would be all over. For them, that was, but not for the families of the victims. Their pain would never stop, and though they would see justice, it would never be enough.

Craig took advantage of Jake's temporary lapse into thought and lunged at the big man. Jake fought to hold onto the pistol as Craig struggled to wrestle it from his grasp. Craig would normally be no match for Jake, but he was desperate, and desperate people do desperate things.

A stray shot could be fatal, and Jake attempted to point the pistol upwards in case it fired. "Everybody, get down," he yelled, and Annie and David scurried toward the hallway.

Craig had a solid grip and was trying to turn the barrel of the gun toward Jake when it fired. Glass shattered as the bullet smacked through lab equipment and embedded itself in the wall beyond.

Chemical fumes filled the air as they fought for control of the gun. Jake brought the elbow of his free arm crashing into the side of Craig's head, and the murderer's grip loosened. One more swing of Jake's fist and blood shot from his opponent's mouth and nose as he crashed to the floor.

Craig lay on his back, unmoving, defeated, and bleeding.

Jake caught the acrid smell of burning chemicals and he whipped around. The broken flask of liquid had spread across the desk and was engulfed in flame from the Bunsen burner. He looked around for a fire extinguisher. There was none.

The sharp smell stung his nostrils and burned his lungs.

Whatever was in the beaker was burning hot, as flames caressed the wall behind the bench, and were becoming dangerously close to a pair of gas cylinders. More cylinders were under the bench, and if the flames reached them, it would be all over.

Thick black smoke wafted upwards, dissipated, and began to fill the room with pungent fumes.

Jake pulled Craig to his feet. "We have to get out of here." He turned to Wolff and pointed toward the hallway. "Move."

"No, no," Craig shouted. "We have to save my father's notes." He spun and glared at Wolff. "Help me."

Wolff dashed over and began pulling the binders and notepads from the shelf above the desk and stuffing them into a briefcase.

The flames sputtered and fizzed. The fire was spreading downward and outward, and Jake found it hard to breathe. He gave one last plea to the madmen and dashed into the hallway.

Annie and David had opened the cell doors and Annie was herding two young boys toward the exit. David followed, with Jake close behind, the flames working their way up the hall behind them.

There was an explosion as they raced through the garage, and then another explosion rocked the roof, sending rainbows of ash and flame high into the air.

The door burst open and they breathed in the fresh air.

CHAPTER 63

Friday, August 26th, 3:25 p.m.

ANNIE RACED across the gravel until she could no longer feel the heat on her back, then turned and faced the inferno. They were safe, but Craig and Wolff would be lucky to make it out alive.

David stood close beside her, his eyes wide with wonder as he observed the out-of-control fire.

Her arm was around another boy, perhaps fourteen or fifteen years old. She had freed him from his prison, and he stood close to her, shivering in the warm air.

Another boy stood close by and was watching the fire in awe.

But where was Jake?

She looked around frantically. He had been behind them when they raced from the barn. She asked David, "Did you see Jake?"

David pointed to the raging fire. "He might be still in there. I never saw him come out."

Annie looked in horror. If Jake was still in the barn, there was no chance he could get out alive. The roof of the garage was buckling under the weight of the burning timbers, and chunks had already fallen loose and crashed into the garage.

"Stay here," she said as she dashed to her right and glanced along the outside of the barn. No Jake. She raced to the left, but he wasn't there either. He was nowhere to be seen.

He must be still inside.

She moved as close to the fire as she could. "Jake," she called, again and again.

No answer.

Flames were licking around the exit door and the metal frame was beginning to melt under the intense heat. The large wooden door had burst into flames and it wouldn't be long before it, too, was totally consumed.

It was too late for anyone still inside.

The large garage door burst forward, and flaming wood and charred splinters flew upwards as a fireball ascended from the roof, far into the sky.

Smoke followed the path of the airborne flames and billowed upwards, expanding and filling the air with soot and flaming embers.

Then there was a sudden roar, like the sound of an angry bull, and the Escalade burst through the door, lunged forward, and ground to a stop beside Annie.

The window zipped down, and Jake stuck his grinning face out. "Anyone call a cab?"

Annie looked at him in disgust, frowning deeply, her hands on her hips. "I can't believe you risked your life to save a car."

Jake jumped out and opened the back door. "Not just a car," he said as he dragged a trussed-up thug from the backseat. "But I had a passenger, too."

Annie smiled through her relief. She couldn't understand why risking your life to save a valuable vehicle was stupid, but risking your life to save a worthless thug was heroic.

She didn't bother to try to figure it out. She was too busy hugging her hero.

~*~

OVER THE CRACKLE and whoosh of a barn being consumed, police sirens screamed as three cruisers roared up the lane and spun to a stop. Uniformed policemen poured out.

Hank pulled up behind the cruisers and jumped from his car. He stood for a moment and observed the fire before joining the Lincolns.

"What happened?"

Jake said, "They had a lab in there. It caught fire when we were wrestling for a gun." He filled Hank in on the rest of the story. "The problem is, all of the evidence went up in smoke, along with most of the bad guys."

Annie sighed and said, "When David and I opened the cell doors, the guard and Dr. Muller were still out cold. We didn't have time to help them."

"I tried to get back to them," Jake said. "But the fire was too fierce. I couldn't even get close." He glanced at the burning building. "Whoever is left in there, it's too late for them now."

Another siren sounded and a fire engine pulled in close to the building. Soon, a futile stream of water was pouring onto the inferno, but it was too late. The building was nearly gutted, and all that would remain would be four charred bodies and an empty concrete shell.

"We may never know the full extent of what went on here," Hank said.

"It may be better left buried," Jake said. "It was a horrifying nightmare, and it's over."

"It's not over for the victims," Annie reminded him.

Hank sighed deeply. "It never will be."

EPILOGUE

Saturday, August 27th, 11:00 a.m.

THE DOORBELL BUZZED and Annie showed Hank into the living room. He settled back in the easy chair as Jake strolled from the office and dropped into the couch beside Annie.

"I just wanted to fill you guys in on what we discovered," Hank said.

"You couldn't have found too much," Jake said. "That barn was destroyed completely."

"Sure it was, but we searched Craig's house, and his office, and we found some amazing information."

Jake leaned forward.

Hank continued, "Apparently, Wolff filled out periodic reports for Craig, and we found many of them in his office, some dating back several months. We were able to piece together a good idea of what was involved, who the victims are, and the reasons they were chosen."

"What about the killers?" Annie asked.

"We'll eventually figure out who the John Does and the other boys are, and in the meantime, David is reunited with his parents."

"It seems we got there just in time to save him. He was spared most of the worst," Jake said.

Hank said, "Yeah, but he got a good enough dose to straighten him out a bit. He was in tears when he finally saw his parents, and vowed to listen to them and do whatever they asked from now on. He's just happy to have escaped. His parents couldn't thank me enough." Hank laughed. "I had to explain to them they were thanking the wrong guy, and it's you two who saved the day."

"Tell us about Cheryl," Annie said. "What'll happen to her?"

"The psychiatrist has made a number of recommendations. He's confident that, over time, Cheryl will recover her memory, and he recommended she not be prosecuted. At the time of the murder, she was unable to understand the nature of what she did, and lacked the capacity to appreciate the criminality of it."

"So, that means …?"

"She won't be prosecuted. And that goes for the girl who tried to kill you as well. I'm sure she'll be diagnosed the same, and after some intensive treatment, she'll recover."

"Cheryl's parents must have been glad to hear that," Annie said.

"Yes, they were delighted, to put it mildly. I told them you'd be dropping by today."

"Wolff told us what he was doing was just the tip of the iceberg, and there are more out there with the same mindset as him. He called it 'the cause.'"

Hank sighed. "I'm sure there are more like him, but

fortunately, details of the procedures they used on the victims were destroyed."

Just then, Matty came charging into the room. "Hey, Uncle Hank." He turned to his father. "Hey, Dad. Catch any bad guys lately?"

Jake grinned. "Yeah, one or two."

###

A NOTE TO THE READER

THIS STORY, although fictional, could have happened. The American and Canadian involvement in trauma-based mind control techniques during the 1950s and 1960s is well documented.

Known as MK-Ultra Project Monarch, the techniques to manipulate people's mental states and alter brain functions included the administration of drugs and other chemicals, hypnosis, sleep, food, and water deprivation, isolation, and verbal and sexual abuse, as well as various forms of torture.

CIA documents regarding the project were ordered to be destroyed, making a full investigation of MK-Ultra impossible, but thousands of documents survived.

Experiments were also carried on in Canada by CIA-funded Dr. Cameron. The Canadian government was fully aware, and later provided another $500,000 in funding to continue the experiments.

The Canadian government eventually settled out of court for $100,000 to each of the 127 victims. None of Dr. Cameron's personal records of his involvement with MK-Ultra survived.

An Internet search will show a myriad of further information pertaining to these fascinating, yet disturbing events in North American history.

CPSIA information can be obtained at www.ICGtesting.com
Printed in the USA
LVOW10s1428050616

491307LV00012B/793/P